Protectin

by Kather

MW01613124

The characters in this book (with the exceptions listed below) are entirely fictional. Any resemblance to actual persons—living, dead, angelic, furry, befanged, or otherwise—is entirely coincidental. While nothing odd happening in Decatur, GA is really much of a surprise to anyone who knows the area, if there is an actual angelic and demonic apartment complex there, the author is unaware of its existence.

To join Katherine Gilbert's More in Heaven and Earth Newsletter and get behind-the-scenes info and updates on new releases, sign up at: http://eepurl.com/dCcccL

To join her reader group and get exclusive details on future and current works, interact with her about her characters and novels, or have a chance to join her review group and get free Advance Reader Copies of upcoming works, sign up at: https://www.facebook.com/groups/1169120069919462/

For all other inquiries and questions, message her through Facebook: https://www.facebook.com/Katherine-Gilbert-Author-102573417043950/

Cover Art by For the Muse Designs

Dedications

For Chris, who helps me keep body, soul, and sanity together
And for my dear sister, Armida, who has always been my comfort
and the angel in my life

<u>Also by Katherine Gilbert</u>
Unearthly Remains

Chapter One

It wasn't every day a girl got to meet an angel, or so the sign on his door said he was, anyway. Even less frequently did it happen in job interviews.

Her potential boss seemed endlessly amused, his smile making small laugh lines crinkle around his enthralling eyes. Linda didn't know that she could blame him.

She doubted that she was really what the retirement village had wanted when they had advertised for an assistant. Her newly-dyed, indigo bob wasn't really septuagenarian approved, however many blue-haired little old ladies might live here. Then again, maybe the 70-and-over set was wilder than she thought. She could only hope to be lucky enough to find out by getting this job.

Thus far, her interviewer — her potential boss — had made no comment. She supposed she was lucky he hadn't just thrown her out.

She'd done her best at appearing normal, other than the hair — her clothes the closest she could manage to professional business-wear without a fashion consultant. Her parents hadn't been big fans of helping her fit in... although she was *not* going to think about the past.

She was aiming for trophy-wife-meeting-her-friends-for-a-casu-al-lunch. That the hair made it feel more like failed-punk-rocker-with-identity-crisis probably wasn't that much of a help.

The strangeness of her hair wasn't really her fault, but she wasn't going to get into that with this gorgeous guy — with anyone, if she could help it. Her history was nobody's business. If she could forget it all herself, she would be a much happier woman.

Thankfully, Mr. Spear interrupted her thoughts. "How did you hear about us?"

At least he was starting her off easily. "I saw the description on Monster."

Weirdly, he appeared to be stifling a laugh. It only went on for a second before he coughed the sound discreetly away, pulling her application toward him. "I see you're not from the area?"

He didn't look as though he was entirely focused on her answers, although he did seem quite concentrated on *her*. It was a little disconcerting but rather nice.

She remembered to smile, doing her best. "No, I just moved to Atlanta. I've been checking the want ads on the computer at the hotel."

Unsurprisingly, he looked at her oddly. "You don't have a cell?"

"I'm afraid not."

She knew what an oddity that made her. Finding an 18-year-old without a cell was probably harder than spotting Bigfoot.

She made herself stop thinking about her parents again and tried to keep up the smile.

Thankfully, he shrugged the issue away, as she watched him politely, dragging herself back from the past, determined to think that things would go her way, wanting to project to him the kind of worker he was searching for — whatever that might be. She needed this job. It was the only real prospect she'd seen. Too clumsy to wait tables, too quiet to be a persuasive saleslady, and too self-aware to strip, she didn't have the education or experience for anything better. She would have to hope that personal charm would work.

Although she'd always felt fairly lacking in this department, she was doing her best to make up for 18 years of gloomy mistrust. She did worry that her attempt at an eager smile was only making her look like an amphetamine-addicted Pollyanna.

When she saw Mr. Spear's obvious attempts to clamp down on his amusement, her fears were proved right. Of course, since the only look she'd ever perfected was the one that said, "Please don't hit me," she was left to work on what was probably a Stepford grin a while longer.

Another minute passed before the man's more polite smile returned, which unfortunately, allowed her more time to gaze at him. He was just a little too beautiful — suited the construction paper sign on his door, the one that announced him as "Head Angel." It wouldn't have been hard to believe.

Everything about him seemed special to her. His eyes were green but with little, lovely flecks of gold through them; his face was model-sculpted, body like some kind of classical statue. Even his hair was pre-Raphaelite, auburn curls a little long, just beyond his ability to control. If the aged residents put up with an "angel" with shoulder-length hair, one who enjoyed lounging around in a comfortable gray t-shirt and extremely worn blue jeans, then she might have some sort of chance of making them forgive her unusual hair.

He was more politely composed when he pulled over her job application again. Linda was just glad he was sitting down, even if he was only perched on the corner of his desk. Just following him into his office had been a menace. Surely angels didn't have butts that nice.

She'd managed — as much as possible — to wipe her mind clean of such ideas by the time his questions continued. That was good, because her thoughts might well have become even less professional, otherwise.

"I see you don't have a home yet?"

Shaking her head, she hoped he wouldn't ask why she'd move to an entirely unfamiliar city with no home or job prospects or plans. It wouldn't look good to be seen as the drifter her life was threatening to turn her into.

"That's good, because we need our tenant manager to live on site. If you're hired, we'll be setting you up in one of our apartments."

A million questions opened up with that fact — rent versus salary, whether she'd be on call twenty-four hours a day, why she'd need to be there if she weren't. They were all the sort of questions she should have asked.

They weren't what actually came out.

"Do you live here, too?"

Her naked curiosity created a desperate urge to kick herself in the head.

Fortunately, Mr. Spear's smile was kind, keeping her from any further thoughts of gymnastic self-injury.

"I'm around."

O-kay. Nothing like having your potential employer be open with you.

Her confusion over this triumph of ambiguity was probably obvious, but he didn't enlighten her any further, and she told herself for at least the millionth time to stop questioning everything. After all, most people lived ordinary lives — *she* was certainly going to from now on, even if it killed her — and most bosses had no intention of answering such intrusive personal questions.

Mentally banging that truth into place, she was ready to hear the rest of what Mr. Spear told her.

He scanned her application, but she had a sense that he wasn't really looking at it. "I see you haven't worked as a manager before."

Shaking her head, she waited, as his indefinable smile reappeared. She felt like he saw everything, which, given her previous life, was not a comfortable idea. Still, his look somehow warmed her.

"I think you'll do for us nicely. Let me tell you a little about us and your duties."

Her eyes growing wide, she managed to repress any squeak of surprise, wondering whether she'd misunderstood. She'd always been led to believe that getting a job was at least a little more difficult than this.

As he began, she tried to listen.

"The Roanoke is a retirement community, of sorts. It's split into two different sections: East and West. Each has twelve buildings. There are two different Resident Coordinators, me and Damian. I'm the East Coordinator."

Linda nodded, trying to keep her thoughts in line enough to follow. Along with a general outline of the complex, which had seemed fairly sprawling, Mr. Spear's explanation had answered another of her questions. It was the name of the West Coordinator, she was guessing, that had been the origin of this inner-office joke. Like Spear's "angel," the sign on the card on Damian's office door read "Head Demon."

She forced herself not to glance appreciatively at her new boss. She was already glad to be on the heavenly side.

Her employer clearly hadn't noticed her mental wanderings, since his explanation continued. "Damian and I handle all major decisions and any of the bigger problems the residents might encounter."

She was managing, if only just, to pay attention — the man's eyes alone entrancing her. Her sigh was wistful. No one this good looking should *ever* have been made a boss.

Really, she was attempting not to be an idiot, but her lack of experience with people, men especially, didn't help much. His voice alone was enough to make her want to whine like a dog looking for a treat. When part of her mind started playing with the word *bone*, she nearly hit herself on the head a few times. Anything to force her well-scrambled brains back into line.

Her mental slap did a little good, at least, some of his explanation sinking in.

"Both of us have a tenant manager working with us. You'd handle all the smaller details as well as any complaints from our tenants."

Well, that told her a bit but had been pretty short on specifics.

She managed to smile politely — or, at least, insipidly — as she worked on phrasing her many questions. "So, there's a difference between the residents and the tenants?" All the duties seemed to overlap greatly, otherwise.

Unfortunately, she didn't get an answer.

"Ah, another one." The man who entered was almost a ringer for Mr. Spear, his voice warm and far too knowing. He was six feet tall, perfectly built, and looked to be made for fantasies of the most lascivious kind. The major difference was that he clearly knew it and expected his glamour to be rewarded.

"Damian," Mr. Spear acknowledged with no sign of pleasure or warmth.

But the "Head Demon" ignored him to make a beeline toward her.

By the time he got to her, Linda was a little stunned. She couldn't quite resist when she was led to her feet, her arms held out to the sides, as Damian inspected her. While she wanted to simply glare, he was a bit overpowering. Mr. Spear, undoubtedly too old for her and probably married to boot, had that distant sort of beauty which made her suspect that many a woman had lived out her life in long, unfulfilled fantasies about him. Damian had anything but. He seemed to project some sort of invisible sign that read, in 100-foot-tall neon letters, "Just Ask — I'm Available." He grinned at her, as she shook her head, clearing it. Available for what, it was probably better not to guess.

He seemed to notice her bemusement, his words nearly a purr of satisfaction. "Look, a new little . . . "

She didn't quite make out the last word, under Mr. Spear's sound of extreme discontentment, but it sounded like "victim."

His grin widened further. "Helper," he finished.

Dropping her hands a moment later, a cat done playing with its new toy, he turned back to Spear. "Too bad about Clarissa." Coyly, his look returned to Linda. "His last . . . helper."

Really, it shouldn't have been possible for a man that flashy to also be attractive. She'd never thought much of that lounge lizard type, not that she'd ever actually been in a bar. *Must be the pheromones,* she thought before pulling her mind back together.

Once she did, she glanced at Mr. Spear, not even certain why she was asking. Maybe it was something about Damian's tone of voice. "What happened to her?"

The West Coordinator grinned. "She's dea—"

"No longer with us," her new boss finished for him, pointing toward the door. "Now, if you'll allow me to finish explaining her duties to my new assistant."

A few moments struggle between the men followed, all of it carried out in an absolute, silent glare.

The break wasn't fortunate, Linda's mind reeling, the thoughts warring with each other:

Did he say dead?

Who the heck is this guy, anyway?

I have to live here? How much do I get paid?

Did he say dead?

What's up with me being attracted to these jokers? I'm never attracted to anyone!

Uh, excuse me—did he say **dead**?

Why the heck would these people hire me? I have no qualifications. I've never even had a job!

Hello*! Did he say* **DEAD**?

Now that inner voice was shrieking at her. Desperate as she was for a quiet, normal life, she found it impossible to ignore.

What's wrong with that? People die every day. It's a retirement home. Maybe she was 80.

Yeah, that's likely.

It was only with serious effort that Linda tugged these mental wanderings back into line. Yes, these guys were a little weird, but not everyone had the blessing of being normal. Maybe the job was being given to her, as well — if she hadn't just made some huge, unfounded assumption — because she was one of the few applicants? It *was* a retirement home, might seem boring to anyone else.

Also, she had undoubtedly misheard those last few words. Clarissa might be . . . desperate to focus on school or deleterious to the good name of the community. Heck, maybe she was dealing drugs. Who cared? Everything there was normal, darn it! Normal!

She was just recovering her Stepford smile, when the silent battle between the men ended, Damian looking a little weary as he shrugged before heading toward the door.

He did glance back once before he left, though, focusing on her hair, his renewed smile knowing. "Why don't you go back to your previous color? We all preferred it so."

When she started shivering, he'd already turned away, leaving her to the terrifying question of how he knew.

It took a while after his disappearance for her new boss to get her attention, something in Damian's eyes much too disturbing for her to just wish away, something she remembered from . . .

No, she was *not* going back into the past, refused to admit that she was trying her darnedest to forget everything he had just said. Mr. Spear had his hand on her arm, before she finally realized that he was speaking to her.

"Ignore him. He has no authority over you." His touch was warm, tender. "You'll work for me."

That was the best news she'd heard all day. As he helped her to her feet, she felt more at peace than she had in years.

"You look tired. Let's discuss the details of your employment in more depth tomorrow." His smile alone was enough to comfort her.

"Until then, I'll show you to your new apartment, and you can get a little rest."

That sounded like a wonderful idea. Apparently, this job-hunting thing really wasn't all that difficult, but it was tiring. The day had taken more out of her than she had realized.

In a daze, she followed along, even her overly bright smile dimming. It took a lot to remember that she should be asking him questions. "Mr. Spear—"

"Geoffrey," he interrupted, leading her into a golf cart and starting it. "There's no need for formality."

Feeling slightly loopy, she smiled. She liked that. She opened her mouth to try again.

Her boss didn't give her the chance. "The apartment's already furnished. Everything's ready for you."

That statement nearly got her worried. She didn't have a lot of good memories of things being specially prepared for her.

Zipping around the circular driveway, they aimed for a building near the office.

"By the way, why do you call yourself 'Linda'?"

She looked at him, her heart thumping — wondering why he'd ask. There was no reason for him to know . . .

For a moment, he was quiet, almost looked worried, as though she'd caught *him* in a lie. It was certainly the other way around.

She had chosen Linda to separate her from the past, as a way to kill the memories; it just seemed so nice and normal to her. Lydia had always been an extremely reluctant freak. Linda would usher her into the world of normalcy she so desperately craved.

It was going to work. She *would* be a new person. She had to be. The horrors she had survived as Lydia couldn't be carried any further without crushing her.

"I saw Lydia on your license," he said finally.

Right, she remembered that. A blink later, the idea was gone, her mind refocusing on his question. She couldn't help how sleepy she was, even that one second of adrenaline fading quickly. Her words reflected it.

"Linda's nice. Linda's normal." Normal was good. Nothing that could be connected with her childhood was either.

She tried not to recall anything like a past, as he pulled up to a building.

There were about three different styles of apartment blocks, interspersed haphazardly. She noticed through her mental haze that hers had the number 8 on it. It would be nice if she could remember where she lived.

She followed him like a puppy, as they made their way inside, stopping in the hallway for him to shut the outer door. Lydia — Linda, if she had anything to say about it— stared at the apartments, wondering which one was hers.

"The tenants won't know about you till after you start tomorrow." His voice was soft, calming. "You should be safe for the night."

She looked at him, confused, until he smiled and added, "No one will ask anything of you yet."

Somehow, she wasn't particularly reassured. Some hidden fears started to wake her up, the lifelong memories of growing up in freakland creeping out of their clamped-down place in her mind. She tried to push them back, craving dullness, managing to conjure up a smile.

He led her past the two apartments near them, up the carpeted stairs to another door, Apartment 885, and turned the key in the lock. "Here you go," he murmured softly.

When she peeked around him into the apartment, she almost wished she was still as sleepy. It might have made everything look far more inviting.

Barely noticing her guide, she wandered around to ponder the new space. A few words occurred to her. One was "sparse." The other was "grandma decor."

She sighed. Well, she'd wanted dull.

The couch and chairs in the living room even had doilies perched on them. All she needed was about a dozen cats, and she would fit right into the original designers' plans.

She almost thought she heard Geoffrey laugh, but it wasn't a harsh noise. "I know it's not much . . . "

She turned back to see him give a shrug, clearly having run out of niceties. Agreeing with him, she sighed before quickly touring through the few rooms she was faced with. At least they were spacious, even if the mostly empty wooden floors gave the place a sort of abandoned, forlorn look. What the heck good all this room would do her she had no idea but supposed it would be better than being cramped. She hadn't had much experience with living on her own to know for sure.

There wasn't much to say to an introduction such as this. The phrase "beggars can't be choosers" was all too appropriate.

Trying to smile at him, she took the key, determined to resign herself to her new weirdness-free life. At least it would be better than her old one. Anything was better than that.

He made no comment, could certainly have no way of understanding her thoughts. "I'll leave you to settle in."

She wanted to say something but was at an utter, sudden loss.

"I'll see you in the office at nine tomorrow." Clearly, he felt he'd told her everything he needed to.

She wanted to make things easy for him, but there were too many questions unanswered. "Wait!"

As he turned back, she had to remind herself that he was her boss. Definitely *way* too good looking.

"The tenants and the residents — is there a difference?" Maybe it had something to do with how active or indigent the elderly residents were?

His head rose, eyes regarding her far more seriously. It felt like quite a while before he answered. "Our tenants are short-term. You'll be helping them come and go."

That seemed odd. Maybe they were only there till they found more permanent residence in Florida?

The silence lingering, his gaze grew deeper, as she waited for the rest. "The others are . . . different."

So many questions, so few answers.

"Different how?"

His eyes probed, the long silences leaving her strangely unsettled.

This one broke a moment later with his deep sigh. "Our residents never leave," he informed her, opening the door. "You're finally here."

Linda blinked. Those last words had been so soft she might have imagined them but was certain they'd been real. Her eyes widened. Given her life so far, she wasn't entirely certain she wanted to understand.

When the door shut, she felt the terror begin, his absence making her desperately uneasy. She ran through the apartment looking for the bathroom.

Once there, she stared intensely at her image in the mirror, her heart thudding heavily in her chest. "Everything is normal."

A small shadow flitted by, seen only out of the corner of her eye.

She dismissed it and repeated the mantra. "Everything is *normal*."

Just believe it, and it would be true. She would no longer be Lydia, would no longer live in a world where weird things reigned. Linda was going to be different.

Chapter Two

Despite all her best attempts to believe in a beautiful new, mundane world, it took Linda hours to settle down. She wasn't helped by the fact that she was still in her interview dress, too lost in the daze of her last few hours to think clearly. And it didn't make her feel any better when she finally remembered that she hadn't checked out of the hotel, all her luggage still there.

Strangely, that memory had only returned at about 2 a.m. The fact that it had been preceded by three hours when she'd tried to convince herself that she was *not* hearing strange noises coming from various areas of her new apartment had done absolutely nothing for her self-confidence.

Still, she'd done her best to live in ignorance, no matter how strange the night had become. That she'd forgotten about her comfortable hotel room and all her most basic necessities was the least of it.

All night long, she'd heard them — the sort of sounds she'd come to dread throughout her childhood, the ones no amount of denial would make disappear. Scratchings behind the walls, voices in the pantry, an assorted odd crash or two out of nowhere. She wanted so desperately to believe that they were all easily explainable — the result of rats, drafts, or unbalanced knick-knacks — but she knew the truth too well. Had she gone looking, she would've found no easy answers, nothing out of place. The long years of terror she'd suffered through already told her that. All she would've gotten for her troubles was an ever-increasing fear of the dark, as well as the lingering chill of the unknown growing once again in her soul.

It always took a lot for her not to reflect on her past, her current situation changing nothing. There were times recently when she'd nearly yearned for a head injury. "Amnesia" was the most blissful word she could imagine.

She'd done her best to get as close to this state as she could, had stayed alone in that bed, staring at the ceiling, willing all those damn noises away as heartily as she could, determined that the shadows around her would *not* force her to investigate. But when a final sound had come from her bedroom closet — a small crash, followed by a muffled, "Oops, sorry" — she'd given up on even pretending to try to sleep.

Even without the noises, it wouldn't have been a particularly restful night — the day before leaving far too many questions. The way she had gotten this job was the least of it, but that alone was just too weird, defied every bit of anecdotal evidence she'd ever heard. While having a hot boss might go along with a Hollywood interpretation of life, it didn't match most people's experiences — but that wasn't the real question. Why she'd been given a job she barely understood — one she was utterly unqualified for — with no real interview, was the true mystery for her now.

All of these worries finally forced her onto one of the grandma chairs in the living room, left her staring at the wall. She'd tried to watch some television, desperate for even the illusion of real company. Still, at this hour, the news, reruns of bad '70s sitcoms, and infomercials with various, rather aged, plastic surgery-or-Botox-victimized actresses hawking supposed beauty treatments had been all that was on. It was hard to say which was the creepiest option.

Although she hadn't liked the silence, she was dealing with it — or, she was now that she'd finally found a way to gain it fully. Even once she'd gotten up, the unexplained sounds had continued, reoccurring whenever she was just about to relax.

It was only once she had given up and announced, "Okay, I get the point! This place is creepy. My life is Hell, and denial is getting me nowhere. Now. Shut. *Up!*" that she gained her peace, the latest round of scratching ceasing in mid-slide.

There had only been one more muffled, "Sorry," from her closet, before she was finally allowed to think.

The silence helped her somewhat, the distracted state that her interview had left her in finally dissipating. Once it did, she realized when her deeper confusion had begun. True, she'd been nervous from the start, her general anxiety not aided by the fact that her hormones had been put on high alert by the mere presence of her boss. That hadn't been her sanity's real downfall, however. That had come with the entrance of Damian. Nothing she'd thought had been entirely clear after that.

This had probably been at least part of the man's intentions, although why he'd wanted to disturb her was a perplexing question. None of her theories seemed to settle it. Clearly, he and Geoffrey had some sort of rivalry going, which she supposed might explain it. Maybe, too, the man just liked to see women fall apart around him.

Heck, maybe I did.

He was gorgeous enough, like some sort of male model just waiting for the next catwalk.

But no — that wasn't really the reason. While her entire body had been screaming, "Yes!" at the first sight of her boss, Damian only left her cold — chilled, to be exact. It wasn't just his last statement about her past, although that was disturbing enough. No, it was something in his manner, his eyes. While he certainly seemed to want to inspire lust in everyone he met, the only message she'd gotten from him was very different, her soul screaming from that first instant. All she could read his invitations as were, "Abandon all hope, all ye who enter here." Clearly, he was a man entirely lacking in mercy.

Compassion was the quality Linda needed the most nowadays — one she'd never really found. Bad boys certainly couldn't attract her. Even her one, brief fling had seemed so caring, although she was convinced he'd wanted her more as a spiritual experiment than anything else. That he'd finally chosen the church had only been a blessing. He had been far too weak a man to ever be capable of supporting her for long.

Not really wanting the lingering reminders, she shook her head. Besides, there was way too much happening to allow herself to get distracted by history.

She rubbed her eyes, trying to focus, but it was hard to stay encouraged. What facts she could put together about her new job only chilled her more.

She'd gotten hired much too easily, for one thing, especially given her lack of skills and experience. In some ways, it almost seemed like this job had been waiting for her, the interview perfunctory, at best.

This apartment seemed to have been set aside for her, too, Geoffrey even hinting that he knew far more about her than was possible in any normal way.

It wasn't like he'd called her references, either. She had none. No work experience, no family, no friends — blanks as big as a desert on her application.

Sighing, she massaged her temple with the heel of her hand. And yet, Geoffrey hadn't seemed surprised by her arrival — kindly amused, yes, but not questioning. It was as if the whole experience had been predestined. A shiver went down to her bones. That definitely wasn't good. Because the last time destiny had been involved . . .

No. She wasn't going there — ever again, if she could help it.

Drawing her legs up toward her body, she buried her face in her knees. Maybe life was stupid and weird. Maybe she'd just have to accept how cursed she would always be. But there were some facts she refused to ever think about again.

Even knowing that there was a lovely, safe room waiting for her in the hotel didn't get her to budge.

It was fear, of course. It always was. The night was too bleak and too unknown to venture out into, and the retirement community had an unpleasant feeling after dark. While there was a decently lit parking lot clearly visible outside her windows, it wasn't inviting. The whole place seemed to pull down its shades to hide.

Maybe it was just the way of older people who were afraid of Atlanta's generous crime rate, but it felt different here, was more the silence of some mythic Western town, as they waited for the gunfighters to stop shooting everything and finish passing through. Heading back into it, even to get to her car, was too big a test of courage for her to endure.

Exhaustion won out over the terror eventually, although even sleep didn't help. She was still sitting in that apartment in her dream — just where she really was. She hated that — was wishing for some, *any*, other image. Even being on a ship boarded by pirates, or trapped in a dungeon, would have been more encouraging. This way, she didn't feel like she had any escape at all.

All her life, she'd had far too many dreams like this, ones that gave her no way out. Apparently, her subconscious's motto was "Screw symbolism." It would have been nice to be able to change.

But no. There she was, curled up in a little ball on the grandmotherly chair, while all around her lounged some of those characters she'd seen in her dreams since she was a child. Fortunately, these were the better ones, but she wasn't entirely happy to see them, anyway.

They were all arguing, but that was typical. As always, the little old lady was leading the offense.

"Here? You let her come *here*, of all places? With a whole *world* out there, you should choose to meet her in the apartment complex from Hell?" Her gesticulations and noise of disgust took up the few seconds she wasn't talking. "Angels!" she cried in exasperation. "Phooey!"

"Look, it's not *my* fault," the teenage girl near her feet sulked. She always sulked. It didn't make it any better that she also looked a lot like an only slightly younger Linda. "*I* was overruled."

A tiger-striped cat rubbed its face on one of the chairs. It too seemed to be part of the fray. "Nice furniture." Its whiskers were nearly embedded in the cushion, as it stroked itself against the fabric incessantly. "Good smell."

Another cat, a midnight black Persian, turned away in disgust to go preen itself in a corner.

The comment only seemed to get the old lady started again. "Feh— smells! Don't get me started." She looked around at the room, sniffing in disdain. "Who decorated this place, a committee for the blind?"

Most of the usual oddities Linda was used to from these dreams were there, then — the friendlier ones, at least. One of the final regulars answered them all soothingly.

As always, the voice came from behind her, his face obscured. "It's not as bad as it looks. This place has its possibilities."

The old lady seemed to be sizing him up for a straitjacket. Linda felt him leaning on the back of her chair, felt it cradle backwards slightly. She hadn't taken in that it rocked before.

"Besides, I can look after her . . . finally."

Somehow, his assurances brought the others' complaints to an end, the dream now almost over.

As she was starting to wake, she felt the man's hand stroke softly over her temple, calming her to her soul. The words, "At last," seemed nearly audible. Then she opened her eyes.

The sun was coming up, but that wasn't what drew her attention. No, it was the sound of small, quickly pattering feet. She sighed. How nice it would have been to believe that it was merely rats.

This possibility dismissed — the dream too odd to focus on — she merely followed the sound of the steps. They'd seemed to be coming from her front door before scurrying through the apartment.

Giving up on skepticism, she followed long and unpleasantly honed instinct by going over to open the door. When she did, she found her bag from the hotel in front of it, the bill on top, paid in full.

Sighing, she brought it all inside with her. Evidently, even her dreams agreed. She was stuck here, so she might as well get used to it.

She did her best, neither entirely accepting the stranger aspects of her situation nor dismissing them completely. Instead, she pulled out whatever clothing was on top and dressed — a bit less conservatively, this time. Geoffrey hadn't said anything about a dress code, so it was difficult to know for sure. Maybe it was really seeing Damian that had made her give up on primness. That man dressed to the nines, ready for his time in the runway spotlight. She liked her own boss's approach better. Dressing down might well be the way to go.

She didn't heed the instinct completely, but she did give up on her more Stepford wife attempts. Although she could wear a skirt and not be too formal looking, her hair didn't make it particularly easy to achieve professionalism, even at her best. It was too short to do much with. Any attempt at a ponytail looked lunatic. All there was to do was brush. She could only hope her indigo locks grew out so it looked like something other than a tween pseudo-rocker's version of a 1920s flapper eventually.

Of course, there was no benefit in worrying about this now, too much else left to occupy her. Even if she didn't want to think about her dream — and she never did — she would have been preoccupied enough with the fact that this was her first day at work, at a job she knew next to nothing about.

Wandering into the kitchen, she was relieved that the apartment looked at least a little better in the daylight. Much as she would've loved to believe that everything from the night before had been her overactive imagination, she couldn't. After all, the sounds had only stopped once she'd acknowledged them. She almost laughed. Maybe there was some sort of message about her weird life there, after all.

She wasn't really surprised to find that there was already food in the kitchen. Her unflappable side reigned briefly, beating down her urge for mundaneness at all costs. It might not be much, but it was enough for a simple breakfast.

As it was, her major hurdle turned out to be the stove. She'd never cooked with gas before — even the appliances looking like they were leftovers from the '40s or '50s. Harvest gold would have seemed trendy in comparison.

She somehow managed not to set herself on fire, as she made some bacon and eggs. That small triumph accomplished, she eventually headed out to work. She even remembered to turn off the gas.

Finding herself in a much cheerier mood, she trotted down the steps toward the front of her apartment building, heading for the parking lot. Maybe it was finally getting a little sleep. Maybe it was just somewhat admitting that life was not anywhere near as normal as she would have liked. Of course, for Linda, even Norman Rockwell looked outré. Lydia was the one who'd learned to deal with life at its weirdest

It wasn't Lydia who arrived at the office half an hour early but a newer version of Linda did, happy to see that her boss was there before her. She hadn't stopped to think what would happen if she couldn't get in, or, even worse, if she'd run into Damian. While that man would clearly be a daily presence, she wasn't ready to ponder the fact. There was far too much else she had to contend with now.

She had primed herself to accept whatever the day tossed at her, far more so than last night. When he looked up to greet her, Geoffrey appeared every bit as casual, and as handsome, as he had the day before. He seemed pleased, and she assumed it had something to do with the fact that her own smile wasn't quite such an effort in peroxide toothpaste marketing. When his gaze traveled along her briefly, she felt an enticing sort of shiver, not the kind she'd had the pleasure of getting used to previously. His glance only took a second, his eyes meeting hers again, his smile deepening.

"It matches your hair." Fortunately, his humor was well outweighed by his warmth.

"Oh," she murmured, looking down. When she'd first acquired the indigo dress, it hadn't been a match. The particular hair color was too new for her to get used to. "Sorry." She shrugged, glancing back to him. "Would you like me to change?"

"No." As they caressed her face, his eyes had the sort of appreciative heat that could light fires. "I like it."

Wow.

It really shouldn't have been possible for her to be feeling any more foolishly giddy about him. Apparently, she'd underestimated his charm.

Whatever he was thinking, his look became less delightfully fiery a moment later. He pointed at the chair in front of his desk, and she was almost thankful. When she was seated, Geoffrey not focusing on her, as he sorted through various papers, he began. "How are you getting along with your apartment?"

Huh. That seemed an odd, all-too-knowing bit of phrasing.

She smiled, appreciating the irony. "I'll get used to it."

"Mm," he commented, finally sitting down.

To her surprise, the forms he'd been shuffling weren't for her. She'd been told that such things were typical for the first day, but, so far, she hadn't filled out anything but a fairly cursory application.

"Most of what you'll need to know, you'll discover by doing. To-day, I'm going to take you on a few home visits and introduce you to some of the residents you need to know."

This seemed a little odd, since he'd already said that the residents were his affair, but she had the sense not to comment.

"This morning, I'll need you to talk to some potential tenants. We have a vacancy that just came open." There was a bit of concern in his eyes. "You'll need to look after the applicants."

His tone worried her. Well, that and the fact that she had no idea whatsoever what she was doing.

She was trying to be professional but had no experience. "How do I do that?"

The sigh he let out said far more than he did. He pushed the papers toward her. "Just give them the paperwork on top of the packets there to fill out. Be friendly. If they ask more questions, go over the first page in the brochure with them."

Shrugging, he seemed to be trying to look reassuring, but his visible worry missed his mark. "Do your best to sound like you know what you're doing. If they catch on, tell them that it's your first day and refer them to me. That should handle most of the problems."

She supposed so. Really, she had no idea, and his uncertain expression wasn't convincing her any further.

She looked down at the "Application for Tenancy" in front of her. "I wish I knew a little more about—"

Geoffrey's hand covered the sheet, pulling it away. "I'll be going over their applications later. You don't have to bother with them."

She stared at him curiously. Why wouldn't he give her more information about the tenants?

He let out a sigh. "It wasn't my intention to . . ." The sound deepened. " . . . have you start out like this. Clarissa . . . "

Again, he trailed off, one finger tapping on the forms his palm hid. "... became unavailable." There was another silence, as she stared at him. "Sometimes, things don't go the way you've planned."

That last confession was nearly a whisper, and it worried her. The part of her mind that was desperate for dull routine tried to theorize; it was willfully forgetting the whole "might be dead" discussion. "Were you close to her?"

He stared.

"I mean, were you two ... ?"

Once more, she was answered by his kind laugh, whatever facts had lowered him into distraction gone. "Hardly."

He pushed the papers back toward her, but only after putting the application on top upside down. Thankfully, he wasn't angry. Even if the two had been together, it wouldn't have been any of her business.

"The names of the applicants are on the forms. Just give the papers out as they come in." He stood up. "If you get anyone whose name you don't have, send them to Damian and Gail. They won't be one of ours."

Apparently, all the applicants had made reservations. She shrugged, guessing that made sense.

As she rose with the various papers, she started to wonder. "Um, where do I ... ?"

"Ah." Getting up to lead her back out to the antechamber of his room, he took the stack she carried from her before placing it all on another desk.

She blinked, not certain how she'd passed by before without noticing. It even had a small nameplate with the name she'd chosen: *Linda Henderson*.

The personalization made her want to cry. It was so normal it could raise puppies by a white picket fence. The thought made her smile, as unlikely as that outcome was. There was also a lovely bouquet of flowers in indigo, white, and royal purple. When she leaned down to sniff them, even the smell of the pollen charmed her. She'd never before been welcomed anywhere, even in her own home.

It took a moment to draw herself away from the sight, her utter happiness clear. "Thank you." Although it wasn't enough, it was all she really had to give him.

To her surprise, Geoffrey didn't seem anywhere near as pleased. His sigh was tight, his face grim, glare focused on the blooms. When he finally noticed her, he shook his head, his words sounding more like a reminder to himself. "They're harmless."

When she just stared, he sighed more deeply, looking only a little calmer.

"They're from the community, not me." He pointed her around to her chair, about to leave. "Just don't eat them."

"Wasn't planning on it," she murmured, wondering what the heck she had stumbled into. More than anything, his glare had worried her, the anger he was only barely masking. Although it didn't seem aimed at her, for which she was thankful, still it bothered her. She almost wished she could pretend that none of it mattered.

She watched him start to go before he turned back to meet her eyes. He was a little calmer. Finally, he returned. When he touched her arm gently, it sent a delightful shiver straight down her spine, her brain suddenly wiped clean of any possible concerns. "Remember, I'm here if you need me." Then, he retreated into his office, leaving her wanting much, much more.

God, that one touch had been nice. She wasn't used to personal contact. In her past, if someone was touching her, something was terribly wrong.

As much as he attracted her, though, she couldn't deny his mysteries. There had been more than enough of them in just the first few minutes of her new job. Somehow, none were as important as another truth that his touch had brought to her mind. It wasn't entirely expected or explainable, but it was much too real to deny. The feeling of his hand against her was familiar — tenderly, achingly familiar, like finding a long-sought oasis only to realize that it had always been her home. No matter what she told herself, for at least this instant, she knew the truth. His was the touch — his was the voice — of that unseen man from her dreams.

Despite its sweetness, this was a difficult moment for her. The woman who was trying to redub herself Linda wouldn't wholly accept the fact, as much as some much-repressed part of her longed to. It was too much to ask of her belief. Already her world view had been pushed way too far, none of her current reality making any sense.

She started fighting the knowledge off, despite herself.

Demons, yes. Angels, maybe. Personal divine protectors from my dreams coming to look after me in the real world — definitely not.

Her gaze sought the door to his office. But that didn't mean she felt any less comforted just knowing he was near.

Despite this strange revelation, the day did go on relatively quietly. Such peace was made all the easier by Linda's decision to ignore any potential new knowledge. There was only so much oddity she was willing to accept anymore.

Her usual, self-constricted limits would certainly be challenged in her new job. As the afternoon approached, she discovered that fact ever more. By then, she'd seen at least a dozen different applicants. Many of them had done her wish for a typical life no good at all.

As she watched the current arrival filling out the voluminous forms, she was trying very hard not to think about them, willing her mind to roam. She'd been happy that some, at least, had been soothingly normal, even if none had been the type of retirees she'd imagined.

In fact, none of them had even been very old. Their hair and dress had all been in some average, current style, their manners either brusque or friendly. But they'd been the sort of people you expected to meet in the course of a usual day in a large Southern city. While they'd seemed surprised to discover their names already on their applications, Linda's inability to answer their questions had finally made them shrug the curiosity away.

Watching them, she'd had to sigh, understanding what they were doing. She couldn't help but envy. It must be so much easier when the weird things in life would just disappear if you looked the other way.

Sadly, that had never been her own experience, as much as she might be trying to believe. The current applicant did nothing to aid her desires, either.

She'd already thought that she'd seen it all — the visitors who'd quickly stopped questioning notwithstanding. No, the weird arrivals had been the ones who'd seen nothing strange in any of the forms' requests. Even if she hadn't yet gotten an opportunity to look the papers over in full — either Geoffrey or another applicant always appearing as soon as she considered doing so — the reactions of the odder possible tenants told her quite a bit. If only she'd been lucky enough to stay ignorant.

She started to think back on these people, as she watched the current one filling in his form. He was probably the weirdest of the visitors she'd seen, but there had been quite a few other contenders.

To say he was hirsute would have been a masterpiece of understatement. Long, coarse, brown hair stuck out from under the cuffs of his oxford shirt. The nest of chest hair that was visible around his collar nearly screamed to have a '70s gold medallion hanging on it. His beard and mustache also seemed to be quickly getting out of control. Every time she looked up, she almost thought they were making ever-increasing forays across his face. The hair on his head was long and shaggy. She sighed, trying not to even think about his overgrown fingernails.

When he turned to a new page in his handful of forms, she caught a glimpse of drawings of the moon in its various stages. He seemed to have circled the last quarter. It was then that she decided to take a little break.

Standing, she managed a smile. "Would you like some water?" Even if it were just an excuse to get some temporary distance, there was no reason to be rude.

The man — Butch, she remembered his name was — looked up for a minute, as he considered. "Ye—" he started, smiling at her, showing a mouthful of disturbingly sharp teeth.

She saw Geoffrey, arms crossed, standing in the doorway of his office, watching the applicant carefully.

Butch let out a small, disconsolate whimper. "No," he whined. Then, he went back to the forms.

It wasn't the first time that day her boss had seemingly stepped in. While he hadn't actually ever entered her office, except to escort the more normal patrons out to show them the available apartment — the weirder ones hadn't seemed to care what it might look like — she had felt his presence constantly, nonetheless. Mostly, it was a comfort. But she wasn't at all certain what it was that caused his occasional glower.

She saw him give one more look back at their current applicant before following her out to the water cooler. She'd been pondering the coffeepot, but decided she didn't need any more help staying awake at night. She almost expected his inquiry, his tone soft.

"Are you all right?"

"All right?" Her high pitch made him raise an eyebrow. She supposed she'd been holding the reaction in longer than she'd realized. "All right!"

He took her by the arm, leading her farther into the building. When she noticed that he'd successfully pulled her away from Damian's office door, where the "head demon" and his assistant were listening avidly, she calmed just slightly. It didn't make the lingering hysteria disappear, though.

"I've seen every applicant from the local freak show in here to-day."

She did manage to keep her voice quieter but felt a little guilty for the term as soon as she used it — having been called at least as bad herself many times — but she couldn't stop, desperate for some benign, boring explanation.

Moved much closer to her boss, her despair grew. "Just what on earth is going on?"

His sigh was eloquent, his hand rubbing briefly over his face. Finally, he took her by the arm, pulling her gently behind him.

Is he going to fire me?

She couldn't have entirely blamed him, had he decided to. She'd missed "professional" by a few thousand miles.

Geoffrey didn't acknowledge Damian or his assistant, who still stared, instead leading Linda into her office and past her latest applicant. He didn't look at Butch, either.

"Mr. Barker . . . "

She heard the newcomer sigh, possibly at his own name, before Geoffrey went on.

No wonder, poor man. Some parents had a lot of nerve.

"When you're finished with those forms, push them under my door."

The applicant nodded, glancing at the two of them before returning to his work. "Denial's comforting, but it's never the answer." His whisper seemed almost a reminder to himself.

Despite her boss's attempts to guide her, she paused and stared at the newcomer.

The man gazed at her with eyes that seemed nearly yellow but also full of knowledge. "Denial only gets you killed."

Fortunately, Geoffrey shut his office door behind them, cutting off her view of the man, making her shiver at his all-too-relevant words. Still, it was only at that moment when she fully realized that she was alone with her boss, her heart rate tripling. She wasn't certain whether it was the lingering adrenaline from the day or his simple proximity — not aided at all by her earlier revelation about him. Much of the feeling, at least, was caused by the latter.

"What do you think this place is, Lydia?" Geoffrey was far closer than he had ever been before, his breath soft on her face.

She opened her mouth to object to the name, but he just shook his head. He didn't seem angry so much as frustrated. "How do you think *you* found it?"

Although his presence was enough to put her on full alert, the use of her real name made the fear she'd barely been repressing start to bubble through her. She tried to fight the feeling, to ignore his words, even though she couldn't deny the thrill of hearing him say that name she was trying not to return to.

But that slight happiness meant nothing now. She didn't want to have this conversation, wasn't ready for it. Denial, that was the way to go, despite the applicant's well-timed warning.

"I found it on the internet." She shrugged, trying to feel brave. "There were probably dozens of other candidates who found it the same way."

To her dismay, he shook his head, moving even closer. Her panicked brain suddenly started quoting Groucho Marx, *"If I were any closer, I'd be behind you."* Her childhood tendency to watch classic movie channels when she was ignoring her fears was catching up to her. If he weren't so unbelievably hot, if she didn't have all the feelings about him that she did, she would've suggested that he take a class on recognizing sexual harassment. It wasn't that the move felt creepy, really. It was more that he just didn't seem to understand the human concept of personal space.

His look was intense, as he answered her suggestion. "There was only one." His gaze seemed to go even deeper. "There's only ever one."

Lord. A deep chill took her over at this point, her terror of all those facts she was repressing starting to come out. Only his proximity gave a little bit of warmth.

"I don't understand." She saw him starting to speak, turned away quickly. "No — don't!" Her hands rubbed at her arms, the chill rising, as she heard his voice trying to begin again, interrupting him. "Don't you get it? I don't *want* to understand."

"Lydia . . . "

The sound was warm, pleading, was the same one she had heard comforting her in her dreams — as well as in the grimmest hours of her waking. She closed her eyes, even as the tone soothed her, caressing away the fear. It didn't have that same effect when he called her "Linda." What a shame normal people couldn't experience that sort of comfort.

They were only silent for half a second before there was a knock on the door. Butch sounded sheepish, as he opened it, setting the forms down on the floor. "Sorry to interrupt."

She heard a whimper and finally glanced at him, saw that he was looking at Geoffrey with the eyes of a scolded puppy.

"It's just that I don't have a number to leave you right now."

"I'll get to you on h-mail."

Linda looked back to her boss, surprised at what she saw, as the newcomer nodded apologetically, backing out, closing the door. Geoffrey's whole aura was shining with a majestic kind of control, telling anyone extraneous to back far away. She was very glad to know that she wasn't one of the people he wanted to distance.

Attempting to take some comfort from this idea, she tried to turn their confrontation around, wishing for the ability to sound flippant again, however unprofessional she was being. "What the hell's h-mail?"

The look he gave her took away her breath, its intensity far surpassing anything else she'd seen. "Don't use that word."

She assumed that he didn't mean "h-mail," whatever that might be.

By this point, she was clinging to flippancy by her fingernails. "Why not?"

His intensity was unnerving her. "It's a word for fools. Only those who don't understand that place use it."

Worriedly, she bit her bottom lip, turning away from him. "I understand it," she murmured.

There was silence, but only for a moment. "I know," he whispered.

She shuddered at its warmth. But she didn't know where to begin to look for sanity after that.

True, Linda had already decided to try to accept a little — *just* a little — of the weirdness in her world; it had been the only approach she could find to get through the night. But the daylight made her want to dream, to believe in a nice, safe, *rational* reality. Despite her experience, it would've been so easy.

Maybe Butch was just hairy. Maybe that guy earlier hadn't had jagged surgical scars around his neck and both wrists, as well as a slightly grayish color to his skin. Maybe she'd just imagined being able to see through that woman in white. Who knew? Maybe she was just crazy.

Her sigh went deep, her eyes closing. Her life would've been so much easier if that were true.

She could feel Geoffrey as he approached again. Now that she thought about it, she could always tell where he was, could feel his presence, if she tried even a little. As his hand caressed her shoulder, her sigh lingered. The comfort of that touch alone cancelled out nearly all desire for logic.

"Don't block the truth, Lydia."

Clearly, he had no intention of working with her rebranding efforts, and she couldn't decide whether that upset her or not, especially as his warning went on.

"It's not healthy. If the door in your mind is closed too tightly, reality will eventually rip it right off its hinges."

He turned her around, gazing at her gently.

"You can't fight super-reality with a pocketful of illusions."

"Super-reality." Now there was a concept. She almost understood but didn't really want to.

Because she had no way to fight, she nodded. While she hoped that normality would come to her someday, she did her best to just move on. Maybe somewhere in the future, she'd find a way to rid herself of this pain.

Chapter Three

Her talk with Geoffrey, such as it was, had left Linda with at least a million more questions than she ever truly wanted answers for. For one thing, she wondered far more fully now just what had happened to Clarissa, the previous assistant. If the woman were dead and there was "only ever one" applicant to replace her . . . well, that didn't leave the new assistant feeling very confident at all.

The first of the questions that followed this unsettling thought rang through her mind: Why had she been chosen? She was very afraid of where any answers would lead.

She was probably lucky that she wasn't given much time to ponder it. Pointing her toward a seat, Geoffrey seemed to have given up on conversation. Instead, he focused on the applications she'd gathered.

Especially given how little she wanted to think into any of it, her mind was easily tempted away from her worries by watching how quickly he sorted through the pile. She recognized all the names of the more normal candidates on the folders that were abandoned immediately in an Out box, apparently utterly dismissed.

"We won't need them," he answered, without her asking.

She wondered whether he were angry with her, tried to make an effort of her own. She hadn't made a particularly brilliant start to her first job, thus far. "Why not?"

He only glanced at her briefly before returning to his sorting. "No one normal wants to live here."

As much as she was coming to reluctantly accept such a truth, it wasn't encouraging, especially given her own constant aspirations.

She returned to watching him in silence, but nothing became any clearer. Of those applications remaining, he fanned them out in front of him and stared at them intently. What he was looking for, she had no clue, especially since he never read over any of them.

There was nothing obvious to distinguish them, at least that she could see.

Whatever his arcane process, he finally picked up that of the last man she'd interviewed before flipping through it quickly, nodding. A moment later, he was on the phone, tapping in a series of numbers before making a very brief call.

The only part Linda could make out went something like, "Yes. Yes. Butch Barker." Her eyes widened when a moment of howling laughter became clearly audible, even to her, although Geoffrey sat through it quietly before continuing. "No phone. H-mail." There was a longer pause this time. "Yes, she's here. I will." Then, the conversation ended.

Witnessing such an interaction certainly only made her more curious, but she wasn't given the chance to ask. Only a moment after the call was over, Gail, Damian's assistant, knocked on the office door.

The girl looked to be somewhere around her own age, maybe a year older. She had bouncy blonde hair, cornflower blue eyes, and the sweetest smile anyone could ever hope to conjure. She seemed ready to enter a Miss Perky competition at any moment — and win.

"I brought some lunch!" she announced, holding up a covered casserole dish. It was such a perfect, Southern "welcoming the new arrivals" move that Linda couldn't do much but sit and blink in awe.

It wasn't given the expected Southern response. Without any answer more than a very terse, "No," Geoffrey pulled Linda out of the office behind him, packed her into the same golf cart as yesterday, and drove her briskly off toward the more distant portions of the community to accompany him on his visits.

She didn't understand the reaction. Even if he had been scornful, there should have been a at least a good "Well, bless your heart!" to answer her — the ultimate Southern euphemism for "What an idiot!" She had no idea of know what to expect from these visits he had mentioned, either. Still, if the day continued along on anything like the same path it had begun, she wasn't likely to end it any more happily than the last.

This possibility did nothing to encourage her, but there was little she could do but follow along. Geoffrey had been almost utterly silent ever since their earlier, aborted conversation. She got the feeling that he wasn't entirely happy with her, which, she supposed, wasn't really a surprise. As an assistant, she wasn't proving at all helpful. Gail, from what little she had observed, seemed to be *much* more involved in her own boss's work. A shudder caught her. Despite her uselessness, she was still enormously glad not to be working for Damian.

This fact brought out another question, the situation not hard to observe. All day long, her boss had appeared instantly to lead her away, every time Gail got too close. When Damian's assistant had introduced herself that morning, Geoffrey had been there, glowering threateningly. When the woman had tried to have a pleasant chat with her between applicants, he had emerged from his office to remind the woman that she was "outside her territory." When Linda had been about to show an applicant who wasn't on her files over toward their office, Geoffrey had quickly taken up the work, not even allowing her to follow his earlier orders on what to do with the misplaced. Now that the woman had tried to offer her lunch . . .

Linda sighed, exasperated. "Why did you pull me away like that?"

His look unreadable but his body language uncomfortable, he glanced over. "She's Damian's assistant. Don't get too close."

Well, that told her very little. She forgot about her own initial reaction to the West Coordinator for a moment, miffed at her boss's dictatorial mood. She'd been prejudged too often not to feel some sympathy — even if she herself hadn't been terribly open to newcomers earlier today. "Just because she works for him?"

He focused on her from the corner of his eye.

"She seems nice."

The pronouncement clearly set him off. Pulling the cart over to the side of the road, Geoffrey cut it off, before turning toward her. His gaze, once again, was very deep. "You like her?"

The question took her off-guard, made her realize that she'd never thought about it. She didn't like the answer, once she did.

Her eyes wandered, not able to keep contact with his intense look. "Not really," she admitted, but she had no real reason not to. It was only a feeling, and she hated not giving anyone the benefit of the doubt. She was still ashamed of her earlier reactions today.

Still, while Gail was more than chipper, seemed to care, there was something behind her smile that gave Linda pause. Pondering it more thoroughly, she almost felt like there was something lingering behind the woman's eyes that was anything but inviting. It watched every reaction, evaluated much too carefully. It was far more than simple interest, was much more calculating. Now that she analyzed it, she realized that it reminded her more of Damian's usual look — a predator waiting for prey. A small shiver caught her, despite the relative warmth of early autumn in Georgia. Maybe the woman was a bit too well suited to her boss.

She didn't really notice until she looked up, but Geoffrey had been watching all of these musings cross her face. Finally, he nodded, turning back to start the cart once more. "Trust your instincts," he reminded her, driving them away.

She supposed he was right. They were nearly all that had saved her before.

This last, disquieting memory accompanied her on to wherever they were headed. Geoffrey parked in front of one of the many units the complex held. It was one of the old, painted brick variety in one of those shades only retirement communities and military bases could get away with.

"We're going to Glory first." Despite his smile, the phrasing disturbed her, since it was how Southerners traditionally referred to dying. "Don't be afraid."

It wasn't an encouraging introduction.

Still, they went into a building marked with a large 1 on its exterior, Linda following him up the carpeted stairs to apartment 111. Before he had a chance to knock, the door opened and a large, powerful-looking woman in a gray taffeta dress glared at him. "You're late."

She proceeded to swat him on the head with a plastic spatula, while he smiled at her adoringly. Linda trembled a bit, hoping the implement wasn't going to be aimed at her, too.

Glory, as she was apparently called, let out a small, "Hmph," before turning back inside. "Get the girl in here before lunch gets cold."

Geoffrey followed his orders, ushering the now-even-more timid Linda inside.

To her surprise, despite its apparently identical layout, this apartment was nothing like her own. It was carpeted, for one thing, not just an occasional rug thrown around. It was extremely lived in as well, with bookshelves that were nearly groaning from the weight of apparently decades' worth of collecting. Everything there was designed for comfort. Linda let out a sigh. If only her own place felt like this, she would be far happier going home.

It was only the soft touch of her boss's hand on her back that got her to move. Glory looked them both over with another small, "Hmph," before nodding them toward the table.

Once they were seated, Linda found her hand enveloped in two others — both large, one soft and pink, the other calloused and brown. Surprisingly, it was Geoffrey's hand that showed no signs of physical labor. She glanced at the man before Glory's stare reminded her to lower her head.

"Geoffrey," she prodded.

"You'll do it better," he answered quietly.

Another, "Hmph," was followed by, "Lord, we're on your side. Now, you be on ours when we need you. Amen." She looked at her guests, her manner that of a grandmotherly general. "Now, eat."

Linda knew an instruction, when she heard one. Besides, since Geoffrey had derailed her only earlier hope of food, she was more than a little hungry.

She was even beginning to wonder if their current destination weren't the real answer to why her boss had prevented her from having any of the assistant's proffered food, when he said, "Gail tried to feed her today."

This won her the intense scrutiny of their host's fathomless black eyes. "Bad business," she murmured before returning to her meal. "You stay away from her, Lydia."

She gave a small sigh. "It's Linda, actua—"

The, "Hmph," prevented her from finishing. "Names are important. I'm Glory. He's Geoffrey. You're Lydia."

Linda was about to open her mouth but was prevented by Glory continuing.

"And don't you forget it."

What did she say to that, especially when it was delivered by a mountain of confidence like this woman? "Um, okay?"

She got the expected, "Hmph," in response. But then the meal became far stranger yet.

There were many challenges to Linda's deep-seated denial that day. Most of them she could find some way to dismiss. She could believe that her boss had simply told the woman that they would be there, that this meal was prepared as a sort of welcome to her. She could believe that she'd just been nervous last night, had imagined all her fears into reality. And she could even make herself think that every potential tenant she'd seen today was entirely normal — if she really, really tried.

What she couldn't explain was the conversation her companions were having. It was in some other language. And it was almost one she understood.

That was an especially unexpected fact. Linda had never been particularly adept at languages. Still, aside from the odd word or two she might recognize — her real name, for instance — there was something about the sounds that seemed so familiar to her. If she let her consciousness drift just slightly, she could almost make out what they were talking about. But every time she made the effort, it slipped away, just out of her reach.

As it was, she was left not quite understanding anything that was said between the pair. All she fully recognized were the words Glory would occasionally direct toward her in English, apparently building off of what she and Geoffrey were discussing. Among these disconnected pronouncements were,

"Appreciate that you're here. You could be somewhere else."

And, "Why would you like Gail?"

And, "What do you think Geoffrey is, a sack of potatoes?"

That last one made her boss blush. But none of the non-sequiturs helped her understand her new life any better at all.

For as long as the meal went on, she wasn't left with any real clues as to how to approach the future, as much as Glory seemed to think she was providing them. Still, when she was told, "Definitely don't eat those flowers," she gave up on silence. There was far too much going on that she just didn't understand.

This last fact ignored that she didn't really *want* to understand most of it, but she'd finally run out of patience, was nearly wailing. "Why does everyone think that I'm going to eat the flowers?"

Glory's sudden, full attention was quite disconcerting. The older woman broke away from her conversation with the coordinator and turned toward Linda, leaning in to look into her eyes. For at least a minute, Linda was caught in their depths, was beginning to feel lightheaded in her disconnection from her surroundings. It was only once the woman pulled away that she could try to blink her way back to sense.

Glory was smiling at her, thankfully. Linda didn't want to know what a real frown from her would be like.

"She'll be fine," the large woman nodded to Geoffrey before rising with their plates.

When he responded with a soft, "I know," Glory smiled.

Linda was left alone with her boss for a minute, while their host disappeared into the kitchen. To her surprise, she noticed four cats staring at her interestedly from the kitchen doorway, all their tails swaying in unison. From farther inside, she could hear another meowing piteously, while Glory told it, "Don't complain, Lucius. There's no point. I know you like that form." If only that were the oddest thing she'd heard that day, she might have been far more contented.

Despite her multiple discomforts, it was difficult to feel very out of place in the woman's apartment. Something about it was very welcoming. To Linda's surprise, the feeling was deepened, when Geoffrey took her hand tenderly.

"Don't worry," he smiled. "It will be all right."

Even though she barely knew what he was talking about, she smiled. She squeezed his hand, a warmth and a truth settling inside her. For the first time, she had a place where she was wanted. That alone would let her see the light.

She felt this newfound confidence doing its work, somewhat centering her scattered thoughts. Geoffrey's touch had that effect, taking away the slight edge of despair and terror that always seemed to stalk her. Maybe that was why he *did* touch her so much; maybe, he understood. There was a sigh, as he drew his hand from hers once more, rising to speak to Glory. Or maybe he just knew that no woman would ever argue about such a tactile approach from a guy as gorgeous as he was.

This latter theory was a little harsh on Geoffrey and was one Linda had to admit he'd done nothing to deserve. True, he touched her more than she'd ever been led to believe was normal in a modern workplace, but he wasn't sleazy about it. Now, Damian — there was a man she could easily imagine feeling up the butt of any woman he chose and expecting her to thank him for it. Geoffrey was definitely different.

Of course, all of these musings ignored her earlier revelation, but she wasn't ready to face that — might never be. Her dreams might always follow one or the other set of the same odd patterns, but there was no reason to think that any of the characters who appeared in them would suddenly make their way into her everyday life.

Such a belief completely ignored the fact that the bad things in her dreams had already attacked her once, but she clung to the denial, nonetheless. Whatever happened now, she was *not* going to think about her childhood.

She could hear Geoffrey saying their farewells to Glory in the kitchen, allowing Linda a little time to think, although not about her past. He turned down the apple pie the woman seemed determined to ply them with, over her decidedly tart objections. The distance was useful now, Geoffrey's mere presence tending to scramble her brains. Not, sadly, that they needed much help.

She listened to him sighing as he was forced to accept to-go boxes from their host, but she thought she could also hear a decided fondness in his tones. It almost made her wonder what the connection between the two of them was. They seemed to understand one another much better than a simple resident and landlord.

She felt a little prickle of jealousy, before she told it to go away. She had no right to the man, was certain that he would turn out to be married with a half dozen kids, his wife and children every bit as shining and beautiful as he was. What he could ever see in an 18-year-old with enough emotional baggage to pack for an around-the-world journey and all the social skills of the desperately awkward and painfully neglected teenager that she always had been was a mystery nothing beyond the most stunning fantasy could begin to ignore.

She was just allowing these unfulfillable fantasies to roam, despite every truth she reminded herself of, when she felt something scratch her ankle. When she looked down, she noticed that the four cats who had been watching her earlier had moved even closer, their tails twitching in unison. A small, deep gray one — the one, she supposed, that had scratched her — seemed decidedly aggrieved. The tortoiseshell beside it was now standing on the gray one's paw.

"Stop that," it said.

Linda blinked. Surely, she couldn't really have heard that. Maybe she was hallucinating. That had to be it.

Still, the gray cat continued to glare at her.

"Don't like her. She takes Geoffrey away."

"Geoffrey was never *ours*," the tortoiseshell replied reasonably, swatting the gray cat's paw when it tried to raise it once more.

Linda was certain she was going to slide off her chair.

The gray cat continued to glare before finally turning its back, its tail now out of unison with the others. "Like Geoffrey's smell. Don't like hers."

"Geoffrey smells like all the others," a black Persian put in dismissively. "I don't see why you're so keen on him, anyway."

The gray cat appeared to be sulking in response.

"I like her," the tortoiseshell said, rubbing its face against Linda's knee.

Even though she was convinced that she'd finally lost whatever might pass for her mind, the move managed to cheer her up. Too bad she had apparently gone insane.

"Yes, you would." The Persian sighed, seeming entirely uninterested. Still, it was sitting on her foot.

A Siamese nearby was watching all their interactions intently. It looked as though it thought this was all being put on for its amusement, in that way that only cats can convey.

It was at this point that Linda covered her face, trying to remind herself to breathe.

Okay, maybe Glory is an old hippie. Maybe I'm tripping from something in the food.

Four synchronized hisses brought her back to herself. She looked at them timidly. "Sorry, I just thought . . . "

She caught herself. Was she seriously trying to have a conversation with cats?

It wasn't that she didn't like animals. It was just that she found it a little unnerving to be have them respond.

Fortunately, she was interrupted in her near-hysteria, when her boss and Glory returned to the room. The look on her face must have told them her mental state pretty clearly, but their host seemed unconcerned.

"Oh, you've met."

Linda nodded dazedly, as Glory pointed to the Siamese, Persian, tortoiseshell, and gray cat in turn. "That's Pasha, Eveningstar, Tiger, and Runt-Runt."

The gray one seemed to be sulking even more intensely. Linda assumed it was the name. She wasn't sure she could blame it.

A black and gray tabby was following on Glory's heels. "That one's Lucius, but he's way too much of a bother for anyone decent to worry about. You'll get used to the rest."

Linda doubted that. Besides, she didn't want to ask. Really, she didn't. A conversation among cats just wasn't supposed to happen during waking hours.

"Um, do they . . . ?" she started but had no idea what to say next. *"I just heard your cats talking about how they hate me"* didn't seem like a statement to be made anywhere outside of an asylum.

Glory didn't seem to notice her distress—or, if she did, she'd apparently decided that Linda would get over it.

She was looking back to Geoffrey, who, aside from a few of the cats, seemed to be the only one gazing at Linda sympathetically. "I'll have Eveningstar and Tiger over there tonight. They're good at that sort of thing." Where — and what sort of thing — Glory didn't seem to feel it necessary to specify.

Geoffrey smiled at Linda as though nothing were amiss. "They're good company. You'll get used to them. I promise."

Linda's eyes widened. "Do you mean that I'm going to be—?"

The Persian interrupted with a sigh, its tail swishing elegantly. "You should be grateful," it huffed. "You can at least bring me doughnuts."

"Don't eat tuna," the tortoiseshell added. "Don't like smell."

"Um, sure," Linda murmured worriedly. "I guess I need to go shopping."

She glanced back up to her more human companions, as both the cats answered, "Yes." Sadly, no one seemed to think she was nuts. She sighed profoundly. *Oh well.*

To her relief, she was somewhat rescued by Geoffrey. He took her arm, helping her up — not that she thought she needed it.

"We should be going." He looked down to the Persian calmly. "Eveningstar, you have to give her back her foot."

Glory shrugged. "Tell the hounds hello for me."

The cat just looked at him in disdain, before continuing to stare at the wall. Geoffrey smiled at their host and then waited. Half a minute later, the Persian let out what sounded like a sigh before casually wandering away.

Linda had no idea what to say to any of this, but she did realize why he was helping her, as they started to move. She was so light-headed with shock that it was a little difficult to keep her balance.

In a nearly impossible gaffe for a Southerner, she nearly forgot to give her thanks to Glory, who watched with folded arms. Geoffrey's smile prompted her. "Uh, yes. It was nice to meet you. Thank you so much for the meal."

Glory observed her for a moment before smiling. "You'll be fine. The girls'll look after you." Her gaze refocused on Geoffrey. "You look after her, too."

To Linda's surprise, he smiled more profoundly. "Always." Then, plastic containers in one hand, Linda's arm in the other, he led her toward the door.

It took a while after leaving the woman's apartment for Linda to start processing anything. By the time she did, they were already back in the cart, making their way toward some other — no doubt con-founding — destination.

"Geoffrey?" she whispered, trying to claw her way back toward rationality.

"Mm?" he answered.

Darn him. He seemed amused.

She let out a sigh. "Is Glory into hallucinogens?"

The cart came to an abrupt stop. A moment later, he looked at her, chuckling softly, before the sound erupted into a full-scale guf-faw.

She sat there, watching him laugh, for several minutes, but wasn't certain how to react to such a response.

He eventually managed to calm down, looking back to her apologetically. "I'm sorry. It's just that that was your best reaction yet."

This assessment, understandably, didn't make Linda happy. Sud-denly, she was wondering whether Geoffrey was every bit as much of

a jerk as Damian. "Do you mean this is all some kind of experiment .
. . ?"

Thankfully, her fears weren't answered. His look changed, became serious and loving. "Never," he whispered, his hand on her face.

A moment later, her heart was thumping in yet another way, as
he leaned in to kiss her on the cheek. It wasn't dismissive, playful, or
paternal, was more the reaction of a lover soothing his upset beloved.
To say it made her pulse race would have been putting it far too mildly. Lord help her.

She was just staring at him, when he finally pulled away, her
mind whirling even more. Some of those cats had been right. He *did*
have a lovely smell.

She tried to catch her breath, as he turned back to the road. Unfortunately for any hope of professionalism, just one thought occurred to her.

"You're not married, are you?" Her life was weird enough without being involved in some strange non-affair thing with her boss.

The man who was decidedly not acting like an employer smiled
at her, holding up his hands, his fingers wiggling, for just a second
before he regrasped the wheel. *No rings*, she noticed, but that didn't
mean much.

"I don't believe in affairs," he answered more seriously, as he ne-
gotiated a curve.

She had to give into these mysteries for now, certain that he
would provide her with no solid answers. Besides, if she really wanted those, she was going to have to accept a lot of facts she wasn't going to like, and she wasn't ready to do that at all.

"Glory is going to give me two of her cats?" She had decided to
focus on something more immediate. It was probably safer. She was
repressing the whole *and they're total chatterboxes* aspect for all she
was worth.

This brought back Geoffrey's smile — always lovely to see, despite her confusion. "'Encouraging them to live with you,' is more the way I'd put it." He gazed at her warmly before refocusing on the road. "Don't worry. They'll be very useful."

She didn't really know what they were going to help her with but decided not to dwell on that mystery. Pondering it would mean thinking about going back inside that apartment tonight — about being left there, all alone, with the sounds and the shadows. A shiver moved along her skin. Maybe it wouldn't be bad to have a little living company, after all.

She was left in her usual state of confusion, as they pulled up in front of another of the buildings, a gray stucco one.

Geoffrey shut off the cart before turning to her. "Glory is a fairly normal resident in appearance."

Linda fervently prevented herself from analyzing that statement.

"The next two will be a bit harder for you to handle."

He got out of the cart without allowing her to answer or beg for a reprieve. It was probably for the best. While she wanted desperately to believe that he was just referring to some physical disability they might have, the day so far had taught her not to go in utterly unprepared. After all, her boss was probably right. Any more fighting, and her mind might get pulled right off its last hinge.

She kept this truth close to her, tried to plant a smile on her face, as they approached the apartment door. This one was on the ground floor, probably only a building or two away from her own. Still, it was only once he looked at her as though she were suddenly juggling gerbils or something that she realized her smile was undoubtedly fairly manic.

She took a deep breath, trying to remain calm. It wasn't easy. Given all that had happened so far, there was no telling what to expect. If some undead guy wrapped in bandages loped his way toward the door . . .

She did her best to repress the hysteria her life was teaching her, as Geoffrey rang the bell. Hard not to notice that it sounded out something that resembled the opening bars of Warren Zevon's "Werewolves of London." Those hours listening to classic rock radio were taking their toll.

Tragically, the person who answered the door didn't make her feel any better. She supposed she should just be glad that there were no trailing bandages that she could see.

The new resident was not the type of monster she had feared, however. They were met, instead, with a wide, but disturbingly carnivorous, smile. Yellow eyes alighted on her boss, and the smile grew even wider. "Geoffrey, darling!" the man exclaimed, pulling him inside. "Get yourself and your delicious little assistant in here."

Hairy. He was just hairy. Nothing more to it than that.

Okay, so his beard, hair, and mustache all seemed to have completed the sort of forays the earlier applicant's had started, matching up with each other to form more a fur mask than anything else. But there was no reason to panic. That was probably perfectly normal, right?

She repeated this mantra, as another voice met them from the kitchen. "You're late, the pair of you!" The fact that she couldn't see the man who said it didn't make her any less nervous.

"Sorry!" Geoffrey called back before turning to the first resident. "Glory kept us a bit."

Both men rolled their golden eyes slightly, as the second entered the room. "You always *were* her favorite."

Despite Linda's efforts, the panic was beginning to truly set in now. She looked back and forth between them, trying very hard not to go mad.

If the first resident had been hairy, the second looked more like a bag of fur that someone had attempted to construct a human shape out of. She tried really hard to believe that they were just suffering from the sort of disease that had put some 19th-century unfortunates into freak shows as "dog-faced boys." Her mind reeled, denial dissolving. But that sort of thing had been eliminated long ago, right?

She decided not to believe in such science, finding this explanation far easier to accept than any of the alternatives.

Geoffrey turned toward her, as she was attempting to keep her eyes from rolling back in her head. "These are some more of our longer-term residents. This is Hugh Baskerville."

He pointed from the first to the second, as she did her best to tuck all the escaping parts of her sizzling brain back in. "And this is Laurence Cheney."

"But my friends call me—"

"No, don't," she begged, knowing what was coming, her face buried in her hand. First, it was . . . well, everything, . . . and now it was Lon Chaney and a Conan Doyle character. *Good grief.*

She knew she was being rude, knew she certainly wasn't proving a good assistant to Geoffrey, but she couldn't quite force herself to look up again. If she did, she was going to see things she couldn't wholly deny.

She couldn't take that. Whatever its dangers, denial felt safe. There was only so much oddity her brain could withstand, before it just started to explode.

She found herself sitting on the couch a moment later, knew that all these men were watching her, knew that she was direly failing whatever test she was being given. But she just couldn't help it. It was too much, was *far* too weird. If only life could be all picket fences and well-tended lawns and SUVs and . . .

Okay, so she really wasn't dumb enough to think such details meant an utter lack of misery, but they just seemed so *nice,* compared to her life. She felt someone sit on the couch beside her, knew it was Geoffrey, even before he spoke.

"Give her a minute," he whispered, tenderly stroking her blue hair.

That only made her sigh all the more. There were times she truly wished she could be a stereotypical vapid blonde.

That wish, of course, was part of the reason why she'd ended up with the hair color she was now stuck with, but she wasn't up to such analysis.

One of the residents sighed softly. "I guess we *are* a bit much for a first day. Especially with our moon phase coming up and all."

She wished she lived the sort of life which made it impossible to guess what they were talking about.

Geoffrey's soft touch finally made her raise her head again, her eyes a little misty, as she gazed at the two residents' worried golden eyes. Their normal clothing only made the situation weirder.

The one who had greeted them, Hugh, dressed much like her boss tended to. The second one was even wearing a business suit. She was trying not to scream.

Fortunately, Geoffrey surprised her out of the impulse, pulling her close, his arms tender, mouth by her ear. Into it, he whispered a series of soft, soothing sounds. Like at her lunch with Glory, none of them were quite recognizable, except for her real name. "Lydia," he would breathe, before those only half-hidden words began again. "Lydia."

It made her real name so darn tempting that she couldn't quite remember why she'd ever chosen another. And it finally made her sanity begin to piece itself slowly back together.

She wasn't certain how long they were like that, knew nothing except his touch, his comfort. Some final spate of words settled inside her as a sort of hope for the future, a thought — even if she had no conscious access to it — that comforted her even more.

She felt his soft kiss there, before he finally leaned back. She didn't really know *what* to think, after that.

Hugh fanned himself with an envelope, his facial fur flying. "My, my," he murmured. She had entirely forgotten they were there.

"Geoffrey, if you're going to behave that way with her, you really need to bring roses." What vague skin was evident on the palms of Lon's hands seemed a little flushed. "You really do know how to raise the temperature."

Linda agreed, knowing she was more than a little pink herself. She looked back to the man who had a hand on her shoulder, saw him smiling tenderly at the residents, and let out a terrible sigh, as a new possibility rose. Maybe Geoffrey didn't play for her team. There was an awful thought. She gazed the three men over further. But, given her usual luck, it made too much sense to ignore.

Such a theory forgot about quite a bit, but it did make sense of the man's decided lack of boundaries. Maybe he just figured that they weren't particularly necessary. Given his inclinations, he could never be said to be coming onto her. It even explained the lack of a ring. Maybe he and his partner just hadn't decided to come out and make it legal yet.

She didn't like the idea, was only soothed away from it somewhat by his continuing, gentle touch over her hair. But none of it made any of the questions which plagued her any easier. Nothing did. No matter how much she pondered it, no simple answers seemed to be forthcoming. All she could really hope was that if these explanations ever did arrive, there might be at least a few that wouldn't destroy her soul.

Chapter Four

The wolf men had proved to be the end of Linda's first-day endurance, her denial already nearly too tattered to survive. Geoffrey, seeing this, apparently, had let her go early, saying they could catch up with the other important residents another day. She was almost weepingly grateful. If they had knocked on another door only to find zombies or mermaids — or God only knew what — she probably would have just started wailing.

Even in this disconcerted state, she couldn't go directly home. For one thing, the meager possessions she had, which hadn't been in the mysteriously delivered suitcase, were still stacked up in her car, waiting to be unloaded. For another, it appeared that she now had talking cats to feed. Unless the apartment's refrigerator proved to be magical — a possibility she didn't even want to entertain, lest it prove to be true — she'd need to do at least a bit of shopping.

She took Geoffrey's directions — given without being asked — and headed toward the nearest Kroger. She'd seen a couple of these stores during her few days in Atlanta, had made a stop or two for snacks, and had noticed that they tended to cater directly toward whatever cultural group predominated in that particular neighborhood. She'd already witnessed the Jewish Kroger — specializing in kosher everything, where the men behind the deli counter wore hair nets for their long beards — as well as one where she seemed to be the only white person and was astonished to find a well-attended sale on products she'd never imagined existed outside of Racist Stereotype World before. Atlanta, sometimes, seemed to have been lifted wholesale out of the most shocking parts of the 1950s. Thus, given her day so far and the neighborhood she seemed to be stuck living in, she was a little timid as to what she might find.

Her fears seemed to be justified, when she noticed a hearse, a really snazzy one, parked at the far end of the lot. It was painted a vivid chartreuse with black flames coursing down its length. When she saw that the hubcaps on one side had the words "Born" and "To" written on them, she felt a morbid curiosity growing. Half unwillingly, she got out of her car and moved closer, wandering around to witness the rest of the owner's message: "See Beyond."

She blinked, almost disappointed that it hadn't been stranger. Apparently, her day had already upped her tolerance for the weird.

This wasn't an encouraging notion for someone as desperately in denial as she was.

She gave up on investigating, coming back toward the store. Even the Neil Young quote, "Long May You Run," written on the car's bumper seemed mundane.

See? Nice, normal people buy hearses and soup them up.

Well, musicians, anyway. She'd never been entirely certain whether the two groups intersected.

She was just coming to accept that more comforting idea when she saw that this particular vehicle did indeed have a casket in the back, a fire-truck red one. It was open — and empty. It was at that point she remembered that talking cats probably didn't like to be kept waiting for their doughnuts.

She made her way hurriedly, if rather timidly, into the store and was relieved to find that it seemed surprisingly normal. Its major odd feature, at first glance, was that there was nearly nobody there. Aisle after aisle seemed devoid of life. She almost went back out to check the hours on the front door but decided that if they'd opened to her, the place must be in business.

Besides, the fluorescent lights shone, and the sound system played Creedence Clearwater Revival's "Bad Moon Rising" at the same level that much worse Muzak or Worst of the '80s was usually forced upon a shopper. Okay, so when she grabbed a cart, the "Thank you for shopping at Kroger's" slogan on its handle had a moon and pentagram pattern intertwined with it, but maybe that was just a new logo she'd missed. She wheeled cautiously into the store. It would be nice if some part of her life would agree to behave.

She decided to pretend that it would, pasting on a smile, attempting to emulate some suburban soccer mom just doing a day's shopping, although the effect was probably ruined by both her hair and her youth. She was soothed that the bread and fruit selections seemed fairly typical, if slightly more wide-ranging than normal. There was even a sort of solitary splendor to wandering through them, gliding past the bakery, the diet foods, the Kitty and Hound Treats counter . . .

Wait a minute.

She glanced back, wanting to tell herself that this neighborhood simply had a lot of dedicated pet owners. Still, looking at the displays, she was surprised to see such a variety of foods. The hound section had meat, organs, bones, and . . . chocolate mousse? Wasn't that bad for dogs? Her gaze moved on to the Kitty side. Catnip, fish, and, on the bottom, three huge trays of assorted doughnuts.

She blinked, trying to nurture her disbelief. Maybe if she kept repeating that she'd merely fallen asleep, the world would agree to play along.

This hadn't happened yet, but there was no reason to give up hoping, even if she knew her dreams were never this far ranging, always stayed where she'd started. Standing, she took a new path, decided — yet again — not to ponder it too deeply. She was there, anyway. If she could just find some assistance, she could go ahead and buy . . .

She let out a minor bleat when she saw a woman behind the counter. She would have sworn that the attendant hadn't been there only a few seconds ago.

Maybe she arrived while my attention was on the doughnuts?

Linda tried a smile, beginning politely. "Do the doughnuts have . . ."

She never got to finish. The woman in blue shimmered at her from behind the counter. The white smock she wore over her clothes seemed terribly disjointed with the rest of the image, like a paper cutout laid over a photo.

"You know Geoffrey?" the woman wondered, pointing at her. Then, her eyes widened. "You're the new assistant!"

Linda didn't get a chance to agree.

The clerk introduced herself, holding out her hand. "Sybil Lovelace."

Linda took it, telling herself that the reason she couldn't feel Sybil's touch was that it was just so gentle.

"I'm one of the residents. You have a cat?"

Linda was almost glad for the opening, as psychotic as this place was making her feel. "I'm, um, being lent . . . uh, keeping one for a friend."

Apparently.

"I've been told she likes doughnuts." It wasn't entirely a lie.

To her surprise, the clerk leaned in toward her, her eyes wide, and Linda told herself that the fuzziness that seemed to surround her was just the result of exhaustion, her eyes playing tricks.

"You have Eveningstar with you?" the woman asked, clearly amazed.

When Linda nodded, bemused, Sybil leaned back, looking her up and down slowly. Finally, understanding seemed to dawn, which was more than Linda could manage.

"Oh, you're *her*!" She was grinning like mad, bending down behind the counter. "I'm so glad! We all knew you were coming, of course, even poor Clarissa."

The woman was retrieving doughnuts from the counter display — handfuls of them, talking all the while. "I don't know if she ever really felt settled, knowing that. None of them really did. Still, the rest at least ended up where they were supposed to go. They were all really nice."

When she stood up, she had a giant silver bakery box in her hands, with the words "Eveningstar's Special" emblazoned across it in little sparkly stars. "But they always knew who was coming, so they never really — oops!"

Sybil had been trying to hand over the box when her fingers seemed to slip directly through it, the container falling into Linda's grasp.

"Oh, darn. I should be used to it by now, shouldn't I?" Sybil looked up, grinning. "I mean, it's been 157 years, and I — Oh. Sorry . . . You don't . . . " She looked Linda over again. "Didn't notice. Tell Geoffrey I said hello!" Then, she disappeared.

"Disappeared." It was a word that got used metaphorically to the point of cliché. But this wasn't that kind. Instead, one second Linda was looking at the woman who was quickly chattering away her every mental defense, and the next, the lady in blue simply wasn't there. She looked down to her hands, which still held the box of treats, proving that she hadn't been entirely hallucinating.

"I'm just tired," she said aloud, as though announcing it to anything that might be listening would make it real. Her eyes were clearly playing tricks on her. That was all there was to it.

She put the box in her cart, moving on. All the things she'd seen today be damned. She was going to live in normal reality if it killed her.

She managed to make it through the rest of the store in a daze, such a state the easiest way to deal with anything she might see. It explained away everything, too: the female worker in the pink dress and apron using what looked like a wand and bright gold light to guide some boxes down from a high shelf; the three small, half-seen creatures with a miniature green cart who cackled happily every time they were near before shooting around the next corner in a strange blue blur; the partial aisle of boxes whose lane marker announced them as "Zombie Training Foods." Clearly, she was half-warped from exhaustion. That was the only plausible explanation.

She bought what she thought she might need in that determined state, used a self check-out to avoid a much-too-hairy cashier, and nearly ran from a woman, all in black, asking whether she had one of their Moonlight Buyers' Cards.

When she got outside, saw someone climbing into the casket in the back of the hearse before an entirely unseen driver pulled away, she took a deep breath, calcifying her belief in normality. Nothing was amiss. Nothing could be. She was just much too tired to be seeing anything clearly.

She drove home in that fervid belief, glad the store wasn't too far away, trying to get her bearings. Atlanta, even the suburbs like Decatur, was a dangerous place to get lost in. She had discovered that on her way there in the beginning, when she had pulled off the interstate to look over her directions, only to find a crowd of extremely interested men beginning to surround her four seconds later.

The roads didn't make it any easier, went off in directions that just didn't seem possible. Two streets that ran parallel might cross over each other two blocks later before running parallel again.

The fact that Atlanta had grown by gobbling up so many small towns didn't even explain it. Decatur, her new home, was no more clear than the rest. All the paths seemed to be carved in some complex and obscure pattern, one not even the best maps helped decipher.

Even half the street names seemed designed to confound. Peachtree Street was completely different than Peachtree Avenue, Peachtree Battle, Peachtree Industrial Way, etc. That wasn't even the worst of it. She'd gotten quite turned around at one point, before she realized that North Roswell Road and South Roswell Road weren't necessarily the same road. Oh, yes — knowing your way around was the only way to survive.

It was probably those survival instincts that got her home, and she was even relieved to be pulling up in front of her not particularly inviting apartment.

When she went in with the first load of boxes, leaving the groceries in the car, she wasn't entirely surprised to find the two cats waiting for her. Tiger was sitting by the door, looking up to her happily. "Welcome back," she said.

Linda managed to bite the inside of her cheek just enough to keep herself from screaming.

Somehow, the greeting was the biggest challenge to her determined denial yet. It was one thing to mentally dismiss the existence of most of the people she'd met that day. It was another to be openly rude. Perhaps because of the absence of such a quality in her own upbringing, she treasured even the most basic politeness. Therefore, if these cats were really here, were really talking, simply walking by them unacknowledged would be hideously uncivil. Especially if they had been sent to look after her, how could she ignore them?

The words barely got past her lips, but they managed to be cordial — even if she didn't make eye contact, moving further in. "Thank you." She could almost believe that she was speaking to herself, if she really tried.

She heard a muted sigh from the tortoiseshell, passed by the black cat without comment on her way to stack the first of the boxes against her living room wall.

Eveningstar, famous cat that she was, was stretched out along the back of the sofa, looking for all the world like she was waiting for a fleet of devoted servants to come peel her grapes. Her golden eyes watched Linda pass with disdain. "Stubborn, isn't she?"

Linda moved back out for another box, only just hearing Tiger's reply. "Give her time. You know what she's come from. She needs to . . ."

Then, she started to run.

Somehow, she managed not to break her neck on the carpeted stairs, whose awful, industrial-patterned covering was much too heavily padded, the stairs themselves too shallow, for their original purpose. How any elderly person was supposed to climb up or down them without falling was a mystery, but, perhaps the fact that she was young was also the reason why she had been given one of these up-per-story rooms.

She knew she was ignoring reality — including the fact that she had yet to see *any* obvious retirees — but she didn't want to face the truth. She didn't want to think about another night in an apartment that demanded she either accept the unusual or face the torment it could give in its disapproval.

She dithered around with the boxes, deciding which one to take next, forcing her mind elsewhere. They didn't all have to come up in one night, assuming that the crime rate in the complex wasn't too bad. It wasn't that bad a neighborhood, but it also wasn't gated like pretty much every other complex she'd come across here. Maybe she'd just take the things she'd miss most if they disappeared and leave the rest till tomorrow. She wasn't certain how many trips up those stairs she wanted to make in one day.

The world seemed to encourage her in these efforts. The sun was well on its way to setting, the evening turning rather cool. Although it was already late October, summer seemed to linger, as it often did in the South.

It was nice, though, she thought, as she hauled another box up the stairs — just in between enough to be comfortable. It gave her a little time to unpack before she'd need her winter clothes.

She was, of course, numbing herself to her real concerns, the mundane so much easier to deal with.

Tiger and Eveningstar watched her silently — for once — as she trudged the package across the floor to abandon it by the wall. She only vaguely heard an elegantly-muttered, "Gratitude," from the Persian, before she made her way down again, but she was getting a little better at ignoring.

She told herself that this was a positive step, continuing the process of unloading for about half an hour more. She was leaving the groceries until last, using them to force herself through the rest of her chores. If there was an absolutely unavoidable task at the end, then she couldn't give up before then, could get through some of the smaller work by sheer mental trickery. It was a skill she'd learned in her formative years, a way to goad herself through the many, awful expectations that had been forced on her daily. She could always make herself keep up if she knew that, at the end of the day, she'd still have to face . . .

She began moving a little faster in her unpacking, doing her best to outrun the memory. But it was only a few boxes later — just a couple left outside — when she realized it was getting really dark.

She shivered, glancing around the parking lot. It was weird how no one ever seemed to leave or enter when she was watching, as though the entire place was abandoned.

She pushed down the terror, starting to retrieve the food, ready to hide for the night even as she tried to talk herself out of her feelings. There were other cars here, several of them. There was no reason to let her fears run away with her.

She managed to bring in the last of the groceries a few minutes later, locking the door firmly behind her. Through her various journeys — a haphazard pile of boxes now braced against the living room wall — Tiger had watched sympathetically, like a mother who knew that her child was maneuvering a difficult rite of passage.

Eveningstar, though, had ignored her, seeming seriously aggrieved that she wasn't being treated up to her standards.

When the last bag was in the human's hand, however, the Persian's head flicked toward her, her eyes widening. While trying to maintain her dignity, she rose, but her gaze was a bit too interested to keep up the front. She began tailing closer, then even closer, stalking what she carried. Tiger sighed in the background, flopping over on her side.

By the time Linda reached the kitchen, Eveningstar was on the counter, golden eyes glaring. "Doughnuts," she demanded.

The return of the cat's speech, after the half hour or more of silence, took Linda by surprise. "Um, what?"

The golden gaze flared even more completely, having a life all its own. "Doughnuts!"

She'd never realized before that a cat could shout. Of course, before today, there'd been other reasons for that belief.

The demand was quickly handled, Linda understanding that there were some requests that shouldn't be refused. She dug through the bag until she found the silver box. By the time she drew it out, the formerly-noble Persian was nearly glassy-eyed and drooling.

Surprised, Linda's hand lingered a moment too long on the sticker that sealed it.

Eveningstar's eyes were glowing like a sun. "*Doughnuts!*"

Linda quickly gave in to the inevitable.

When she opened the box, she practically expected the cat to dive into it. She seemed to be considering it strongly. Finally, the small black head rose toward her, eyes intent. "Feed," she ordered.

Linda could have argued. Maybe she should have. She'd had a rough day, had rented an apartment to a werewolf, gone to the Kroger of the Damned, and was now living with two talkative — and demanding — cats.

The look of imminent doom that was promised in the feline's gaze if she ignored this particular order, though, made her back down, her inherent niceness taking its place. She lifted a doughnut and was then witness to what a kitty crack addict might have looked like.

The pastry was gone in only a few bites. Linda was just glad that she'd been left her fingers, although perhaps they weren't considered as tasty.

Perhaps not, since Eveningstar was licking the sugar off of them thoroughly.

"Next," she commanded.

The order was duly followed, the cycle repeating for several minutes, until all of the treats were gone.

Finally, the Persian licked off the last of the sugar, sighed at the empty box, and jumped down from the counter, looking as though she'd never been the least bit inelegant at all.

All of this left Linda blinking, only the arrival of her other feline roommate distracting her.

"Supper?" Tiger inquired softly.

Linda shook herself from watching the Persian's elegantly disdainful retreat, and dug farther into her bags to find the cat food. Looking around, she noticed that kitty bowls had already been set out — a good thing, since she'd forgotten to buy them herself — and began to dole out some of the food.

"Is this okay?"

Tiger, unlike her companion, hadn't made too many requests.

The tortoiseshell stared at the label then sniffed the food before digging into her meal. A couple of mouthfuls later, she raised her head. "Good choice." Then, she went back to eating.

Somehow, in only a very few minutes, Linda had been thoroughly trained. "It's okay?" She filled a water bowl that spelled out the cat's name in paw prints before setting it on the floor. "There's nothing particular you want me to get for you?" It didn't really seem fair, given the other cat's treatment.

"Not—" *Munch.* "—picky," Tiger assured her.

Linda just watched, like an overeager waiter.

After a few moments, the cat raised her head and looked around. They could just see Eveningstar preening herself unconcernedly in the other room.

Tiger looked regretfully at the food she was temporarily abandoning before jumping onto the counter, her voice dropping. "You'll need to put down some for her, too." Her head turned toward the doorway. "She'll get around to it eventually." With that, she returned to her meal.

"Oh. Right." Linda followed her orders, trying to make sense of it all. Being a new cat cohabiter was confusing. She wasn't certain that having them tell her exactly what they wanted made it any less so.

She was just setting out the second set of filled bowls, the darkness outside now total, when she heard a knock on the door. It startled her, no one ever having come by before, the silence of the complex sometimes almost frightening. She couldn't just ignore it, as much as she might want to. She was the new tenant manager. If one of the tenants had a problem . . .

What she would do if this happened, she had no idea. She didn't understand — or wasn't admitting — the true nature of the place, didn't know any of the rules, and was only now realizing that she didn't even have Geoffrey's phone number in case she needed him.

With a sigh, she went over, gazing through the peephole. Maybe friendliness alone would help.

What she saw on the other side didn't seem particularly frightening. Given some of the residents she'd encountered so far, that was a relief.

She opened the door to a lovely, young, blonde woman — probably no older than she was — dressed all in black for a night out. Her pale skin glowed, her blue eyes sparkling.

"Uh, hi," Linda greeted her, a little stunned. Except for the clubbing outfit, her visitor suited every definition of wholesome middle-American girl she had ever seen. Then again, so did Gail. Apparently, that wasn't much to go by.

The newcomer's smile seemed truly kind. "Hi! You're the new tenant manager, right? Lydia?"

Linda was about to correct her — wondering whether the entirety of Atlanta, or at least Decatur, had gotten some memo about her and her real name — when the girl started peering into the apartment. "Can I come in?"

Linda was about to agree, when she heard a loud hiss behind her. Tiger, who had seemed perfectly contented with her food only a moment ago, was now standing like a statue, glaring at the visitor.

Linda guessed that was a no.

She didn't have to say it, either, the new woman retreating a step. "Oh, the—" Her visitor stopped, looked back at her, smiling again. "—cats." The woman shrugged. "We don't always get along."

Apparently, Linda thought, but decided not to voice it, turning the conversation. "Can I help you . . . what was your name again?"

"Oh," the blonde looked genuinely surprised but still friendly. "You can call me Cee."

Linda heard Tiger growl behind her, but Cee went on. "I'd heard you were moving in today. I just wanted to see whether there was anything I could do to help."

Her outfit didn't entirely back up this claim, but Linda let that fact go. "Um, thanks, but I was going to leave it for tonight. Are you a resident?" And, if she was, given the cat's reaction, was Cee really one that she should be talking to?

Cee gave another pleasant laugh. "I've been around for a while."

That answered nothing, as the small bit of the more Lydia side of her noted.

Her visitor didn't seem to notice her skepticism. "Well, if you're all settled, how about if you come out with us tonight? There's this great club in town, The Masquerade, and I know it can be lonely on a first day here." Her smile, her eyes, made Linda want to agree. Cee moved a little closer. "Why don't you see if we can cheer you up?"

Have I been unhappy? Suddenly, Linda couldn't entirely remember.

She blinked, trying to object. "I'm not dressed for a club." She probably wouldn't have the right clothes, even if she looked.

Cee was nearer now, though Linda couldn't remember her moving. "Of course you are," she soothed. "You're just right. You look perfect." There was a pause, her eyes shining. "You *are* perfect. You want to *be* perfect." Her white smile widened. "We can help."

The smile was convincing. Linda felt herself wavering, wanting to go. She'd never been to a club before, had never really been out at all. She had no friends, nobody to talk to, to hang out with. Cee's dark blue eyes were so enchanting. A night out would be nice, would take her away from her troubles, her pain, her . . .

She only came out of the spell slightly when she felt a sharp stab to her foot. Looking down, she saw that Tiger had her claws dug deeply into her ankle, the wound bringing up blood. Behind them, she heard Eveningstar's soft words. "Good work, but let her go. She needs to understand."

It took another moment before Tiger's claws retreated. She sat staring at Linda, her eyes evaluating. "All right, but remember that." She looked toward the wound before starting to lick the blood off her claws.

Okay, so that hasn't gotten any more normal.

Linda, despite her best efforts to believe only in the dullest reality, was gazing over her visitor once more. She didn't want to leave with Cee, just wanted to go and hide in her bed — like that had helped her last night. Or ever. Still . . .

She noticed that Cee's eyes were wide, gazing over the blood that had seeped from Linda's wound. That didn't exactly encourage her further, but she was beginning to give into the inevitable.

Linda grabbed her purse, took a handkerchief from it, and wiped the blood away. Then, with one look back to the ever-watchful cats, she made a decision. "Fine." She locked the door behind her, leaving her feline Cassandras behind it. Whatever was going on, she apparently had to see it all the way through.

Cee seemed only too thrilled to have convinced her. The blonde decided that they should take Linda's car — telling her not to worry about getting Cee home. There were people at the club for that.

Cee apparently wasn't one for silence, chatted like a happy sorority sister for the next half hour. All the way, she told Linda how wonderful it would be, how lucky she was, how much she would love it. The girl's chattering was only broken by an occasional direction. It was only when her inner Lydia pointed out that she was entirely lost that Linda started to panic.

To her relief, Cee didn't lead her into some blind alley or abandoned street. Instead, they pulled into the parking lot of what looked to be a huge old factory. With all the other young people who surrounded it, either looking cool or trying to, she knew they had arrived. Whatever was at this club, she was now there to discover.

Linda began to wonder, too, as she let herself be led by her cheery tour guide, through rooms marked for Heaven, Hell, and Purgatory, whether she were even old enough to be here, but nobody actually stopped them. A band with some name that was barely a single entendre was setting up, but the background music was already soul-penetratingly loud.

For a while, Cee left her to her own devices, which included getting a ginger ale from the bar. Not only was Linda not old enough to drink, she didn't think it a good idea. She'd been led here for some, specific reason. Even the cats had let her come, as little as they apparently approved of Cee. Getting wasted, as alluring as that idea sometimes was, could make her miss any chance for escape she might have.

Linda could barely think through the noise of the room, had no idea what was going on, but could feel the dread growing slightly, as the club filled up. Most of the crowd didn't notice her, although a few tried to pick her up, while one or two others seemed to want to start a fight.

There was a certain crowd, too, always in black, that seemed particularly attracted to her, gazing at her wounded ankle, as they came closer. One even leaned down to sniff it. She almost got up and left but decided she would have to ride it out. For one thing, she didn't know where she was. It was going to take some serious map wrangling to get her back home. She sighed. It was one of those times she really wished she had a cell phone.

She was abandoned to questionable music and random partiers for at least an hour, then, stewing ever further with each passing minute. Her third ginger ale, which had been a bit stale to begin with, was definitely wearing thin.

Finally she felt something, a presence; she didn't really know how. But she supposed that she would take any break in the tedium, just now.

She turned to watch Cee coming toward her, a tall, stylish blond man in tow. He had an aura of power, Cee's looks at him showing her awe, her fingers clinging. He seemed to expect to always have such admirers, barely noticed the girl. Without even appearing to realize they were, the crowd parted for him.

His smile, when they reached her, was seductive. "I'm glad you came." And that alone, in this place, was probably a come-on.

Linda didn't really know what to make of him, except that he was trouble — trouble in casual designer clothing. His hand abandoned Cee's clinging embrace, caressed against Linda's arm, before she could move to stop him, his look enticing her. When his next words were, "I've heard so much about you," she only sighed.

Apparently, everyone is getting that memo.

She didn't respond to his pick-up lines, but she did allow herself to be led. His whole air said that he expected such capitulation, and the ever-more-annoyed Linda just wanted to know what this was about so she could go home. She hadn't been raised to be a party girl, had none of the skills, and she didn't know anyone here well enough to put in the effort. While Gerrard, as he claimed his name was, was undoubtedly gorgeous, so was Damian. She might not want to run quite as far from this man, but he wasn't exactly giving her any friendly vibes.

Geoffrey could have her with a smile. Gerrard couldn't manage it with an all-expenses-paid trip to Fiji.

She didn't know why the man would want her in the first place, of course. She certainly didn't seem to be his type. As they moved farther through the club, others in his group followed him, all of them apparently models. She never had been one of the beautiful people, and the indigo hair didn't help.

Still, she went, growing more irritated all the while. When they moved through a door onto a back fire escape, she nearly lost her patience — but that was when she realized they were alone.

She wasn't certain when the man had lost his entourage, hadn't even noticed. Given the crush inside, there should have been at least a few stragglers hanging around out here. Instead, Gerrard sat on steps that seemed newly cleaned and entirely devoid of watchers and smiled at her.

Reluctantly, she propped herself against the railing. The part of her that wanted to believe nothing weird existed — the self-named Linda — noticed that his smile was attractive. The rest of her — an eyebrow-quirking Lydia — just wanted to punch him in the face.

He seemed to have picked up on her annoyance, at least a little, his smile humoring her. "I know you find it late. You probably have to work tomorrow."

He said it as though he had never had to countenance such concerns at all and gazed down at the stairs, probably playing coy. That Lydia-like urge to punch him was growing stronger.

"I needed to see you first, though, before *Geoffrey* does his thing." He said the other man's name with a tired sort of disdain. When his smile broadened, she started to catch sight of something. "I need you to know who I really am before he poisons you against me."

Christ. She leaned down, staring at the man's mouth, barely having noticed his words, her patience exhausted. To his evident shock, she pulled back his lips.

Great.

"They're fangs," she growled.

He pulled away from her, looking abused.

"You're a goddamned vampire, aren't you?"

He blinked. "Well, um, yes?"

Linda glared.

His caressing tone returned. "But I need you to understand . . . "

That was it. *No. More.*

She stood up, annoyed beyond belief—all of that foolish determination to ignore everything odd entirely dismissed, hopefully for good. "See? You see what I'm up against?" she screamed.

He leaned back, looking weirdly terrified.

"Everywhere I go, something creepy wants me."

He was actively cringing, as she threw her head back to shout at the sky.

"*I hate the supernatural!*"

Chapter Five

The night didn't appear to be going the way Gerrard wanted. Maybe that wasn't such a surprise.

Lydia was incensed. She was done with being "Linda," had finally abandoned that whole "There's nothing weird out there in the world! Really!" nonsense. She was going to be herself, full force, and the world could like it.

She was glaring down at her would-be escort now. If the vampire's look of terror was anything to go by, it wasn't a sight for the faint of heart.

Lydia could care less about his feelings, her fury utterly aroused. Standing over him, hands on her hips like an annoyed and lecturing teacher, she continued her tirade, her eyes burning. "Look, I've tried to avoid you all, really I have."

Her tone sounded perfectly reasonable to herself, but the vampire's growing grimace seemed to indicate otherwise.

"I didn't want to have a demon in my basement when I was growing up. I didn't *want* to be dubbed the neighborhood freak because my stupid parents painted upside-down pentagrams on my backpack. Do you think I had *fun* when they sent me to my first day of kindergarten with a few devil-worshiping sigils shaved into the back of my head? Huh? Do you?"

It wasn't that Gerrard was professing such a belief. The master vampire looked more like he was trying to think of someplace he could conveniently cower until this terrifying threat went away.

By this point, Lydia's rant had caught the attention of his underlings, but they weren't exactly coming to his aid. Her gaze skewered the first one to exit the door onto the stoop.

"Okay, so I've survived all that. I've gone through years of my parents' crazy rituals trying to dig up every terrible netherworld being up to and *including* the ghost of J. Edgar Hoover."

Cee, the last one unfortunate enough to make it out the door, was pinned by a truly deadly look from Lydia.

"Do you know how bossy ex-FBI directors can be?"

Cee shook her head but seemed more than ready to run.

"He wanted me to turn my second grade teacher in as a communist!" Lydia's venting was now aimed at the sky. "He wouldn't even listen when I told him I had no idea what the USSR *was*!"

Some part of Lydia — a part that wasn't currently ranting — could see that her strange litany held the creatures of the night spellbound but only in the way a cat might watch a mouse who'd suddenly dressed up in ballerina pink and was dancing the flamenco. Well, if the mouse also had a very large hatchet aimed directly for its head. Running still seemed like the vampires' favorite option.

Gerrard tried to reassert control, using his most persuasive voice. "Lih-dee-ah," he called, like Dracula crooning to his brides.

It only won him her attention. He barely managed to swallow his, "Eep!"

Lydia glared at him before relenting somewhat. "Yeah, you're right, you're right. I made it through all that. I got rid of all the . . . "

She trailed off for a moment, her eyes closing, holding back the memories. "Anyway, I got away. I finally come here. And what do I get?" Her look returned to him, no friendlier than before. "*You*."

All the vampires leaned as far away as possible. A few of the more cowardly scuttled away.

Cee, however, had made her way toward Gerrard, her hands on his shoulders to support him as though he had just lost some sort of epic battle and was barely holding on.

It was only as the final surge of adrenalin started to wear off that Lydia took in the effect she'd had, and a small fear started deep within her. This was not a position in which sensible people found themselves.

This truth only sank in more deeply, as she came back to reality. What was she doing, anyway? She had not only just confronted a posse of vampires on their home turf but had then also screamed at their leader for a good few minutes. She almost felt like she should blush. Unplanned dental exams probably weren't high on the usual list of vampire manners, either. She let out a snort, annoyed despite her peril. Maybe she should have spent that time at the bar figuring out her way home.

It was just as she started to wonder how she was supposed to get out of here alive — wholly alive, at least — when she felt a hand on her shoulder. Thankfully, she recognized it. That was when she knew she had been saved.

"Nice work," her new employer whispered, possibly too low even for the vampires to pick up.

How he had known where she was, that she was in trouble, how he had managed to appear behind her on the small space on the fire escape without her noticing, she had no idea. But Lydia, thankfully, wasn't the sort who needed such mundane explanations.

There was another moment of blessed silence, as her rescuer and the head vampire stared at one another, Lydia closing her eyes. She was okay again. There was a sense of peace just having her employer here, being near him at any moment. This feeling, maybe not so strangely, she knew. This one she had already been comforted by in all the worst moments of her life.

She let the unusual happen, for once, images of that terrible battle in the basement of her childhood home flooding through her mind. Then, she closed them off once more.

As he always had been before, Geoffrey was with her. His hand squeezed warmly. His presence was all she required to find immediate peace.

She opened her eyes to witness this confrontation, only half-remembering what the vampire had been trying to tell her. He had regained much of his apparent composure after her tirade, Cee's touch barely needed to support him. "Geoffrey," he acknowledged, with relative calm.

"Gerrard," her employer returned. His tone, even in the one word, was far less tentative. When she looked back, she saw that his eyes were burning, protective. But the gaze seemed to melt into something infinitely sadder, when it turned to the vampire's companion, even if he said little more than before. "Clarissa."

The name, the look, showed his feelings, Lydia's heart tugging. For the first time in all her thoughts of the mysterious tenant manager she had replaced, it wasn't brought on by fear or jealousy.

Geoffrey's whole gaze showed the truth, his eyes those of a teacher or parent whose desperate attempts to save a child from herself had finally proven useless. He looked as though he were staring at her grave.

Lydia glanced over the petite blonde and saw that she, too, understood. Cee — Clarissa — looked like a girl who was facing the person who had offered her a full scholarship to Radcliffe, knowing that she had instead decided to take up stripping at Big Ed's Playland and Adult Toy Emporium, all because it sounded like more of a cheap thrill. She couldn't even keep her former employer's gaze, would probably have been blushing, had her choice to be undead not made that impossible.

Geoffrey's hand warmed over Lydia's back, soothing away the torment that so clearly flooded from Clarissa, swamping anyone around her. It just hurt to see anyone brought so low.

Lydia suffered along with her, despite the girl's earlier actions, the fact that the blonde had tried to lure her here with the probable intention of making her one of their kind. It was a fate the Lydia had never envied. Still, looking at the chastened vampire and her obvious seducer, all she could really feel was pain.

The four of them were the only ones left on the stairs by this point, the rest of the vampire's followers having quietly fled. Gerrard was holding his own, or seemed to be, as he tried to explain to Geoffrey.

"I just wanted to talk to her. I wanted her to understand us, before you . . . "

That was as far as Geoffrey let him get, his look infinitely frosty. "Told her the truth?" he finished. His regretful eyes trailed over to Clarissa, whose head was turned far away. "All she needed to see was your previous work to understand that."

His opponent apparently wanted to argue the point, but Geoffrey began to lead Lydia away. She wasn't sad to go.

As they moved slowly down the steps, Gerrard's voice reached out to her. "Lydia, truly, I mean you no harm . . . "

She had to sigh. A lengthy knowledge of modern vampire lore wasn't really necessary to see the pattern here. As sorry as she was for Clarissa, she had no desire to join her.

"Save it, Fang-Boy." The warmth of Geoffrey's hand over the small of her back sent a tender sort of quiver through her. "I'll never be interested in what you're selling."

With that, the vampires let them go. Lydia knew she should be rather surprised. Given her confrontation with them earlier — as well as vampires' usual, territorial reputation — she had expected a fight. But the other black-clad members of Gerrard's troupe merely stood around the outskirts of the building, watching.

She had no illusions about what had caused their cautious reaction. It was clearly not her who made them move away in respect.

The two of them eventually made it to her car without incident. Only then did she ask. "You didn't drive here, did you?" It wasn't a particularly necessary question. He had been with her too quickly, in her first moment of need, to have done anything so mundane.

He just smiled at her, one of those looks that made something within her ache with both tenderness and desire. "I made other arrangements." As usual, that didn't answer her question, but she was beginning not to care about such facts.

She let this detail go, then, holding up the keys. After the day she had survived, she was in no mood to maneuver Atlanta's arcane roadways. "Have a license?" she wondered.

He smiled again. "I can manage." With that non-answer, he took them toward home.

They drove in silence, Lydia no longer surprised that he found their way so effortlessly. She let him get on with it, leaning her head back against the seat, closing her eyes to ponder all she had seen. A rather slaphappy laugh emerged, her words half-murmured. "Werewolves and vampires and . . . angels? Oh my." Then, she fell asleep.

The ride didn't take as long as she was learning to expect in Atlanta, where five miles was typically a minimum of a half hour trip. When she looked up, they were back at her apartment.

To her surprise, Geoffrey actually joined her inside after that, no arguments, no retreat. She understood his silent point. It was time that she faced at least some of her reality.

What she didn't expect was to find the cats sitting there, waiting for her at the door, their tails swishing in unison. From what she had seen so far, they usually liked to lounge.

Upon seeing Geoffrey, though, they didn't question. They just sat there, staring from one of them to the other for a long moment, before they wandered away. Their only comment was Eveningstar's murmured, "About time, too." With this tacit permission, the pair entered.

Geoffrey locked the door behind them, as Lydia made her way toward her bedroom. While she knew that she should sit on the couch, maybe lead him to the dining room table, she was too emotionally ragged for either option. Propriety be darned. She collapsed onto her bed, taking up a study of the ceiling.

Geoffrey stood beside her, gazing down quietly. "Questions?"

Well, there's a brilliant understatement.

Still, most of the new knowledge wasn't up for debate. She thought through the various supernatural creatures she would've sworn not to believe in before, images of the tenant applicants she had gone through earlier as well as what she'd seen at the grocery store filling her mind. Werewolves? Check. Ghosts? Yep. Vampires? Oh, yeah. And they were every bit as Euro-trashy as she would have expected. Add in a few talking cats and there was probably very little that *didn't* exist. So much for her earlier Pollyanna hopes.

She sighed a little but decided to get over it, realizing there was nothing to be gained from this "let's pretend" nonsense. She wanted to cover the basics, instead. "What's the real difference between the tenants and the residents, except length of occupancy?" It would be nice if she understood something about her job.

"Nothing much." He was pacing very slowly.

Lydia was at least glad that the light coming from the living room allowed her to watch such a *great* view. Thankfully, he didn't seem to notice her appreciation.

Definitely for the best.

She was broken from her desires by his voice. "The tenants have short-term issues. Many of them are new to their conditions." There was a quiet sigh somewhere over in the far corner of the room before he executed an elegant turn to resume his walk. "It's difficult for them to get used to the new rules."

She nodded, imagining it would be, focused in on an example. "The new tenant you chose today, Butch . . . "

Her boss interrupted her quietly. "Not his real name. None of the werewolves are allowed them anymore."

Well, that certainly made more sense of Lon Chaney and the Baskerville hound. She remembered that hound treats were part of the local Kroger's many odd selections and almost laughed but pulled her mind back in time. It didn't seem like such a funny situation. "Why not?"

Geoffrey's sigh was longer this time, his pacing paused as he stared out the door toward the living room light. He seemed saddened by the whole topic. "They aren't human anymore. They're something else. If they do things correctly, they can build a new life for themselves, can have new jobs and families, but their old ones are lost to them." His lovely green-and-gold eyes rested on her, making her heart thump again. "That's why they need a place to adjust."

She could understand, unpleasant as it was. She didn't really want to admit that she was doing much the same thing herself, her mind revolving back to the hounds. It would be difficult to tell your family: "Guess what? I'm going to become a wolf once a month." Her heart ached further at their situation. While the hounds she'd met earlier didn't seem to support the whole "ravening for human victims" image the movies sometimes gave of werewolves, that wouldn't be an easily acceptable fact in most parts of society. Assuming they didn't just decide the person was nuts.

She let this truth go, wondering about only one more thing, for now. "And h-mail?" That had possibly been the least explicable part of her experience with the tenants.

This question was answered, in perfect, horror-movie timing, when a howl started up, somewhere in the complex. It was a lonesome, mournful sound but regulated, nonetheless, seemed to have a message to give.

Geoffrey smiled. "Howl mail." He looked at her. "Wolves know how to find their own."

She saw no reason to question. It was more his tender look that made the ache start in her again. She tried to ignore it. "And the residents?"

He broke off the gaze, resumed his pacing. "There are some who can't move on, for different reasons. Some have families they want to watch, even if they can't interact with them. Some are trapped in some way. Some have business. Others are here to help out the tenants or have simply become too contented to ever want to leave." He was far away from her now, seemed to be lingering there. "We look after them, bad and good."

Lord. That brought up a whole other issue, one that was even more unbelievable than the rest. She was thinking about the signs on Geoffrey's and Damian's doors but tried to push the issue away, not quite ready to approach it, another question arising. "I met a woman at the store today, at the kitty treats counter."

She thought she heard him sigh, but it was too quiet to be sure.

"She told me that . . . " She didn't quite know how to put it into words. "Well, she suggested . . . "

She didn't get much further, far too flustered by all the ghost woman had insinuated.

Geoffrey stepped in. "Sybil," he whispered, walking toward her. "She's a nice enough girl, just a little talkative."

This didn't answer her real questions, but Lydia supposed she should've gotten used to that. "I noticed. But she mentioned—"

"It's her way of coping," he informed her, completely interrupting her again. "The trauma of her death still haunts her. She can't get past it, not enough to move beyond this world, anyway."

Lydia fell quiet, only half-wanting to know.

He filled her in, despite her reticence. "Stepfather. Axe. Lots of blood."

Shuddering slightly, both from the images and the overwhelming sense of sadness that seemed to be rolling off of him, she just watched.

"It wasn't pretty," he ended quietly.

She had to swallow back heavily, horrified enough for poor Sybil but also worried for Geoffrey. His eyes looked like he'd been witness to torments far too searing for human comprehension, like the traumas of the world were a permanent part of his soul. "You were there?"

"I saw it." For a human, it wouldn't have been a real answer. But for an angel . . . ?

She had to take a deep breath, preparing herself for the deeper question before her. Even as she watched the man standing beside her bed, he seemed impressive, beautiful. There was a sort of light all his own that surrounded him. But it was the immense sadness in his eyes that made her nearly rise, made her want to hold him close, to open every part of herself if it could soothe away even the tiniest portion of the suffering he'd witnessed.

She already knew that he'd healed her torment thousands of times in ways she couldn't fully comprehend. Always, in her most horrific moments, he'd been there, comforting the ache, revealing the inner strength she needed to recover from the most brutal attacks. Still, it wasn't merely any sort of gratitude that pulled her toward him. Seeing him there, meeting him in the flesh, brought out an immense desire to hold him, to know once and for all that he was close. Maybe she would even be capable of giving him something in return. Her hand reached out. Maybe now . . .

She didn't get the chance.

Geoffrey returned to himself, taking a step toward the door. "I can explain more of what you need to know tomorrow. There's too much to tell it all at once."

He seemed about to leave. The very idea made her mourn. Her desire to be close to him wasn't merely about his physical beauty, although there was certainly plenty of that. She wanted to be useful to him — as an assistant, maybe as something more. Sybil had even suggested that . . .

She let out a sigh, her eyes closing, as she realized that he'd sidestepped her questions yet again. He was a pro at that.

She didn't want him to go, though. Okay, so it was thoroughly inappropriate for him to be here in a darkened bedroom with her in the first place, but her life was far too weird — in far more serious ways — to worry about so minor a point. Besides, she didn't really want him to see her solely as an employee.

He appeared to be waiting for her agreement before he left. He stood a step away from the door, his back to her.

She didn't give it. "You're an angel, aren't you?"

He looked up to some point she couldn't see, and a golden light suddenly seemed to surround his auburn head.

"You and Glory both are."

He glanced back at her.

She found the strength to say the rest. "So Damian is really a . . . ?"

He actually laughed. It was the first smile she'd seen from him in a while. "Choosing a name like that, was there ever any doubt where he came from?" He shook his head, glancing to the side. "He has a ridiculous weakness for pop culture."

It was Lydia who was laughing now, especially given how outdated the reference was. Still, she supposed, to such beings, time was probably a fairly relative concept. Sybil had even suggested that she'd been dead for 157 years. If Geoffrey had also seen that incident . . .

Lydia let the idea fade quickly; it added just a bit too bizarre a twist to her life.

Okay, so things were strange enough as they were. Her past was best not mentioned. Geoffrey was an angel, literally, and she would've been weepingly happy to hear him whisper sweet nothings to her for eternity — maybe this time in a language she could understand. And naked — naked would be good. All of that she could handle. A several thousand year age difference, though . . . not so much.

He said nothing to answer her wishes, probably fortunately. His gaze made something within her warm, his look worried. "Are you frightened?"

She knew what he meant. She'd spent the entire day — a lot of her life — in permanent freak-out mode. But she wasn't doing that anymore. There was no joy in that.

The part of herself that was so determined to ignore all the weirder realities of the world had been safely subdued, was currently tied up and forgotten in some small space within her, abandoned along with her attempt to reinvent herself as "Linda." With any luck, she'd stay there. Who had she been kidding?

"No," she answered finally. The only real fear she had was in never knowing his love.

This was a sudden — and undoubtedly ridiculous — notion, in many ways. Primary among them was that angels getting it on with humans was considered a less-than-positive pastime by most Western religions.

Of course, most religions she knew would also be more than happy to take a girl who said that a demon lived in her basement to the nearest mental health facility and leave her there, so they weren't high on her list of favorite people. Maybe none of them really knew what they were talking about.

He smiled at her. It was a look that was guaranteed to get her heart thumping, especially in a darkened bedroom. Then, sadly, he turned to go, his voice soft. "See you tomorrow."

She knew she should let him. It was the only sane option. He was her boss. It was already late, and she had to get up ridiculously early the next day and try to remember the new rules of life for every type of supernatural creature that no one besides her believed were real — and for her, only just recently.

Besides, her next thought wasn't an appropriate one to voice to him. She wasn't even certain where the idea had come from, besides her constant desire for him. She gazed over him, the curiosity rising.

Oh, to heck with it.

"Um, Geoffrey." Looking into his eyes made her blush furiously. Maybe one aspect of Clarissa's new life did make sense. "Angels are supposed to be sexless, right?"

She saw one of his eyebrows rise and was caught between wanting to laugh hysterically at his surprise, hide under the covers in mortification for ever having thought of it, and continue to stare at him with a sudden, and really earthy, curiosity as to the answer.

He didn't say anything, making it seem much harder to get the next words out.

"So, um . . . " She looked down at the crotch area in question. "Do you have . . . ?"

He just looked at her for a minute, but he was smiling slightly. Finally, he walked back to where she lay. When he leaned down, her heart started thumping so heavily that she was certain even the probably eavesdropping cats could hear it.

Her pulse raced faster, as he slowly traced her indigo hair back behind her ear. When his lips came closer to it, she thought she was going to hyperventilate, his voice warm and caressing. "Would you like me to show you?" And then she felt the sort of flush Clarissa would never be able to manage again.

In some ways, it was an obvious answer, but "Yes, please!" just wouldn't come out of her lips. Nothing would, her body too overwhelmed by his presence. Had he turned on such tempting charm

with her the day before when she'd been trying to remold herself into
. . . well, something vapid, she might have gone up in smoke. If this
were what he was like as a tease, God help any woman who got more
of him.

Lucky wench.

He continued to stand beside her bed for a second or two after
that, his lips curved, fingers caressing gently down her neck. A moment later, his gaze turned serious, his hand lost in her blue hair,
cradling her head. "Never forget the truth, Lydia." His eyes connected with hers so deeply it was nearly frightening but so sweet she
didn't want it to end. "Never forget how long I've been with you."
Then, one last, lingering gaze left behind, he retreated for the night.

It was a tangle of raw but dementedly happy nerves that collapsed on her bed that night. She didn't think she would ever sleep.

Sometime later, around early morning, Lydia woke to discover
herself in bed in her pajamas. She sat up quickly.

The living room light was off, only a soft glow, reflecting down
the hall from the kitchen, illuminating the room. She gazed down
at herself. She couldn't remember having changed, having even gone
to bed. There was a deep sigh. *Damn.* It would really suck if the last
thing that had happened had been her falling asleep in the car on the
way home.

She looked at Eveningstar, who was curled up at the end of the
bed, acting as Lydia's own personal foot warmer. "Was it all just a
dream?"

The Persian's tail swished once before settling back into place.
"You tell me, Miss Angel Bait." Then, she ignored Lydia and went
back to sleep.

Lydia fell onto her bed with a *whump*, sighing deeply, not at all
astonished that, even if it had only been an illusion, Eveningstar had
seen it. Now that she thought about it, the cat and her tortoiseshell
companion had long been in her dreams. As had Geoffrey. Her sigh

deepened. It appeared that, no matter how much new weirdness she accepted, there would always be at least another few mysteries waiting just around the corner.

Chapter Six

With a start like Lydia had had that night, it was a surprise how quickly she got back to sleep, the shocks of the day immense. Knowing that Geoffrey had been in her bedroom left her with a warm sort of comfort. She wanted to believe that their conversation had happened, that he had left her with such a very intriguing reminder. Even if it hadn't been real, one odd fact *was* clear. She had no idea how she'd managed to get into her pajamas.

The possibilities that mystery left open got her mind racing. She knew she should probably find it creepy, but oh, she didn't. Only a bit of disappointment lingered. If her apparently angelic boss had changed her clothes, it was just typical of her luck that she'd been unconscious when it happened.

This was Geoffrey all over, as far as she could tell. There were always hints of sensuality about him, many moments when he treated her more like a potential lover than an employee, or even a friend. Maybe that was all part of the angelic service — although it put an entirely new twist on the whole "guardian angel" thing.

It was with these odd, if intriguing, questions that she eventually made her way out of bed the next morning. Try as she might, she couldn't get the cats to confirm or deny any of her theories. For once, they were perfectly silent when she pleaded with them. Even her offer of doughnuts only made Eveningstar's left ear twitch. They clearly had no intention of telling her the truth.

She made herself breakfast, focusing on *not* thinking about the possibility of Geoffrey's hands upon her. She didn't find it remotely unnerving that he might have touched her while she slept. It was clear that he would never do anything she wouldn't want, her comfort with him total. While Damian probably wouldn't be deterred by fully spiked and plated battle armor, the angel she was so attached to was, thankfully, not the same. She knew without question that it was not only her body she could entrust to his care.

Such a truth ignored the fact that she wanted very much to do far more than simply "entrust" herself to him. Lounging before him in the world's least-subtle nightie, begging him to take her, might have more accurately expressed some of her desires. Still, she imagined that it wouldn't have been a particularly convincing enticement. She had never even been in a real relationship. Seduction wasn't exactly her forte.

This sad fact determined her mood. She made herself an egg in toast but only managed to pick at it, while the cats sat evaluating her from across the dining room. They were probably wondering why she'd stopped pestering them.

Then again, they probably already know.

Omniscience was definitely their neatest trick.

It was a little unnerving to know that your cats were far more knowledgeable than you were. She tried to console herself with the fact that they were no ordinary animals. Given her limited experience with anything but the weirdest of worlds, it probably wouldn't have taken much to understand a lot more than she did, anyway.

She was just starting to doubt herself again, stabbing distractedly at her breakfast with a fork, when she heard Eveningstar sigh deeply. When she glanced toward the pair, she could have sworn that she saw the Persian roll her eyes at Tiger before muttering, "This again."

The black cat smoothed herself elegantly along the floor, her chin propped on one foreleg. The looks both of them gave her suggested the sort of endless patience mixed with eternal condescension that only felines could produce. Whatever their other interests, they were clearly ready to wait.

She decided to take the hint, stowing the fears away once more. Doubting herself would get her nowhere.

She scarfed down most of the toast quickly before rising to drop one of each of the last two pieces into the cats' half-full dishes. The only way she was ever going to understand the man . . . angel . . . whatever . . . was by being around him. She checked the cats' water bowls, grabbed a jacket, and headed out the door.

She found Tiger looking up at her, as she was about to close it.

"Have a good day," she purred.

Lydia decided to accept that as a positive sign.

She returned the good wishes before heading off to the office. The air outside had taken on a slight chill overnight, suggesting that it was October, after all. At the top of one of the closer trees, a couple of leaves seemed to be pondering the merits of taking on Fall colors, while the rest of their compatriots continued to ignore such strange diversions. It was the start of the type of autumn day she'd always enjoyed being out in, a soft sort of weather containing no extremes. She let it calm her, preparing for the morning's work. Events were bound to become strange soon enough. Just enjoying the normality of the morning was a pleasure.

It was when she was most of the way across the parking lot near her apartment that she saw one of the hounds waving at her. Laurence — Lon, she supposed — was dressed for a day's work, looking not the least bit strange, except for the fact that he had quite thick hair growing on the back of his hands. She could see it even from a distance, could only imagine what it would look like, otherwise.

"Getting used to it?" he called.

Her smile was mostly genuine. Okay, so maybe normality wasn't the right word, but "normal" had always been a highly relative concept.

She responded that she was working on it, to which the wolfman chuckled, getting into his car. Where he worked, she could only guess.

"Tell Geoffrey to keep you close!" she heard, just before he shut his door.

She had to laugh at that. If only he knew what she wanted.

She waved at the werewolf, as he drove by, but had to blush, as she turned down the main road toward the office, remembering. Given the way Geoffrey had held her when she'd been introduced to the hounds, the pair would have had to be mentally deficient not to have noticed her feelings for the man. Heck, even the cats got it — but she supposed they weren't the best examples of incomprehension, anyway.

She made her way carefully down the hill, as she pondered Geoffrey's possible feelings for her. Her own for him weren't really in doubt. True, she'd just met him, but Lydia was wise enough to realize that such a fact only applied in a more mundane sense. She was mostly accepting that reality wasn't as unyielding as people pretended.

She was supposed to learn more about "super-realities" today, if Geoffrey's hints last night were anything to go by. Whether that whole conversation had happened in the physical world or not, she accepted its basic truth. Despite her occasional wishes, her dreams never lied to her.

That fact left one obvious conclusion, but it wasn't one she was ready to address. That Geoffrey was an angel she could handle, oddly. She'd mostly felt that from the start. That he was somehow connected to her — obvious as it was — was harder to believe. As ungrateful as she was certain it was, she didn't want him as just her protector.

She was caught deep within these desires, and the many questions they produced, when she realized that she'd arrived. That wasn't the cause of her sudden disturbance, however. She was halfway up the stairs before she discovered the source of that inner tingling of panic. She was only two inches away from someone who was watching her intently.

Gail's friendly smile froze Lydia to the depths of her soul, before she even finished looking up completely. The woman's blue eyes were bright but chilling, like a sunlit iceberg awaiting an unsuspecting ship.

"I see you're getting into the swing of things." She beamed. "Have you become one of us yet?"

Lydia wanted to scream — sudden, searing memories assaulting her. She could feel the doorknob digging into her palm.

There had been something in Gail's gaze, something Lydia had seen far too often in her parents' eyes whenever they were hiding their real intentions. It was a look that worked for all the world, made anyone with absolutely no ability to read beneath the surface say, "Aw, see how much they love you?" She shuddered. It was the look they had given right before—

She couldn't finish the memory, wouldn't let herself, responded out of instinct, understanding that there was no true friendliness being offered here. Her voice was hoarser than any clueless observer would ever understand, spitting out the words. "I'll never be one of yours." Despite all her usual desire to be nice, she made her way quickly past this pretty poison, slamming the door in Gail's face. Then, she was blissfully rescued from any further persecution.

Geoffrey's presence just inside the office, her immediate retreat into his protective embrace, saved her from her next would-be tormentor. Damian was standing not five feet away.

"What a rude little pig you've hired," the Head Demon observed in the friendliest tone imaginable. "She doesn't even know how to treat the other managers."

Geoffrey's arms spasmed slightly, as he held her more tightly.

"Whyever do you think she's worth it?"

The Head Angel kept her from having to endure any more of these pleasantly vitriolic assaults by leading her into his office, the door shutting firmly behind them. "Ignore them," he whispered, holding her close. "They don't matter."

She shook slightly against him, the unexpected adrenaline of her memories wracking her.

"*You* matter."

She wanted to say something, wanted to explain. It wouldn't have made sense to any outsiders, certainly. Gail's words were only friendly and welcoming, Damian's insults on her conduct understandable.

But no normal observer could see the past, the one that continued to batter Lydia in blood red flashes. An altar, but not to anything holy. Vows she could not force her mouth to say. A human-sized slab of slate-colored marble. An intricately carved, deadly sharp silver knife. But mostly she remembered the brand, the torment of it searing into soft human flesh. All of it went back to those words.

She shuddered uncontrollably in Geoffrey's arms. *No! I will never be one of theirs.*

She couldn't help it, could do nothing to stop the sobs, that hideous old wound making her whole shoulder nearly writhe with pain. She would've felt like an idiot for such a reaction had she still been trying to ignore all the truer realities of her life, but such a greeting from the demon's assistant would have done far worse to that foolish, Linda side of herself. Only the stronger part of her soul could remember such torment and survive.

"Shh," Geoffrey soothed, his hand stroking tender circles over the once-abused skin of her shoulder blade. Even if her clothes hid the spot, she knew that he understood it was there. "You've rejected them."

She hid her face against his chest.

"They can't have you, unless you accept."

She wanted to believe. It was what Lyle had told her, as well.

Lyle hadn't been Geoffrey, though, hadn't even been close. He might have saved her, had definitely seemed like a blessing at the time, but his love had never been real. To him, she'd only ever been an interesting spiritual experiment, a living expression of his desire to be an exorcist. He'd been gentle and kind with her, had even been the only man she'd slept with, but it hadn't been love. He'd only been interested in what he could discover, and she'd been desperate enough to be grateful for anything that looked like a friend.

She'd been easy to win with even mild concern, then, so long as it had been remotely genuine. And it had. Lyle had seen her through that awful night in the basement, the one where she was supposed to—

She couldn't finish the thought. He'd even been the one to sear the blank brand over the demonic one, to blot it out, as much as that was possible.

But the first was still there, still marked her in ways she was certain she could never escape. Gail's words just reinforced the fears, making her shake all the more. That she was allowed to work for an angel was a miracle. She was lucky that he would even acknowledge her.

Her boss, her protector, continued to hold her close, soothing away what could be reached of the many torments of her life. "You're safe now."

His breath was warm against her, her arms surrounding him further, wanting to convince herself that he was real.

"They can torture your body. They can abuse your mind, heart, and soul." He embraced her even more completely, making her feel protected from any such fate. "In the worst cases, they can even rend you limb-from-limb. But they *cannot* have your soul, unless you let them."

One of his hands moved under the collar of her jacket and dress, soon covering the scarred flesh on her shoulder, warming her to her core. "Unless you relinquish it, that belongs only to you and God."

And you, she wished. But she could only think it, too afraid to speak the desire aloud, so fearful that her need for him could prove far too greedy. It had started too long ago now to stop.

He'd been with her on that awful night, his spirit part of her, as she'd managed, somehow, to stop the ceremony. It was he who'd given her the strength and courage to survive the hatred her parents called love, the torture by her peers. It was his presence that had taught her beauty existed in the world, even when she'd been given no signs of it. It was he who'd shown her life's meaning.

Maybe he was an angel, was only meant to observe. Maybe she wasn't even meant to meet him now. But nothing, besides his wish, could make her let him go.

That was what she hoped, but she feared a tendency far less beautiful within herself, the love and belief that flowed through her from his embrace almost too immense. If she let herself, she could desire him in the most selfish ways, already did on a level every religion said angels weren't supposed to know. If she weren't careful, she'd beg for him.

She stayed close, taking in his scent. She already had him in a way few others could ever understand. She'd have to learn to content herself with that.

She was trying to convince herself of this truth, as the moment went on, now lovingly tender. In the peace between them, she started to realize that, whatever she might want of him, all that she couldn't possess, she did have a part that was, somehow, hers alone.

She understood it, although it would be difficult to discuss. Mostly, it came down to this: being with him was like being with herself, with those deepest parts of her that were most essentially of God. The being she was so far inside herself that she could never explain it to anyone else was connected to him. Thankfully, at least some part of the reverse was true, as well.

Maybe it was just the bond he shared as an angel with all those he oversaw. Maybe it was the little piece of heaven he brought with him to share with the world. Whatever it was, part of it was hers. She breathed a sigh of peace against him. There was pleasure enough in that fact to live on for now.

She'd stopped crying a while ago, yet he hadn't let her go, undoubtedly knowing that she wished to stay near him. The place where his hand soothed against the burned patch on her shoulder felt especially good, warmed something deep inside. Even if it reminded her much too strongly of her desire for him, she'd happily take whatever he could give.

She wasn't certain how long they stayed like that, too lost to such peace. Unfortunately, they were eventually interrupted by a rapping on the door.

She could have sworn that she heard Geoffrey sigh, as he slowly let her go. He spent a minute arranging her collar before issuing a rather hoarse, "Come in." By the time the door opened, he appeared completely professional, but his hand did brush lengthily along her arm on the way back to his side.

Lydia had a little trouble following after this, too many emotions confronting her. The terror of her memories had probably dislodged some of her brain, but it was really Geoffrey's amazing soothing that had temporarily robbed her of her ability to speak or think.

His spiritual presence during her earlier years had been enough to see her through a life spent on the very precipice of Hell. Being in his arms, having his hand touch her wound, left her nothing but a speechless wreck. Her thoughts turned. Heaven help her, if he ever kissed her. She'd probably go up in smoke.

Her mind was decidedly distracted. Only his glance brought her back to the scene before her, and rightly so.

A young ghost girl was in his office, sighing — if such a term could be applied to anyone in her state — asking them to come visit her mother. She was very faint, only a small smudge of smoke, human features rippling over the surface for a second or two before disappearing again. Had Lydia witnessed her yesterday, when she'd still been trying to deny the truths of the world, she'd probably have convinced herself that she wasn't seeing the girl. But she wasn't heartless and oblivious enough to do so anymore.

Geoffrey was listening wholly to the child, barely even seemed to remember Lydia. Some selfish part of her wanted to feel sad about that, but she understood that there was much more going on. He was very worried.

She focused on the girl, chastising herself for her distraction. There were times when it was okay to be brain-boggled by a gorgeous angel and times to work. This, certainly, was one of the latter.

Geoffrey had heard the entire situation by the time she was paying attention again.

"We're going to be there in a minute," he assured the girl.

She started to fade away.

"But first." Lydia had thought herself forgotten — although she couldn't blame him — until he pointed toward her. "This is Lydia. She's the new tenant manager."

The small cloud of smoke puffed toward her slightly, and she managed not to back up by reminding herself that she'd no longer live in "Linda's" willful ignorance.

Geoffrey looked at her tenderly, pointing toward the fog. "This is Allison."

A small face rippled across the smoke for a moment before it was lost once more.

"She and her mother, Mandi, are tenants of yours." His gaze was very serious. "We need to go visit them."

Lydia couldn't do much but nod. She was really feeling her lack of experience.

"Meet us outside the door. We'll help her."

He seemed to be more hopeful than confident, but she didn't want to do anything to undermine him. All she could do, as the small cloud faded away, was smile. It was time to learn what her job really entailed.

Chapter Seven

Lydia wasn't entirely eager to discover what lay ahead of her but was determined to be useful now. Geoffrey closed his eyes before leading her out of the building. She followed his example in ignoring Damian and Gail, who seemed to be saying less-than-pleasant things in the most blandly friendly voices about the ghost girl's mother. It was only once they were well away from the office, walking toward the nearest apartments, that he finally spoke.

"Mandi's husband is one of Damian's tenants. Until she can move on, Allison is trapped here with her, and Matt gets to stay, but she's having trouble understanding." He sighed, continuing before she could ask. "Sometimes, hope is a trap."

Lydia didn't ask more, fearing what they'd find at the apartment, following Geoffrey up the front stairs. The small puff of smoke was waiting, as was another familiar face.

Sybil shone bluely at them, her hand on the little patch of fog in what seemed to be a comforting manner.

"Geoffrey." She smiled. Then, looking further, she positively gleamed. "And Lydia!" She surveyed the pair speculatively, murmuring, "Hm, not yet." Her gaze travelled along Lydia more thoroughly, her voice then rising. "But you've accepted more! How wonderful!"

"Sybil." Geoffrey's voice was quiet, nearly the sigh of an old friend who knew better than to try to make any significant changes. His eyes said that he would've been amused had he not been so worried.

"Oh. Yes." She gazed down to the smoke tenderly, her hands on what might be shoulders among all the ether. "Let's go talk some sense into your mommy, dear."

To Lydia's surprise, Sybil suddenly seemed far more capable, guided the puff of smoke through the front door of the apartment, as Geoffrey unlocked it.

"Mandi, darling!" the ghost woman called out, as Lydia and Geoffrey took the more traditional route inside behind her. "Please come out. Little Allison is worried about you."

Lydia had little idea what to do, so she stood beside Geoffrey, watching quietly.

It took a moment, but a woman did appear, fully formed if rather fuzzy around the edges. She was dressed like the ideal soccer mom, just like Lydia had always envied growing up. She had no doubt that all the woman's, probably still living, friends had been the same ones she'd had since her sorority days.

She looked like a prize, if only the shade of one, anymore. She also looked rather angry.

"Becka, I'm sorry. I don't have any time right now." She didn't even seem to notice the living beings in the room. "Allison won't put on the dress I bought her. Matt's going to be very upset." She crossed her arms, looking aggrieved. "She knows we've got to make a good impression for his boss." Her foot began to tap. "Why does she always have to act like this?"

She began wandering around the room, straightening things. But none of the objects she seemed to be touching were actually there.

It was, to put it mildly, a rather eerie scene. Despite her attempts to stay calm, a feeling of terrible unease started deep within Lydia's soul, as she began to fear the truth. She glanced over to Geoffrey, saw how tight his entire body was, a wounded sense of sympathy rolling from him as he watched. For all he concentrated on what was happening, he did take Lydia's hand, and she began to realize a deeper fact. Just being witness to this would definitely require someone's support.

She looked back to the room, feeling sick, wishing she could stop this, but there was no way to now; that was all too clear. What Mandi was going through was only a reenactment.

She didn't even see her daughter — or the small puff of smoke that represented her spirit — in front of her, seemed to think that the girl was off in her room in a house they no longer had the physical bodies left to inhabit.

It didn't take much analysis to realize what was happening. These were the moments right before the woman's death. This was the reality she couldn't break free from.

The prim ghost continued to lecture whomever she had been talking to, the earjack for a cell against her cheek, as she straightened objects in some other time. "What about the charity ball?" She seemed to be listening, as she rubbed a spot off of something invisible. "No, not that night. Matt's . . . " There was the slightest of pauses. ". . . got a meeting then. Oh, the Bevenshires will be there? He might be able to shift things around. They've been so good to us, after all. I don't know any other chairmen like . . . "

It was torturous watching the events unfold so slowly, suspecting where they would go, but that didn't stop them. Mandi's head turned suddenly, the fear not entirely hidden in her eyes. "Look, honey, I've got to go. Matt just came in." Her hand reached for the button, her eyes seeming to meet with someone's who wasn't there anymore. "Yeah. Uh-huh. Bye."

She walked forward. "Matt." She was kissing the air nervously. "I've got everything ready. You don't have to be nerv— um, no not nervous. Of course not. *I'm* nervous. That's what I meant. I'll just . . . I'll just go check on Allison."

It went on from there, relentlessly. Nothing could stop it, not the past. No one in the room even tried. Sybil, Geoffrey, and Lydia could only watch in horror, the little cloud of smoke seeming to shiver, while first one red mark, then another appeared on Mandi's ghost, as her invisible, angry husband struck out his revenge. For what, it wasn't entirely clear. But Lydia supposed that was never really the point, anyway.

She was more than questioning her job — the moment everlasting in its pain — by the time the horror eventually ended with the image of an open red hole in the woman's chest. The angel had Lydia's shaking hand held firmly in his own, fingers entwined, as both of them tried to get through it. She didn't need to be told the rules. Once something like this started, it was apparently impossible to break in. The only thing you could do was wait it out — and pray.

It did end, finally, thankfully, for all those who had to watch.

Just as Mandi's image was about to fade, the little cloud of smoke spoke. "Mommy? Mommy, please, answer me."

There was a shimmering to Mandi's outline, as her daughter's pleas went on.

"I don't want to stay here, Mommy."

An image of the woman grew more solid.

"Please, Mommy, take me away."

They all waited, holding their breaths, at least for those such conditions could still apply to. Finally, the last image faded, replaced by the sight of that same woman, now dressed in white. She sat on the floor, her knees tucked up toward her, fingers playing with something they couldn't see. When she broke her silence, it was with a sigh. "I'm sorry, Allison. It isn't supposed to be like this." She looked away. "It isn't supposed to happen like this at all."

Sadly, Geoffrey let go of Lydia's hand then, but she understood his intent too well to question. He was soon in the middle of the room, kneeling before the woman's ghost. A golden light extended from his back into the shape of a beautiful pair of wings, his eyes the kindness of heaven. "What did you think would happen?" She shimmered for a minute, glancing away. "How did you think it would end?"

The woman didn't answer, but she didn't disappear, either. Lydia hoped that was a positive sign.

Geoffrey's voice was loving, powerful, entirely irresistible. "Amanda." She gazed up to him, looking for answers. "He never loved you. You knew that. He was just the fantasy your parents and friends wanted."

She didn't resist this truth, as saddened as she seemed.

"Nothing you could have done would have changed it, once it started."

Lydia wondered about this fact but was in no position to comment. Besides, she saw his point. The only way Mandi could have changed the situation was either never to have entered it or to have escaped. And she knew from experience that the latter path didn't just take courage. It required the kind of luck only God could create.

Geoffrey's words did seem to bring about the proper end, finally. Lydia was deeply thankful. Although it took more discussion to force her to accept, half an hour later, Amanda did. Her daughter in her arms, they eventually faded away. Then, all that was left was an angel, a human, and a much older ghost in a now-empty room.

Lydia didn't really know what to say after this, watching her boss and Sybil exchange glances. Sadly, his golden wings had faded again, something of beauty lost with them.

She supposed that there was a lot to ask, but so much seemed obvious. There was only one thing she really wanted to know, a new fear beginning. "Do I need to do this a lot?"

She hadn't realized how pathetic she would sound, until she spoke. Sybil and Geoffrey looked back to her, smiling sympathetically. "It gets better with time," he claimed, but something in his eyes suggested that he was really trying to convince himself.

The immense sadness Geoffrey held was on display once more, but it was shown only to her. To her surprise, she heard a small giggle.

"Oh dear," Sybil murmured, looking embarrassed. A second later, she was beside Lydia, holding out a plastic bag with two doughnuts in it. "Give these to Eveningstar. Apologize that it's not more. It's just *so* hard to carry more than that at a time."

Lydia wasn't surprised, had no idea how an ethereal being carried anything physical, anyway.

Sybil smiled. "Must dash! The counter needs tending." She waved. "Bye, Geoffrey!" Then, she disappeared.

Lord, what a morning.

Lydia, now speechless, collapsed gently back against a nearby table, careful not to crush the doughnuts. The cat would kill her, if she did.

Geoffrey was smiling, as he approached. For the first time that morning, he looked genuinely amused. "How do you like the job?"

Darn him. Lydia glared. Were angels even supposed to *have* a sense of humor?

"I'll get used to it," she muttered. It was that or leave him. The latter wasn't an option.

He just smiled before pulling her close, cradling her head to him. "I know." He kissed her temple. "I'm here." Not surprisingly, that made all the difference in the world.

The time they stayed like that was blissful, although, sadly, not eternal. Eventually, Lydia pulled away. It wasn't that she wanted to, more that she was afraid of bothering him. He had already seen her through so much horror in her youth, had clearly been witness to more than any living person could handle. Having to coddle her constantly would only prove an extra burden.

She told herself this, smiling almost shyly, as she gazed at the floor. Besides, there was another reason to move on. She wanted to be useful to him, to earn her place by his side, and she couldn't exactly do that, if she simply kept glomping on him all day.

He was watching her with that curious look, the one she could never quite read — although maybe she was just afraid to — as she glanced over the room. Except for the generic furniture, a nearly perfect match for the pieces in her own unit, there was no decoration to be seen. Anyone could easily think that it had been vacant all along.

She tried to repress a sigh, as she realized that yesterday she would have believed that lie instantly. "I guess we have another apartment to rent."

She more felt than saw Geoffrey smiling at her, the warmth within her tangible. She cherished it but tried to focus elsewhere, new possibilities unfolding. There was no telling what sort of creature they might have in here next.

She had seen only a little of her duties, as the angel put his hand on the small of her back, walking with her toward the office once more, but she wasn't really settled. Even this last half hour had confused her, her participation not necessary. Geoffrey had done all the work. True, Mandi and Allison had been her tenants, but that fact had been the beginning and end of any supposed usefulness; her thoughts turned. Why on earth was she here?

Not surprisingly, Geoffrey picked up on her questions, responding quietly, as they made their way through the parking lot. "Tenant managers have a lot of work. Mostly, they're here to help."

She guessed that, from today, if nothing else. His hand, thankfully, was still on her lower back, although its warmth did undermine her concentration a little. She tried her best to pay attention. "You interview the applicants, when they first arrive. You'll show them the apartments, once they're accepted. After that, you're the liaison between me and the tenants. If they need help you can't give, you'll come to me."

Given the fact that she had done precious little to help anyone thus far, she might well be taking up a great deal of his time, but she didn't say it. She was a little afraid she might talk her way out of a job.

This possibility didn't seem entirely likely, but Lydia wasn't taking any chances. Having finally discovered the physical form of the loving presence that had guided her all of her life, she wasn't ready to give him up that quickly.

As always, Geoffrey seemed to know her fear, chuckling warmly. "Don't worry. You'll get the hang of it soon. The individual needs of the tenants won't take long to understand. You were born to do this."

Yesterday, Linda would have run a mile at that statement. That was all the more reason for Lydia to take it as a compliment now.

She was basking in the pride she felt in his voice, as they came back to the office. Gail was sitting on the front porch, her arms crossed over herself, shaking her head at them, pouting prettily. Lydia followed her boss's wise example and simply ignored her. There was nothing to be gained from humoring her now.

Damian's presence just inside the door was far more formidably frosty. "Well, well, look at you."

His gaze raked over Geoffrey disparagingly, and Lydia actually felt a slight tug at the back of her dress. Maybe he had guessed her desire to claw the Head Demon's eyes out. Apparently, he knew her well.

"Did it make you happy to banish yet another of my tenants?"

An icy staring contest began between the men, the Head Angel continuing to hold his assistant back from defending him. Finally, he did answer. "Yes." Then, he led her into her office.

Lydia found herself unclenching her hands a little, as he guided her over toward her desk, trying hard to calm herself, wondering why she felt such a need to defend him. He wasn't weakling enough to need whatever aid *she* could give. Besides, she suspected Damian always needled people. It was probably the least abhorrent thing he did, especially if he really was a demon. She shouldn't let it get to her now.

Her rationalizations didn't really work. Feeling the demon's eyes upon her back gave her chills, his arguments continuing. "You really aren't fair. Gail works so hard to help her tenants, unlike your new piece of trash."

The venom with which he pronounced the slur was new. Lydia felt herself shivering, despite her boss's presence beside her, had to force herself to sit down calmly, meeting the demon's eyes.

"She doesn't even care about her job. She's too stupid to understand the rules, too ignorant to even believe in them." He took a step closer to her office, his eyes burning a terrible sort of fire; they seemed to have connected with her soul, the scar on her shoulder sending out sudden, jolting shocks of pain. "Look at her, sitting there, breathing, pretending she can seduce you, when my Mas—"

She didn't even realize what kind of a trance she had been in, until the demon broke off in a hiss unlike any sound she had ever heard a human being make. She had to blink hard, before she understood what had happened.

The angel had said nothing, only pointed toward the doorway, but the instant he had, a flaming, sparkling network of silver-blue lit up the formerly empty space. She couldn't even focus on all of it clearly but somehow *felt* the patterns the symbols formed.

There was a shudder, now one of relief. They were the exact opposites of the ones she had seen that dreadful night in the basement, the ones that had nearly killed everything. These held beauty and hope and love, and they had sent the demon nearly flying across the room.

She watched, amazed. It wasn't entirely the effect of the symbols that had rid her of her tormentor. Damian couldn't get far enough away, was clearly forcing himself not to flee, every ounce of courage used to hold himself against the far wall of the outer office. Gail, who had come back in to watch the show, lingered warily just out of his reach, seemed about to retreat into her own room, her eyes wide, shaking visible. The veil of heavenly protection allowed Lydia to watch without too much trembling. But it was what was happening with the demon that nearly sent her into a retreat of her own.

She would have had difficulty explaining the impact of what she saw, none of it particularly obvious. Although slightly narrowed, Damian's eyes remained the same deep, enchanting shade of blue, the white of them clear and without imperfection. His face, too, while slightly contorted — *was that horror? pain?* — was utterly lovely, a trap for the unwary. It was more what was happening behind his gaze that terrified her. It was not a sight for anyone with a heart.

He was glaring at her, hissing. If the eyes were the windows to the soul, this was a view into Auschwitz or a Klan lynching. All the hatred, all the evil, all the pitiless, willful violence the world could ever hold reeked back to her from them — and they left no mystery at all about the fate the demon would like to see for her.

She didn't know how she continued to watch but knew better than to look away, shuddering though she was. Just like earlier with Mandi, she was a witness. And, like Geoffrey, it was her job to know the truth.

It was the angel's intervention that gave her strength, as well, although she didn't recognize it for several minutes. It was only once Damian started to pull himself together, to hide away the realities of his soul, that she realized her companion's hand was on her shoulder, stroking warmly, soothing the ache.

His voice delivered the final blow to the demon they worked beside. "She's mine, Damian." She looked up to him. His eyes were glowing. "Mine, hers, and God's." His touch sent a welcome sense of life deep within her. "None of you can ever have her for a second."

That claim nearly made Lydia want to weep with joy. She didn't let herself question how far it went, not wanting to ruin the moment.

Once the demon seemed more himself — if still positioned far across the room — the angel returned to Damian's previous complaint. "Matt is only where he asked to be. Don't worry," he went on, refusing to be interrupted. "There are plenty of psychopaths out there ready to take his place."

Such a reassurance brought a smile to the Head Demon's face; it wasn't a pleasant sight. "Yes, there are." Then, gathering together what he could manage of his dignity, he retreated into his office with Gail.

As intra-office relations went, it hadn't been the best of mornings. Despite her efforts, Lydia found herself shivering, looking up to her boss for comfort. "Is it always like this?" Given the number of tenants there must be, and the fact that they all had to move on, it wouldn't make for quiet working conditions.

Geoffrey, thankfully, smiled at her. "No." But she could see the concern he hid, a sudden fear growing. She could only hope that it wasn't the truth.

She stared out at the glowing pattern across her doorway, its shade much lighter than before but its presence tangible. She didn't really want to voice the thought but knew that ignorance would only endanger her further. "That was about me, wasn't it?" She felt Geoffrey's hand stop moving against her shoulder and knew she was right. "It's me he wants."

For a long time, Geoffrey didn't answer, fingers perched lightly upon her back. Finally, he sighed, kneeling down beside her chair, pointing toward the flowers that adorned her desk. "Gail brought them," he warned her, and she knew her look showed her feelings.

Despite their origin, she couldn't bring herself to throw them away, their beauty overwhelming. They even went with the now-altered name plaque on her desk that read *Lydia Henderson*. Apparently, like with everything else, he knew she was no longer desperate to rebrand herself.

Her heart ached, as she looked the blooms over. In her whole life, no matter the intent, no one had ever brought her flowers.

"Do you know what they are?" he asked softly, and she shook her head, not even certain of the purpose of the question, just torn over how to feel. He pointed toward a large flower with lavender petals and a purple center. "This is an anemone." His finger moved to one whose petals were some lovely mix of lavender, indigo, and purple, with yellow and orange stamen. "Autumn crocus." Then to one she thought she knew, its petals white and inviting, stamen large and yellow. "Calla lily." Last, over to the one she had almost admired the most, its petals mostly indigo with a white and green pattern near its bold yellow stamen. He looked at her. "Nightshade."

Finally, she started to get it, shivering slightly. "As in 'deadly nightshade'?"

He nodded.

A poison. She had to grimace. No wonder everyone in sight told her not to eat the flowers.

"They're all poisonous," he sighed, gazing back to them. "Beautiful and fatal."

The first part of that was certainly true. That old desire for normalcy made a brief reappearance. "But they're so pretty!"

She blushed, even as she said it. *Dumb. Dumb. Dumb.*

He just laughed lightly, undoubtedly knowing her thoughts, before his own sobered again, returning to his earlier words. "Hope isn't the only trap."

No, she supposed not, was embarrassed to have said it. Of course, other than that particular symbolism, she wasn't certain why the demon's assistant had given her such a present. Despite everyone's fears, she had never intended to start munching down on them, and it wasn't like they killed with their scent. Why welcome her at all, if they hated her so much?

Her confusion must have shown, Geoffrey smiling softly before the look faded once more. "I had a previous assistant. Ivy."

What an appropriately botanical name, Lydia mused, though she didn't interrupt.

"Gail told her the flowers were edible."

A cold fear started within her.

"She believed her."

Two responses to this horrible truth appeared within Lydia simultaneously. One, she wasn't at all proud of. She spoke the other, her concern genuine. "Did you save her?"

The angel sighed. "Barely."

Did he just shiver?

"But she wasn't quite the same afterwards."

Lydia couldn't help it, the second thought breaking through. *Ivy must have been dumb as a post.* Why else would anyone start munching down flowers, especially when *Gail,* of all people, gave them to you? She only just managed not to say it. Maybe not being the same again would improve her.

Geoffrey looked at her, and the heat rose up her face, ashamed to have been so catty, even in her thoughts, her analysis turning inward. Given all the crap she'd convinced herself to believe as recently as yesterday, it certainly wasn't like she had any room to judge. No wonder everyone was so worried that she would just start chomping.

She had to rub at her forehead, as Geoffrey's silence gave her time to pull herself together, reminding herself of the truth. *Pretty poison.* It was a rare person who wasn't tempted.

She was herself again when she looked to him, was warmed by his understanding smile, but the concern in his eyes remained. When he asked, "Do you want to know what they mean?" she understood why the worry was there. She should have known there was a deeper message to be found.

She was well aware that she just hadn't wanted to think about this truth, but ignorance could be deadly. She knew that too well.

Had she not understood her parents' plans for her, she would be both dead and in Hell right now.

Not knowing enough about flower language to translate on her own, she needed the help. She took a deep breath, bracing herself, nodding. Might as well get it over with quickly.

He was gazing into her deeply, clearly preparing her. That wasn't a good sign.

She tried to smile, and he turned back to the flowers, pointing at them in the same order as before. "Unfading love. Cheerfulness or abuse not. Majesty. Truth."

Okay, on their own, they should have been comforting, but the source of them was disturbing. After all, there were certain situations that people called "love" that were far better off fading, anything to do with Damian or Gail definitely among them. The trauma she'd just witnessed poor Mandi reliving was another hideous reminder of that. Her parents had always expected and demanded her outward cheerfulness, as well, had accused her of hurting and using them, if she showed any kind of sadness, whatever their myriad insults, attacks, and plans. And that thing they had called up at the ceremony that had branded her had been a type of royalty, if only in Hell. As for the truth . . .

She was shivering heavily by the time she looked toward the angel, finishing out this idea. "Do I really want to know?"

Unfortunately, it wasn't Geoffrey who answered. To her shock, she discovered the demon standing just outside the barrier that protected her. "You already do," he smiled worryingly. Then, he left the building, slamming the door behind. The reverberation shivered lingeringly through her heart.

She came back to herself a few seconds later to find Geoffrey holding her hand. She looked up at him, frightened.

His gaze was beautifully strong. "You have me," he reminded her.

She grasped his hand more tightly in response, praying for his strength, fearing she would need it. She'd clung to his presence once before and survived. Maybe this time, she'd be lucky enough to make it through with a little more sanity intact.

Chapter Eight

The morning, thus far, had been awful, too many messages received, the fear welling further by the minute. The past was catching up, making Lydia shiver. Despite Geoffrey's promises, she feared she might find no way out this time.

She tried to distract herself by helping the applicant who sat before her desk. Even if she feared she might be falling back into her old ways, she didn't want to think yet about all Damian's hints might mean.

The day had continued on a bit too quickly from the moment of the demon's departure, a dozen possible tenants soon arriving, leaving her little time for analysis. As before, she wasn't certain how they had heard about the opening. Geoffrey had left her a stack of applications with names, only this time with a difference. She was finally allowed to read their contents.

She had to admit that she was almost glad she hadn't before. They would have sent that poor idiot, "Linda" side of herself screaming off into the woods.

She'd already been through three werewolves, four ghosts, and a succubus ready for a career change, among a dozen other major shifts to her world view. Even had it started in a much more settled manner, it wouldn't make for most people's typical day.

The distractions were probably helpful now, the revelation that the flowers, which were still on her desk despite all her more sensible mental lectures, had brought to her far more than she was capable of handling. For anything like acceptance, she would need some time alone. Maybe the cats could help her understand.

The truth, her future, seemed obvious enough, of course, but even Geoffrey had encouraged her not to focus on it yet. Among other things, she had clients to help. There was only so much time left to panic about the possible fate of her body and soul.

She engaged in this odd sort of work therapy with abandon, then, watching the woman before her filling out her form. Although Lydia was starting to understand the basics of most of the other applicant terms she had seen so far — WW for werewolves, GH for ghosts, SC for succubi, as well as, as she had finally figured out, RV for revenant — CP had her stumped. Like the succubus application, it seemed to ask a great deal about the tenant's sexual history, although this one focused more on abstention. Like the WWs, there were questions about physical changes, but mostly whether they had ever happened, whereas the werewolf application assumed they had. She just managed not to shake her head. Yes, it was a mystery, indeed.

She gazed the woman over once again, hoping for clues. There wasn't much else to do till she was finished. She was lovely, was probably around Lydia's own age, with dark hair and eyes, was certainly far more beautiful than Lydia had ever hoped to be. Her accent was definitely European, the name she had put down Irena Simone. Of course, if the WWs were anything to go by, that might be made up.

Lydia smiled, trying not to appear too curious, as the woman looked back to her. She was supposed to be helping, not snooping. There was no point in taking her fears about her own safety out on the applicant's privacy.

Her perusal of Irena thus far — and it was difficult not to stare, she was so beautiful — had already brought a distinctly pink tinge to the applicant's cheeks. Lydia looked away, giving her more space. She supposed attractiveness of that sort would mean that you were always stared at, would probably be quite uncomfortable, after a while. Still, as she started a rather distant examination of the short carpet, it did occur to her that such constant attention should also make a woman a bit more used to it. Perhaps Irena was just shy.

Lydia wasn't exactly unused to being stared at herself, but the scrutiny she gained never seemed admiring, or even entirely friendly. Of course, the blue hair didn't help — most people who would sport such a style probably *wanted* attention — but the stares far predated her current image. Even back when she'd been blessed with a more normal look, she'd seemed to gain all the wrong sorts of interest. Her eyes returned to the beautiful woman before her, starting to understand. Perhaps that was another reason for her discomfort.

She glanced over an earlier application, trying to give the woman her space, mentally and otherwise, attempting not to remember the events of the day so far. She nearly snorted. Like that was possible. Had she only been witness to a beating, however ethereal, it would have been bad enough. But to have been forced to watch a murder . . .

She took a deep breath, as Irena turned a page, continuing to fill out her forms, the silence giving Lydia room to think. It wasn't a pleasant occupation. For much of her life, she had wished for love, not necessarily of the romantic sort, though that would have been nice, but just the true concern of another human being. In her childhood, she had considered once or twice that being pretty would have helped.

It wasn't so much that when she had looked in the mirror, she'd believed herself to be hideous. It was more that she hadn't had much idea of what her appeal might be. No one had told her she was anything but a burden — or a freak. Despite her attempts to believe, it hadn't done much to help her develop any sort of self-love.

She had fought this truth for some time, still did now. Her half-lingering desire to be the ever-normal Linda, a girl who could fit in anywhere, showed that. Certainly, she had never been one of the pretty, popular girls, the ones who always seemed to have everything. The shudder returned. Then again, given what she had been forced to observe earlier today, that might not always be the panacea she had thought.

It was easy enough to believe in this idea, was certainly well preached. Be beautiful, and the world will be yours. Be feminine and alluring, and every obstacle will evaporate. The popular girls in school had seemed to back it up, were never denied anything they had wanted. The freaks like her learned early on not even to fight. Teachers, administrators, parents, other students, all of them would side with the pretty ones in a heartbeat. The unloved had no place at all.

She knew she was being naive, of course, knew it even as she thought it, fighting down her self-pity, but today had brought the lesson home far more fully than before. Amanda and her daughter had been lovely — sweet, agreeable, and model-perfect. It hadn't saved them, might even have made their situation more difficult. Had Mandi been less of a catch, Matt might never have wanted to hook her, and she might be around to tell the tale.

Lydia pondered this insight for a moment, then shook her head. Such a theory only told half the story, if that. It hadn't been Mandi's looks that had killed her, wasn't her blonde hair that had put her in harm's way. That had come down, entirely, to her husband's degraded soul. It had been his hands that had brought her to her end.

Lord. She rubbed her forehead for a moment, wondering how she had gotten here, but she could see the mental breadcrumbs if she tried. Although tempted, she managed not to stare at the current applicant, one truth emerging. Beauty didn't bring happiness. Her gaze caught the flowers before she forced it away. Sometimes, the attention it did give, you were far better off without.

She left these obvious truths behind, then, her musings turning sideways, back to what was becoming their constant home. Her boss might be made to inspire classical statuary, but he wasn't without his worries, either. She didn't even know how he managed it. Geoffrey had had to encounter such ugliness for so long, had witnessed . . . God only knew how much. *Literally.*

She laughed slightly, her head shaking, irony rising. The whole angel thing was proving more difficult to accept than she had guessed.

It wasn't that she was denying any longer, however, that course well in the past. For one thing, it wouldn't do her any good. Her heart froze suddenly, gaze on the flowers again. If Damian's insinuations meant anything, too . . .

She could hear the pounding in her head, but it was better than the memories, than the fear. She couldn't — wouldn't put it all together, didn't want to know, repeating an old comfort. They were gone. The house, her parents, that . . . thing they had conjured were all gone. The pounding grew even louder, as she fought to ignore the obvious. They couldn't come back. They *couldn't*. The "RV" of the revenant's application seemed to jeer her, until she buried it under a succubus and three werewolves. Besides, she had Geoffrey to look after her. She would NOT think about this now.

A bit of the comfort of denial was making its reemergence, despite herself, but she just wasn't ready to deal with the truth. Witnessing a phantom murder, as well as interviewing a fair chunk of the paranormal community, was enough Halloween fodder for one day. She felt a staple drilling into her palm and let go of the papers she hadn't realized until then she was damaging. Demon problems would just have to wait till she was ready for them. Another millennium or two would be nice.

She blinked a few times, trying to rid herself of as many of these fears as she could, staring instead at the previous applications, wondering about her current visitor. CP . . . CP . . .

She picked up a pen, ignoring the fact that she was probably just being nosy, and began to ponder the possibilities, feeling her foolishness, as she tried to keep the pad as far away from Irena as she could. Her pen tapped against the sheets, until the woman looked up and Lydia smiled, forcing herself to at least be snoopy in a quieter way.

Most of the rest of the abbreviations were of one word. She started to scribble:

Captain.

Uh-huh. Of what, stupid? Undead European cheerleading? She glanced up at Irena and felt even more ridiculous, before trying again.

Chaplain.

She almost laughed, imagining. *Our Lady of the Weirdos, we beseech thee . . .* Um, no.

Culpepper.

That's a name, idiot.

Cupholder.

Now, she was just getting ridiculous.

City Preacher.

It was two words. It was much the same as chaplain. And it was incredibly, incredibly dumb.

Cult Provider.

Yep. That's likely. moron.

She took a moment, working with the letters, even as part of her mind realized that she'd been carrying around the two doughnuts for Eveningstar in her pocket for several hours. She took them out at last, laying them carefully aside. If they were too badly crushed, the Persian would be *pissed*.

She picked back up the pen, trying not to tap it again, letting her mind roam. She didn't notice Irena finishing the application, holding it out to her.

"Cat Person." There was a moment before Lydia realized she'd said it out loud. Then, it was her turn to blush.

Irena was staring, understandably, her beautiful, dark eyes wide. Lydia wanted to pound herself repeatedly on the head. It took a lot of will to accept the papers from her, even more to speak. "I'm sorry. I'm new."

Her mind filled in the next bit: *Some excuse, moron.*

She saw Irena blush and felt even worse. A lock of blue hair fell in her face, as she lowered her head in remorse. Who the hell was she to judge somebody else? She was clueless, useless, and probably demon bait. "And I'm unbelievably rude."

Her fingers were wrinkling the paper now. She tried to stop herself, not wanting to damage the woman's hard work, too.

To her surprise, she heard a laugh, warm and amused. *Definitely not Damian or Gail, then.*

It took a lot of courage to look up, but, when she did, she found Irena shaking with repressed mirth. "Sorry," she managed finally. "I'm just not used to anyone saying it without a pitchfork."

Despite herself, Lydia was hard-pressed for a response. Although immensely relieved that she hadn't offended, she was still disgusted at her own brusqueness. Besides, it was a strange conversation to be having. "Do they still have those?"

In spite of the topic, Irena smiled. "You'd be surprised."

It didn't seem a likely way to form a bond, but it worked, somehow — mostly, Lydia decided, because of the cat person's humor. She hadn't really remembered that from the classic movie channel showing she'd once seen, but, then again, *The Wolf Man* hadn't exactly prepared her for the hounds. Perhaps Hollywood wasn't as well versed in its supernatural facts as she had imagined.

This wasn't really a surprise — as happy as she was *not* to find a besotted vampire camped out beside her bed to stalk her while she slept. But any further conversation between the pair was temporarily interrupted by Geoffrey.

To her relief, he was standing in his office doorway, arms crossed, smiling. "Lydia's new to this world," he informed the possible tenant. He said it with enough warmth that she could tell he wasn't angry with her.

She tried not to read his statement as, "She's as naive as the day is long," but knew it was probably true. When he moved forward to collect the applications, the warmth deepened. It was comforting to know he forgave her, whatever her faults. His regard only made her want to work to improve herself all the more.

"There are still a lot of God's creatures for her to meet."

Irena, fortunately, continued to laugh. The way her dark eyes shone as she looked back at Lydia made her seem even more beautiful. "Don't worry about it. *I* wouldn't believe in me if I weren't me." Even her shrug was elegant. "I don't take offense easily."

Given the little Lydia knew — well, the little she *guessed* — about cat people, that was undoubtedly for the best. Having a giant panther stalking you, even if you *were* the Queen of the Idiots, would definitely suck.

Irena seemed more at ease than she had before. Lydia guessed that it came down to Geoffrey's presence. Heaven only knew, he relaxed her. Well, among other things . . .

She probably didn't hide the blush, as her boss flipped through the applications neatly. They landed in three different piles, Irena's alone in hers. It took only a moment, as he glanced through it, before focusing back on her. "The available unit is 951." She seemed to ponder this a moment before nodding. "You can move in as soon as you'd like."

As had happened with Butch the previous day, the decision process was far faster than Lydia could follow, but she saw no reason to ask any questions.

Apparently, Irena did, although she seemed a bit apologetic. "The previous tenant . . . it wasn't a zombie, was it?" She stopped for a moment, gazing at her lap, apparently searching for words. She went on, before Geoffrey could interrupt. "It's not that I'm prejudiced, you know, just that . . . "

Geoffrey didn't appear to be thrown, smiling. "Don't worry. They were ghosts." Irena's relief would have been comical, had her fear not been so obvious.

Lydia understood none of this interaction, but she was growing used to that. Maybe he would explain it to her later.

This was her hope in many areas, but she didn't get very far in pondering any of them, a diffident murmur sounding from the doorway.

When she looked up, she saw Butch, making what was probably supposed to be a polite noise for attention but sounded more like a rather submissive whine. He cleared his throat, staring at the floor. "Sorry. I didn't mean to interrupt." He looked like he expected the traditional rolled-up newspaper to be aimed at him any second. "I just . . . "

"That's all right." Geoffrey met him at the door, leading him in, but even his angelic reassurance couldn't entirely settle the man.

As Lydia watched, she began to suspect why, the werewolf shying away from their newest tenant. He wouldn't even meet Irena's eyes. Despite her determination to treat these people well, Lydia almost laughed, guessing the obvious. Dogs and cats — not the most traditional of buddies.

Her boss didn't seem to notice, leading the man toward the cat person. "Butch, this is Irena. You'll be in 953, across the hall from her." He smiled over to the woman. "Irena, this is your new neighbor."

Uh oh. Lydia was certain that she was right, when she saw the beautiful woman's eyes almost burning. For a moment, a low sort of growl rumbled in her throat. Even Butch looked surprised. But to Lydia's shock, he didn't seem shy anymore.

It was Irena's turn, apparently, quickly looking away. "Sorry. Haven't eaten in a while." She nearly scurried toward the door. "Can I see the apartment now?"

Butch watched her go with a low whine.

Lydia's confusion wasn't answered immediately, Geoffrey placing the keys in her hand, sending her to follow Irena with a look. She felt him pat her back reassuringly on the way, and a sigh left her. At least he wasn't angry.

To her relief, the cat person wasn't, either. She just seemed immensely distracted. They were nearly to the apartment building before she spoke, having only answered Lydia's multiple attempts at polite inquiry with a murmur or two. Her toes scraped at the gravel distractedly, more like a little kid than the elegant woman she had been a few minutes ago.

"Is Butch by himself?"

Lydia blinked, discarding the *"How would I know?"* that played in her mind. She didn't know why she was feeling so querulous today, although she supposed a witnessed murder and a demon threat might be somewhat involved in the answer.

Instead, she tried to remember what she had peeked at of the man's application. She really only remembered that question, his name, and the moon chart. She shook her head for a moment, as Irena gazed up at her. She looked partly like Eveningstar expecting a treat and partly like a cautious stray, ready to run. Nope, Lydia didn't get it at all.

It was difficult not to wonder, but she came to no real conclusions. Maybe the woman planned to play tricks on him? Hopefully, she wouldn't be too bad, if she were one of Geoffrey's choices. "I'm pretty sure," she answered finally.

"Mm," Irena murmured. It sounded like a purr. It was also the last thing she said for the next 15 minutes.

Lydia tried to be professional, confused as she was. She finished finding her way back to what had, only this morning, been poor Mandi's apartment and showed the woman around. The fact that it was very similar to her own helped.

As far as she could tell, Irena took in none of it, her far-off stare focused blindly on the floor. Lydia suspected she could have said, "And here's your kitchen. Be careful of the elephant," and gotten at least as much response. Then again, given the weirdnesses that were now commonplace to her, maybe she just hadn't discovered her own kitchen pachyderm yet.

She forced herself not to shrug. If Irena had any questions later, she could ask. Presumably, Geoffrey knew what he was doing.

It was only as she was turning toward the door that final time, asking, "Is there anything else you need?" that she got any sort of response.

Even then, it was only to see the woman stare in surprise before smiling an, "Oh." The look only deepened after that. "No. Nothing."

With this, Lydia considered herself dismissed. She left the woman with an invitation to come ask if she changed her mind, wondering just what the heck the last half hour had all been about.

As she moved toward the parking lot, she tried to shrug it off. Cats had their own rules. Cat people probably weren't any different.

She meandered her way back toward the office, but her mind was roaming. Despite her efforts, her progress was slow. She didn't even hear Hugh and Lon approach. "Cat got your tongue?" the latter inquired, and she began to wonder whether all werewolves were quite this perky.

The last one she'd seen certainly hadn't been. Her arms were crossed over herself distractedly. "Just confused," she muttered. A second later, she imagined the responses this might bring and held up her hand. "Don't say it! I know." The shrug finally emerged. "Permanent condition."

They both laughed with her. Or, at least, she hoped it was "with" and not "at."

Despite the short amount of time she had known the hounds, she was comfortable in their presence. They might understand a heck of a lot more than she did, but they didn't seem to dislike her for the fact. Besides, they were cheerful. Given some of the events of the day, that was a blessing.

It was Lon who answered, brushing a strand of hair away from her face. "And what has you confused this time, my pet?" She heard Hugh chuckle at her other side. "The job? Your tenants? The fair Geoffrey?"

Even she had to smile, although she decided to take the opportunity to ask, ignoring the last implication, knowing it was only too right. "The tenants. Or rather, two tenants." She stopped before they did, looking at them, as they turned to her. "There's a new were—."

She paused there, wondering if there were some sort of term they would prefer. She had already blurted out, "Cat person!" in a thoroughly indecorous way. Manners, with the supernatural and undead, were going to be a whole lesson in themselves.

Lon just laughed, leaning in, an inch from her face. "Weeeeerewolf?"

She smiled, seeing that, at least here, she wasn't offending community standards. She'd take all the small victories she could get.

Hugh was still chuckling at his partner, as he leaned back, filling in the rest. "If you mean poor Butch." She heard a barely-repressed guffaw from Lon, Hugh just smiling. "Be patient. He's new."

"And smitten," Lon finished.

This was news to Lydia. She glanced back and forth between them. "With who?"

Hugh's brows went up, as his partner laughed again, filling her in. "With our fair new catwoman, of course." He waggled an eyebrow at Hugh. "She might just return the favor, as well."

Oh. She was staring off into the distance. It had been *that* type of growl.

"I almost thought she was going to ea—" She'd nearly said "eat him," but held up her hand, closing her eyes. "Please don't finish that!" She'd been enough of an idiot for one day.

She wasn't spared, however. The hounds were howling — well, nearly — their amusement too great to contain. She almost wanted to point out that the pair were clearly different species but decided against it. After all, she was in love with an angel and the probable obsession of a demon. Normality wasn't exactly her forte.

It took another minute for the hounds to settle, Hugh, at least, attempting to hide his mirth at her amazement. She didn't know whether she should just thank them and go before she made an even bigger fool out of herself, or whether she should stay and try to be polite. As she pondered it, Lon took a deep breath, trying to regain his control at last. "Anything else you need to know?" The "You poor, naive soul" there was only implied.

Part of her wanted to just go, knowing Geoffrey could probably answer all her questions, but decided against it. She still felt foolish and guilty for blurting out Irena's status like that, didn't want the angel to start to wonder why he protected her. If there were any more mysteries she could have solved without displaying her ignorance to him, it might be best to do so.

Hugh, at least, was waiting when she looked up, had apparently anticipated more.

She gave in. "Irena asked about the previous tenant." She believed the woman's claim that she wasn't prejudiced. Geoffrey wouldn't have chosen her, had she been hateful. "She wanted to know whether it was a zombie."

Okay, so it wasn't a question, or could have been at least three. Hugh, amazingly, picked up the right one, pointing to himself. "Sensitive nose," he explained. "The scent of the dead, even the undead . . ."

Lydia, fortunately, had no idea, but she could imagine, given her previous demon encounter. "A bit smelly?"

Hugh smiled, but Lon, surprisingly, was serious. "Or worse." She just stared at him, wondering. "It makes you hungry."

She couldn't help it. Her eyes widened.

His own just closed, head shaking. "Eating people — very, very bad."

The hounds were quiet now, their eyes haunted.

"I imagine," she answered dumbly, then shook her head hard, her eyes shut for a moment. "Sorry. No, no. I don't." How could she ever claim to?

When she looked back to the pair, she knew they saw the truth of her sympathy. Lon tried to smile, but it fell flat quickly. Whatever he was remembering, she was happier not to know.

"It's the beginning of the madness." Hugh looked over toward Damian's apartments. That alone told her more than she wanted to understand.

To think that there were creatures who might be eating people in the demon's units was not a pleasant insight. She shook it off, her gaze showing her sympathy. "I'm sorry." Whatever the hounds — whatever all of the tenants and residents went through — she truly had no idea. There were too many ways to suffer to begin to imagine them all.

Hugh and Lon seemed to understand her concern, each patting her on an arm. "Don't worry about it, love," the former smiled, having apparently pulled himself back from his musings. "You don't have to understand everything to help them out."

That was one of the more comforting thoughts she'd had all day.

She started to leave, then, little else left to say. As she walked away, she heard the same sort of "Oh," Irena had given.

She turned back, confused. "Have I got a 'Kick Me' sign on my back or something?" Maybe Damian was capable of magically transporting hackneyed practical jokes?

"Hardly." Lon grinned.

Hugh shook his head, coming up to her. "It's Geoffrey." Before she could misinterpret, his smile deepened. "He's left his mark."

This was a much-too-evocative statement, especially coming from a werewolf. Lydia had to shake her head.

Lon, still laughing, joined on her other side. "It's a pentagram."

Her eyes widened, remembering too many of those.

"A right-side-up one." His gaze chided her, and she had to shake away the irrational fear again. Some memories were hard to forget.

Once she came back to herself, she did wonder, though. She tried to look over her shoulder to where Lon's hand had touched her back, just over her heart. It was a dumb move, no way to see anything. "How can you tell it's his?"

Hugh smiled at her. "It's glowing."

Her eyes widened, dumbfounded, remembering the pattern of protection over her office door earlier that day. Apparently, she wasn't the only one to have witnessed this particular ability.

The wolves took that moment to leave her, hand-in-hand. "Goodbye, my dear."

"Send Geoffrey our love!" Lon added, waving. And all she could do was watch them, stunned.

It had, she decided once mental activity began again a moment later, been a long day. Hauntings of murder, demonic threats, cat people, werewolves . . . all of it confounding.

She held her hand over her heart, as she stood there, and could nearly feel the warmth of Geoffrey's protection glowing inside her. He always did that, always looked after her. Her eyes watered a little. And she loved him. Not for this or anything else, but for him. Too bad he was an angel and what she wanted was never meant to be. As much as she might wish it, there was no reason to believe otherwise.

She wandered back toward the office, while this gloomy thought pervaded her, wishing there were some logical way to hope, but none she found seemed likely. As her past had so thoroughly proven, she was not meant for romance. It wasn't in her stars.

Every experience of her life said so. Normal women, if television were anything to go by, got asked out on dates or at least ended up in some type of relationships. Not her. The one guy she had been vaguely involved with . . . well, it hadn't exactly been conventional.

A laugh emerged, but it was a little mournful, the memories of the night the demon had come for her always too fresh. Lyle had been much more interested in the demon than in her. Their one time together had been more adrenaline than anything else. It wasn't like he had really been all that attracted to her.

It hadn't been that Lyle wasn't interested in women, either, although from what she had seen, he'd certainly tried to repress those feelings in his quest for the priesthood. That night had just been . . . odd, if she was being polite about it. Thankfully, he hadn't been an opportunist, and it wasn't that quashing demons was exactly one big turn-on. It had been more that, in those few moments of heart-quaking relief after the worst had been over, they had each been faced with an altered universe — all his original beliefs in his battle to defend the light reconfirmed in the most searing ways, all her lifelong terrors about the fate of her soul finally allowed to rest. Facing an evil that intent, that rancid, had definitely left its mark. And not just the physical ones. The need to connect with someone else, to confirm that the earth continued spinning, that life was not just some painful illusion, had been the only hope of sanity, for a while.

Her hand rubbed lingeringly over her heart, as she felt the blessing her angel had left on her back. It alone gave her some sort of hope that the stain the demon had left might not doom her permanently. But the questions were not easily answered.

She had not been in love with Lyle, not even that one night they had spent together. He had stood by her, yes, had done his part in saving her soul, but he had done it as a sign of his loyalty to God, not her. While the gift he had given in helping to free her had been immense, her feelings were more gratitude than anything romantic. That one night was an exception. It wasn't like there was any chance it would have continued.

The laugh burbled up without warning. Besides, having her one sexual experience become the cause of her lover's immediate, and massive, crisis of conscience wasn't exactly a panty-dropper.

The relationship between them, then, had never really existed. Even that more normal side of her hadn't wanted to keep in contact with him, once he went back to the church.

Sadly, that was the closest she'd ever come to love. Not exactly the stuff of legends. Well, not romantic ones, anyway.

It wasn't that Lydia could blame the man — or any of the others she'd known. Even before the blue hair, she'd been too different. Her parents' demonic plans for her aside, she had always been a supernatural magnet; her caustic laugh returned. It figured that some lecherous vampire was the best offer she'd had in a while.

This wasn't the whole of her lack of appeal, however. She found herself pondering it, dawdling on getting back to the office. It just wasn't like she was all that great a catch. She was weird, at least half-traumatized by her childhood, didn't have even the most basic social skills. And it wasn't like she was immensely hot enough to make up for any of these other deficiencies. She was, as she always had been, a freak.

She kicked a pebble across the lot, approaching the office's front door. How she was lucky enough to have Geoffrey willingly look after her was a miracle, required an angel's patience. Her desire for anything more was a fantasy she would simply have to nurture in the dark.

"Glad you know," sounded behind her, in the one voice, besides the demon's or her parents', she wanted to hear least.

She froze, as much as she wished to run, Damian crowding her even further, whispering in her ear. "You can never have him. He'll never be able to claim you."

She didn't know exactly what he meant by this but wasn't able to concentrate on figuring it out. His presence alone made her shiver, every cell of her body trying to crawl away from him, frozen as she seemed to be. All she wanted was for him to go away.

Damian, of course, wasn't leaving. He ignored her disgust, or rather, he fed on it. His hand stroked the air, near the spot on her back where the demon had marked her that night. To her surprise, she could hear Geoffrey's protections burning him, could smell the singed flesh, but her tormentor didn't move away.

"Geoffrey's a dreamer, if he thinks he can save you. You belong to my Master." His hand pressed even closer to her skin, the sound and smell of the burning increasing. "He'll pay you back soon for his exile."

He was trying to touch her, she knew, was trying to bring out the demon's mark once more. The fact that she had willingly burned off her own flesh just to try to cleanse herself of its defilement meant nothing to him.

Despite the sense of terror and physical illness his presence brought out in her, her outrage rose, not willing to let him think he could claim her. No. She was *never* willing to go back.

Unfortunately, telling him this proved to be nearly impossible. It was like one of those awful nights she'd suffered through so often in her childhood, her entire body paralyzed, as she had lain in bed, some terrible presence of evil swarming through her room, doing its best to claim her at last. Try as she always had, she could never scream, could only lie there in horror, as that *thing* menaced her soul.

Her mouth opened, doing her damnedest to form the words. Still, just as she had found then, she couldn't get out the sounds, only her lips working: "Leave me alone. Leave me alone." It was the best she was able to do.

She needed to fight him, knew she was losing, couldn't let him undo what had cost her so much pain to perform originally.

She closed her eyes, as Damian's hand pressed closer, her lips working faster, trying to find the will to reject him or run away, a thousand images from the horror of that night assaulting her. As they flowed through her more quickly, the rage grew greater — her fury at her parents for wanting to sacrifice her to that thing flowing hotly through her bones. It grew inside her, melding with her blood, started to burn. *No!* She would not be a victim again.

The words began to grow into a faint whisper of defiance. "Leave me *alone.*"

Damian just chuckled at her resistance, his hand almost touching her skin.

The revulsion that flooded her with that thought finally aided her, the need to be rid of him, to be safe, pounding through her soul. Her anger exploded with it, voice ripping from her, now a screeching demand. *"I said to leave me alone!"*

What followed after this left her reeling. A shockwave of silence made her totter, nearly fall.

Geoffrey caught her. She opened her eyes to discover a parking lot that was empty except for the two of them and the many lights dancing before her eyes, Damian nowhere to be seen.

Glancing around, confused, she nearly fell again, looking back to the angel. "Where . . . ?" she began, but he only looked into her, concern and . . . something else burning in his eyes. If he hadn't held her up, she would have collapsed. She had no idea how he had gotten there or what was going on.

He left her in the dark, for now, simply putting his arm around her, turning her toward her apartment. "Let's go home," he whispered, leading her along. Apparently, there was nothing more to be said.

The journey took longer than she would have suspected, her legs immensely shaky. She couldn't understand how such a small confrontation, as hideous as it had felt, could have drained her so thoroughly. Even in her childhood, those nighttime paralysis episodes had only left her feeling miserable and sick but not so indescribably weary.

The lights that swirled before her now seemed unbearably bright. She tried to force herself to speak, but the exhaustion made it difficult. "Wh-wh-at ha-hap-p-pened?"

The effort made her sag further, Geoffrey now mostly holding her up, her mind spinning. She might always have been shy, but it really shouldn't take *that* much effort to talk.

"Shh," he calmed her, but his own tension was much too clear, his body the one rigid thing keeping her standing. "Not yet."

He was probably right. By the time they got to her building, were faced with the stairs, she nearly keeled over. He let out a sigh before picking her up, carrying her to the apartment in his arms, or, at least, she assumed so. She seemed to black out a little by then.

By the time she came to, she was being placed gently on the sofa, the cats letting out a series of hisses and cries that sounded nearly . . . well, catlike. When Geoffrey moved away, she let out a whimper at the loss of his warmth, squirming onto her back. Not that she could blame him for leaving. She clearly wasn't going to be the life of the party anytime soon.

She heard the door close, as the cats jumped onto the couch, beginning to crowd her. Their hisses were starting to sound almost like words by the time they took their places, sprawled over her.

They didn't seem any more pleased, though. She had nearly blacked out again by the time they started to purr; she hadn't realized that cats could reach that volume. It was rather soothing. It made her want to . . .

She nearly fell asleep — or possibly passed out — by the time Geoffrey returned. One particularly loud purr woke her, as the angel sat down, lifting her head to place it on his lap. It wasn't just her lack of strength that led her not to protest.

Now, she couldn't deny it. This was nice. He stroked back her hair, humming softly, back to the language she couldn't quite decipher.

She listened all the harder. When she nearly made out two of the words — "angel" and "mine" — the cats' volume increased so much that she became certain the neighbors would complain. But then she started to feel much more peaceful than before.

She didn't try to understand, just lay there for quite some time, draped over by purring cats, plopped warmly onto Geoffrey's lap. She wasn't actually sleeping, more just existing in heavenly peace.

When something like real consciousness began to build again, her thoughts were a little shaky, moving to earlier in the day. A bit of guilt peeped out. It took a while to voice the thought. "Left . . . doughnuts . . . in . . . office," she managed at last. She would be lucky if Eveningstar didn't claw her to death.

To her surprise, not a single such weapon emerged, although she did feel the cat twitch slightly where she was flopped over Lydia's stomach. A moment later, there was a snort from the feline. "Be quiet, or I'll cover your mouth."

At least she could understand them again. Still, that was when Lydia knew this must be serious. Anything that could make

Eveningstar deny doughnuts would have to involve the crack of doom.

This possibility began to worry her, as Geoffrey continued to stroke soothingly along her temple, his sigh quiet. His touch alone was blissful, made it hard to concentrate. "Do you know yet what you did?"

The question didn't help to settle her entirely, but it did open her eyes. It was the sort of thing her mother would have asked her frostily. The answer usually involved not genuflecting properly to the picture of the anti-Christ, or something of the sort.

She saw both cats glare at the angel, their purring increasing, and found it hard to speak again. Her guilt was always strong, even without a cause. "D-do?" She might never have a chance to be precious to him, but it hurt her physically to disappoint.

His sigh increased, the cats glaring. "It's not . . . " He paused, as she worried.

Eveningstar let out what sounded like an, "Idiot," half-masked as a meow. That was odd. She wasn't usually that subtle. But Lydia soon wasn't able to think so far.

Geoffrey's sighs were almost shuddering now. His hand caressed across her brow before coming to rest beneath her chin. That alone made her shiver a little — in a very pleasant way. A moment later, he leaned down, his lips pressed to her ear. "Do you know what I would do if I ever lost you?"

She wanted to sort through the statement. Truly, she did. But Geoffrey's fingers were stroking softly along her neck, his head pressed to hers. Hoping for rational thought was kind of deluded.

The fear did emerge, though. "*Can* you lose me?" He was an angel. If he meant that the demon could still claim her . . .

His breath shuddered against her, his hand reaching down to find her own. He had to extract her arm from beneath the cat, but he managed it without too much feline fuss, entwining their fingers together.

"I can lose you *like this*," he whispered, squeezing her hand. She was certain she felt his kiss against her temple but was too afraid to believe it was true. "I could lose this lifetime with . . ."

Tragically, that was as far as the statement was allowed to go, a pounding knock sounding on the door.

Lydia jumped slightly, as Geoffrey sighed, pressing his face close to hers for a moment before slowly sitting up. "Come in," he acknowledged hoarsely. But he didn't let go of her hand.

She didn't know what to make of any of this, as much as she would have liked to, but it wasn't like she was trying to get away. Since he hadn't moved, she continued to lie there, listening to the cats and Geoffrey's sighing, as the lock turned.

A moment later, Glory entered. One look made it clear she wasn't happy. And a six-foot, two-hundred-pound head angel in a bright red dress was nothing to mess with, when she was pissed.

Glory made this instantly obvious. The door had closed behind her solidly, her face glowering like a disappointed mother, arms crossed. "Well?" she demanded, staring at Geoffrey.

To Lydia's surprise, the other angel didn't seem the least bit apologetic. "She banished him." His eyes were surprisingly dark, when she turned back to watch him. "Damian deserved it."

"Wait. I what?" the blue-haired woman wondered, only to let out a small, "Meep," at being on the receiving end of Glory's stare. That wasn't a sight for the faint of heart.

"Shh," Glory commanded before glaring back at Geoffrey. Clearly, Lydia was entirely secondary to the conversation. "Care to explain that again?"

Lydia wanted to back up that request but had the sense to stay quiet. She turned her head, watching Geoffrey, who wasn't flinching under such cross-examination.

"I *said* she banished him." His tone was almost petulant, and Lydia began to feel a little like a contested doll. The thought disappeared, as Geoffrey's eyes burned. "He was trying to renew the mark."

That wasn't anything Lydia didn't know already, but it made her shudder, nonetheless. Somehow, hearing the demon's intentions spoken as a certainty made the peril seem far more real.

It took a second to really focus back on Glory, whose worried look flashed back and forth between the pair on the couch, her eyes narrowing. "Did he succeed?"

Geoffrey's hand was underneath Lydia, warm against her back, his eyes still bold. She knew he was renewing his own mark, her whole body heating, healing. "*No one* will." He looked down to her tenderly. "Not while I exist."

It was a lovely moment, his gaze saying so much. Lydia barely dared to hope that any of the messages she imagined were real.

The intensity was broken by a small, "Hmph," from Glory. When Lydia glanced back, Glory had propped herself onto the side of a large chair, her arms crossed, as she watched Geoffrey sarcastically. "All right, Romeo. And where were you? Jerusalem?"

This seemed to be an old joke between the pair, even if there wasn't much humor there now. Strangely, too, Lydia realized that she already knew the answer. "He was with me." Her gaze met Glory's. "He was beside me the entire time."

It was what had given her the strength, she was sure, to rebel against the demon. Something inside her sank. Just like with Lyle, that one night. He, too, had reminded her that she could be herself, his presence making her realize that there might indeed be a future outside of Hell.

Geoffrey's look soured slightly, possibly as a result of the head angel's increased glowering, and Lydia winced, glancing back at her boss, her voice becoming smaller. "Or should I just shut up now?"

To her surprise, Geoffrey smiled, the look warming her in any number of ways.

It was Glory's turn to sigh, the male angel eventually answering the unspoken question in her stare. "Damian will return soon enough." His head nodded toward the window. "*That* will subside."

He gazed back to Lydia lovingly, just as she gasped, seeing that she hadn't been hallucinating earlier. The whole parking lot was a sparkling, multicolored blaze.

When he kissed her temple this time, she was certain it was real. Geoffrey's voice was confident. "Anything else I can handle."

Okay, she was definitely distracted now, the angel she was in love with nuzzling against her. She only heard Glory sigh. "You?"

His lips quirked against her cheek. "Us," he amended.

Glory seemed a bit more satisfied, finally relaxing, as she stood up. But whatever acknowledgment she might have given was more than a little lost on Lydia.

She only caught the sound of the door closing, Geoffrey kissing slowly along her face. Suddenly, she wasn't so sure that her hopes were all that foolish.

Some small part of her mind knew Glory had gone, even thought the cats might have departed. There were a lot of questions, her mind struggling to voice them. "G-Geoffrey," she managed, just as his lips kissed a soft, tender spot along her neck. But the groan she let out was echoed every bit as loudly in the angel.

She didn't have a second to analyze — or doubt — after that, soon caught in a kiss unlike any she had even imagined before. It wasn't chaste, wasn't subtle, was more a plea from the angel's deepest soul. She didn't know for what and barely cared, moaning softly, as her fingers roamed through his hair, begging him to stay close. He didn't seem likely to disappoint.

The intensity of the connection had her spellbound, incapable of focusing anywhere else. It wasn't anything like she had experienced that one night with Lyle, his most fervid kisses seeming paltry and meaningless in comparison.

This touch lit her soul, made her recognize a bond far beyond any she could explain, one that existed on both the most expressively physical and achingly spiritual levels. It wasn't the kiss of someone assigned to look after her or someone who had only a general interest in her welfare, was utterly giving and incredibly possessive, all at once. And it made her wonder, for the very first time, whether it were possible that she might be supposed to know true love.

She had rather lost track of time when the angel finally pulled away, his fingers now stroking lightly over her throat.

She sat up, facing him, as he held onto her hand.

His eyes were burning, not giving her time to question or doubt. "I am *not* Lyle," he whispered fiercely before pulling her back in to him for one more deep, singeing kiss. He seemed to force himself away from her only by sheer will. She certainly wasn't going to be helping, far too addled by love and passion. "Don't ever think that . . ."

His breaths were harsh and unsteady, both his hands holding hers. He broke himself off, eyes closing.

She could only watch, stunned, amazed by his beauty, body and soul. Finally, he kissed her palm fervently, before rising, slightly awkwardly, from the sofa.

He just stood there for a moment, his breathing audible, the change between them leaving her a little stunned. He wasn't looking at her, as he spoke. "You should be safe, for now. I'm going to . . . "

Once more, he stopped before finally turning back to her. His look was a bit more normal, but his eyes still shone. "I'll see you tomorrow." Then, to her dismay, he finally walked away.

Dear God, she wanted to stop him. Heck, she wanted to tackle him, and given the fact that at least part of his body had seemed exceedingly rebellious at the thought of leaving her, she might even have been successful.

But whatever had allowed him to kiss her like that, there was clearly some other force telling him he had to leave. She didn't understand, or even much sympathize, but she trusted that there must be a good reason. Whatever her fears about her place in his life, she knew that he was always looking out for her. If he didn't want to stay to enjoy whatever meager charms she might have, despite his body's obvious pleas to the contrary, she would respect the decision.

She looked over at the cats, who had parked themselves on a side table to watch the proceedings interestedly, as she heard the door close softly. "Angel — human," she pointed out, a little incoherently. "Probably not meant for . . . "

She was interrupted by Eveningstar's elegant sigh. "Tell yourself that," she murmured, placing her chin on her paws. But Lydia tried not to listen. Her own personal Greek chorus of cats could only ever explain so much.

Chapter Nine

It proved to be a long night, sleep quite elusive, despite her exhaustion. The restlessness Geoffrey's kisses had caused was only the smallest part. Apparently, banishing demons with only your voice was fatiguing work. *Who knew?*

Lydia lay in bed, trying to ponder all that had happened on just this one day but found it difficult. She couldn't even begin to think about those kisses, for fear that she might hear mental sizzling, her relationship with Geoffrey a matter for when she felt stronger, other events taking precedence.

Most of them, surprisingly, she could handle. That Geoffrey was definitely an angel, could put disturbed souls to rest, was established, as shocked as she might have tried to be over the matter a few days ago. That werewolves and cat people existed — and that they might even have the urge to mingle fairly intimately . . . ditto. That she was the favorite target of some stupid demon . . . yeah, yeah — been there, done that, bore the demon brand. Her eyes widened. But that she had the power to *dispel* a demon . . . No. That had definitely not been the story of her life.

Given what she had managed that one other, terrible time, this should have been surprising, but today's incident wasn't the same. Then, she had had Lyle with her, throwing every anti-possession prayer he'd ever researched at the thing, the night the culmination of all his years of study. As far as she could tell, she had just been along for the ride, her major contribution coming in the form of constant, silent pleas for her soul to any listening, benevolent deity. She had really only been there as a sacrifice. It didn't seem likely that anything she had done had had that much effect on the proceedings.

Today had been very different. She couldn't deny it, no matter how comfortable it might be. Somehow, with just the power of a wish and a strongly worded, if prosaic, command, she had made

Damian disappear. If Geoffrey were to be believed, which there was no reason not to, the demon wouldn't even be able to return for a while.

Her head shook, amazed. No, it didn't make any sense. No one voice could hold that kind of power.

She was flicking at a mote of dust that was shining in a moonbeam from her window, the strange light show she had somehow brought on earlier today finally having dissipated. She didn't get that, either.

She left the tortured dust speck alone, crossing her arms over herself. Maybe it had just been Geoffrey's invisible presence with her, but he had specifically told Glory otherwise.

Lydia's look widened further. *"She banished him."* Those had been his words. *She.* But how on earth could she possibly . . . ?

This question remained unanswered, a loud thump sounding from her closet, followed by a muttered, "Sorry." It wasn't the first such noise of the night, certainly not the first since her arrival.

She almost welcomed the distraction, no amount of analysis likely to settle her, a more immediate mystery almost a comfort. The cats, she knew, were elsewhere, Tiger consoling Eveningstar in the living room over her missed doughnuts, even as the Persian pretended not to care. Besides, the voice that had also apologized to her that first night had definitely not been the cats'.

She stood up, the day making avoidance of the absurd impossible, and stomped toward the door, remembering the tenants she had met. She might as well be acquainted with the entire bestiary now.

She acted on this resolve, the silence that lingered after the loud *thump* of the closet being slid open making even the cats' murmurings pause. They seemed to be waiting for her reaction.

She wished she could give them one. All she was able to notice was that there was a five-foot-tall scale-model of one of Mad King Ludwig's castles in her closet. It was still under construction — by a small blue creature with large yellow eyes. It looked rather petulant at being caught. "I did apologize," it pointed out.

She should have been shocked. She knew it, even as she raised an eyebrow, one hand propped on the closet door. "And you are?" After a day like today, she wouldn't have been the least bit surprised to find a cross-dressing Yeti in the fridge. Small blue castle makers seemed rather tame.

Her new blue companion sighed rather pathetically. She hated the part of herself that noted that its fur matched her hair. "Alvin," it pouted. It began to scuff its foot against the floorboards, like a rebellious little kid. "Not supposed to get caught."

This told her nothing except one taboo and its parents' lack of naming sense. She continued to stare. "Are you a tenant?" She hadn't realized she was subleasing.

"No," it sulked, watching its own feet, which, she noticed, were strangely disproportionate. "'M an imp."

She let this explanation go as being as good as any other she had gotten this day, focusing on other issues. "And you're using my closet to build a German castle, because . . . ?"

Now, it looked a little miffed. Maybe its guilt was wearing off. Maybe she had asked the wrong question. Apparently, he seemed to find her rather obtuse. "I'm an imp, aren't I?"

She blinked, seeing no reason to question the fact, her silence forcing him on.

"What? You were hoping for one of those guys who just hides your stuff?" He shrugged. "Where's the art in that?"

"Where indeed?" she murmured, crouching down to be closer to his level. Not that it really helped. It was hard to see eye-to-eye with a creature that only stood five inches off the ground.

"Listen," Lydia began. The cats had come in to watch, making her wonder whether this were some sort of initiation. Then again, knowing those two, any spectacle seemed welcome. "I'm new here."

The imp gave her a *well, duh* expression, and she was certain that she saw Eveningstar's tail twitch.

"How about if you explain to me what imps do?"

He looked at her as though she were crazy, and she realized that it probably wasn't a fair question. *"What do humans do?"* would have been rather difficult to answer, too.

"I mean, why are you included in the apartment?"

It didn't help. Alvin only blinked. "Um, I'm in *training*," he said, as though explaining something to a small child. It disgruntled her that she probably deserved it. "Where else do you think imps come from?"

That did it. Lydia flopped onto her butt, looking over to the cats. "Help?"

The feline pairing gazed at each other, before Eveningstar settled herself, head on her paws, letting Tiger do the work. "She's never met an imp before," she explained.

It didn't get them any further. Alvin was incensed. "Of course she's met an imp! *Ev-ery-body's* met an *imp*!"

Tiger blinked, once. Lydia was amazed at her patience, as she tried once again. "She doesn't *know* she's met an imp."

"Oh," he sniffed. "That's different." He plopped down on the floor, which made him seem even tinier. "Whaddya wanna know?"

Well, he seemed more helpful now. She supposed that was a start. Still, finding the right question was difficult. You didn't just walk up to a wolf, for instance, and say, "Tell me about your entire species." Well, you could, but it probably wouldn't respond. Unless it were like the cats. Anyway . . .

She pulled her mind back into gear with some effort, trying not to worry about whether the shocks of the day were causing her to lose whatever tenuous grasp on sanity she might ever have held. "So, imps hide things?" she tried.

"The artless do," he shrugged dismissively.

She attempted again. "So, you . . . "

Try as she might, nothing came after that. Finally, she lowered her head into her hand. "Listen, I'm an idiot, okay?"

He didn't look surprised at the information.

"I'm a two-year-old. I know nothing."

He just watched.

She leaned forward, begging. "*Explain it to me.*"

For a moment, she thought even this request hadn't worked, Alvin looking her up and down. "Babies are big these days."

She blushed but said nothing, since he finally started to talk. "We're imps, y'know?"

She refrained from giving the obvious answer.

"We give life its little ration of chaos."

Her silence made him continue.

"We persuade. We hide things." He pointed at her. "Left your keys on the counter last night, and the next day they're gone?" The shrug returned. "Imps."

Okay, it was actually starting to make sense, in a psychotic sort of way. She shook off the minor desire to run, trying to press further. "What do you mean you 'persuade'?" There weren't too many imp conversations she could remember, up to now.

"Oh, that."

She had to wait. Alvin, apparently, liked an audience.

"The little voice that says, 'Don't do your homework. Go get some ice cream.' That's imps. Or, 'Why should I go home for Thanksgiving? I don't even like turkey.'" The shrug was ubiquitous. "Imps."

In Lydia's case, it had been more the black candles and prayers of gratitude to the devil she had objected to, but she supposed hers was a special case. She tried to focus. "Isn't that just laziness?"

"Pff. Modern talk." His head shook. "That's imps all the way."

She took his word for it. After the lessons of today, she certainly shouldn't judge. Still, it did seem odd, his being here. Geoffrey's ten-

ants and residents were supposed to be . . . well, not necessarily beneficial but at least benign.

She asked, even though she knew she would offend him, needing
to understand. "So . . . imps make minor trouble?"

She predicted correctly. "Hey, good imps aren't troublemakers."
He answered her pressing look. "Sometimes, people need a break in
their work, so they can refocus more clearly later. Sometimes, people's families are jerks they should stay away from."

"And the keys, hiding things?" she prompted.

"Some days, being late could save your life, keep you out of a
horrible accident. Maybe you need to remember to have some spare
keys made, 'cause you're about to lose the main ones." The yellow eyes
glowed, as he defended his work. "Things happen."

Okay, she guessed she could see that, and it made a lot more
sense out of the creatures existing on Geoffrey's side of the complex.
Her earlier run-in with the demon came back to her. "But bad imps
exist, as well?"

He shrugged. "Bad *everything* exists, sister. Get over it."

"Alvin," Eveningstar purred. She was strategically cleaning her
paw, one very dangerous-looking claw extended.

The imp cleared his throat, his cheeks turning a little purple, as
he changed the subject. "But don't blame all that loud music at three
in the morning stuff on us. That's the misery demons."

Lydia was glad she was feeling better adjusted to her life. She
would have been gibbering otherwise. "Misery demons?"

"Yeah. You know, you just got your two-year-old settled down,
when 1000 decibels of 'Sweet Home Alabama' starts blaring. There's
suddenly loud jackhammer sounds coming from above you, just as
you're about to get to sleep, after four nights of intense insomnia."
He looked at her like she would surely understand. "Misery demon
stuff."

She didn't say anything but could see her own inexperience. The only thing that had kept her awake at night had been her parents' black masses — or the things they had conjured. She shuddered slightly but tried to hide it. Maybe apartment living was different.

He didn't seem to notice the gap in conversation, his gaze wandering back up his handiwork. "The worst imps get is hiding the stuff you need." The shrug returned. "Maybe a nasty suggestion or two." His look was apparently caught by something on the structure. "Most of us are pretty helpful." He stood up, starting to fiddle with it. "We just need the practice, so no one sees us."

Lydia managed not to discuss his own minor failings there, feeling lucky once again to be on Geoffrey's side of the complex, glancing over the imp's masterpiece. It was amazingly white. Disney would have been jealous. "And the castle helps the imps' cause in what way?"

"Hey, it's not a cause, sis—"

He was stopped in mid-point of his finger by the sound of Eveningstar sharpening one of her claws strategically along the wooden floor.

He cleared his throat, turning back to the structure. "I just got bored with the whole hide-and-whisper thing. You got a problem with that?"

One long, scratching sound later saw him adjusting a turret on the far side of the closet.

Lydia smiled. As creatures went, he was the least of her problems. "Not at all. I like art."

She stood up, brushing off her hands on her flannel nightgown. It wasn't sexy, but . . . well, sexy hadn't been a priority, up to now. "Let me know when you finish."

She heard a, "You should be so lucky," as she closed the closet door to leave him in peace, but she was certain that she also saw a smile.

There was nothing for it now. No sleep was coming tonight. She wandered into the living room, deciding to try watching a little television. It was a meaningless activity but better than thinking about what the demons might have in store for her. And that said nothing about how overwhelmed she was by those kisses . . .

She was just sighing at the memory, when she heard a small tapping noise. She turned her head, listening to where Alvin's work on his castle had just become much louder, but knew this wasn't the source. She followed it, tired of fighting knowledge, not realizing that she was trailing cats. She only discovered the latter fact, when she heard two loud hisses, as she rounded the corner to her dining room. Unfortunately, it didn't take long to see why.

There, at her patio window, was Gerrard, that bloody vampire. Her eyes narrowed. She had never realized that a bloodsucker could look that pleading.

She could have ignored him but was darn tired of backing down from her problems. Besides, given Clarissa's request to enter the other day, she hoped that the permission part of vampire lore was true. If the woman were just terribly polite, it might be a problem. Then again, she had the cats with her, and Geoffrey was only one thought away.

This last fact settled her, giving the strength it had all her life. She marched over to the glass door, sliding it open to glare. "What do you want, Fang Boy?" It was just her luck that she was apparently caught in visiting hours.

The elegant blond man winced slightly, as though the name hurt him physically. *If only.*

"Lydia, my dearest," he began, reaching out to her.

"Touch me and lose a hand, Scissor Teeth." She was tired of every demonic little Tom, Dick, and Hairy thinking that she was something to be caressed.

Geoffrey would have been another story, of course, but Geoffrey wasn't here.

Gerrard, sadly, was, his gaze all wounded lover, begging for forgiveness. She didn't want to know for what.

"Please let me in, Lydia." His voice was soothing, wheedling. "I just need you to hear me."

It was in this moment that she decided that maybe being a vampire meant losing at least a few important brain cells. The simplest concepts — like "no" — just didn't get through.

She considered calling Geoffrey but decided that this loser really wasn't that much of a threat — not if he was still in the cajoling, feel-sorry-for-me stage. "My ears work just fine with you outside, and I'm not interested, anyway." She started to shut the door. "Just go away."

His hand stopped it from closing, although he was very careful not to extend his fingers past the threshold. She hoped that was a good sign.

He was nearly pouting. "Geoffrey has poisoned you against me, I can see. I had hoped you would be fair enough to hear my side, too."

The slur to the angel annoyed her enough, but the injured bad boy act was just downright pissing her off. "Which part of 'Get lost, you lecherous, bloodsucking fiend' are you failing to comprehend?"

He looked wounded by her distrust, but she didn't let him go on.

"Okay, let me try again. I'm not into fangs. My blood is my own. Underwire nightdresses and bathing in virgins' blood — no thanks."

None of it appeared to be working, Gerrard seeming almost comically pouty. "All right, try this." She leaned a little closer to the door but not too near, ready to slam it, if need be. "Go away, you scheming, abusive freak."

The door closed. And locked. He still didn't go away.

She could swear that she saw a tear, one lone, pristine tear, trail picturesquely down his perfectly-sculpted face. Sighing, her arms crossed, a cat on either side of her, she glared at him, knowing he could hear her through the door. "Are you that confident or just really into rejection?"

It was amazing how glamorous his model looks made his sheer put-upon world-weariness.

He turned and stalked languidly to a lawn chair on the cement outside her door. How he managed that walk alone astounded her. *How can anyone move in leather pants that tight?*

She hadn't really even noticed the balcony there before and wasn't happy for it now. Despite how grimy the abandoned object was, he managed to prop himself on it as though he were waiting for a photo shoot, gazing out into the night. "I'll wait here and hope you'll listen," he announced. One slight head tilt, and he had managed to aim his profile rather sublimely against the porch light. She would have sworn he was waiting for a flashbulb.

She could have left him there — or called Geoffrey to get rid of him. She definitely considered both; despite her hopes of safety, she didn't want to turn her back on him. But the whole kissing incident earlier with Geoffrey had left her with too many questions to bring the angel into this situation, unless it were truly necessary.

Her gaze probed the small woods that bordered the back of her apartment, her mind turning briefly. She didn't know what was living in them, although it was a cinch that they had seen a werewolf or two. There was a deep sigh. Maybe it was just her night to confront the unearthly.

She pulled in a chair from her kitchen, then, opening her balcony door just slightly. She had Geoffrey on a sort of mental speed dial in her mind, just in case. "You're never invited in, so don't even bother, but you can say your peace, if it'll get you to buzz off."

He looked so handsomely grateful; she supposed that was meant to be its own reward. It didn't work on her.

"Don't you want to know why I was so desperate to see you, my Lydia?"

"Do I get three guesses?"

He looked beautifully hurt.

"You have a grudge against Geoffrey and want to steal his assistants?" She went on, as she watched his mouth open. "You're a compulsive collector of women with supernatural connections? I'm your favorite blood type?" He was clearly about to interrupt again, when her eyes rolled. "And I'm not 'your' anything. Leave the theatrics to someone who cares."

His blue eyes shone at her, none of her denials deterring him in the least. "But you're listening to me, my . . . "

She started to rise, closing the door.

His hand shot out in front of him, palm up. "No, wait!"

She did, but her irritation was growing. Just what he thought he was accomplishing, she had no idea.

She watched him for the next minute, as one perfectly manicured finger tapped on the arm of the deck chair, his expression confused. "Why don't you respond to this?" he murmured finally.

She knew he wasn't expecting a response but wasn't in the mood to coddle him. "Because it's trite? Because using a smile to distract from a waiting knife still isn't appealing? Because the cow doesn't get along with the butcher, much less beg to be made into sirloin?"

Strangely, this actually made him smile, a more genuine look this time. She wondered whether it was just another ploy. Everything seemed to be, with him.

"You're a strange one," he murmured.

"Story of my life, pal."

He laughed softly again. "For the last thirty years or more, all they've wanted is tall, dark, and tortured."

She sniffed. "More like tall, light, and pouty, but whatever gets you through the day."

Surprisingly, he was smiling, his gaze more real, as he stared down at the concrete. "Before that, it was all the suave aristocrat thing." He winced slightly, clearly lost in his own thoughts, as she finally sat down, waiting for the rest. "I hate capes."

"Uh-huh." She had a feeling that she had set off something intensely boring, but he clearly had no desire to leave yet.

"And before that!" he pointed at her, growing more animated. "It was all 'I vant to suck your bluhd!" He shook himself a little, remaneuvering his tongue around his mouth. "Hungarian accents are a bitch, when you have fangs."

"I'm sure," she murmured, staring at the ceiling, not at all sure where this was going and even less certain that she cared. "Look, it's getting late. If you could go now . . . "

He didn't take the point, sharp as it was. "You have no *idea* how refreshing it is to talk to someone who isn't interested in becoming like me to save my soul, or looking for a quick thrill with the undead, or searching for an immortal unlife." He shook his head. "I tell you, you can't imagine the type of groupies we get." His gaze met hers. "Do you have any idea how boring it gets wearing nothing but black?"

Style With Mr. Fangs: there was a way she hadn't wanted to spend her evening. Her eyes rolled. "Why don't you toss in a few pinks to liven things up?"

"I'm a vampire," he shrugged, gazing at her uncomprehendingly. "We're all fashion victims."

This was truly getting her nowhere, her head rolling back before she refocused on him. "Look, Gerrard . . . "

When she looked at him next, his eyes were suddenly intent. "*Lydia.*"

She only glared, certain that he was trying to hypnotize her. Hadn't he gotten the point?

He only closed his eyes, though, shaking his head. "You have to be careful."

"No kidding," she muttered.

His head shook again. "Not of me. I just . . . " He sighed, gazing away. "I took the wrong approach with you at first, I admit. I thought you were like Clarissa."

Given what she had seen of that particular vamp fangirl, she wasn't impressed. "Gee. Thanks."

His eyes closed more tightly, before he refocused on her. Surprisingly, his gaze was much more tender. "She's not a bad girl. She's gentle and good."

He didn't seem to be mentioning her IQ. Eating poisonous flowers, becoming thrall to a vampire . . . Was being gullible a requirement for this job?

She blushed slightly, trying not to apply the lesson, focusing back on the point at hand. "So you corrupted her?" She was quite certain that was what Geoffrey thought.

There was a long, tired sigh, as the vampire stared at his entwined hands. "She was bleeding to death." Something about his nails seemed to fascinate him. "I didn't want her to die."

Lydia didn't really know what to say about this new revelation. Partly, it seemed like death would be extremely favorable to living an undead life drinking blood for millennia. Just living in the same body forever seemed rather horrible to her, as accustomed to and relatively comfortable with her own as she was.

Partly, too, it seemed a ridiculous stereotype, the eventual end to every vampire saga. But she also had to wonder at another, horrible thought. If Gerrard weren't lying — and he didn't seem to be now — Geoffrey's assistants certainly seemed to get into deadly danger on a fairly regular basis.

It didn't take long to understand the rest, her blood boiling a bit. Given what Damian had tried to do with her today — the plans he seemed to have for her — it wasn't hard to guess who was at fault for this trend.

A deep shiver caught her. It seemed there was a killer in the office. But she supposed that wasn't exactly a shock, for a demon.

There were a lot more questions to ask the man now, his own conduct less than perfect. However, his voice broke off many of them. "You need to watch out for them. You can't banish him forever. If they win, we're all in trouble."

Despite the seriousness of her fears, her eyebrow raised, understanding whom he meant. "A vampire who's afraid of a demon?"

He sighed, looking away. "I'm not that bad a guy." He went on, before she could point out the obvious. "I didn't cross most of my followers over. I just provide leadership."

Her gaze cut deep, but only to find his shrug.

"We can't help it. It's the way we work."

She wasn't certain how to take this claim. Today *had* certainly started to teach her that these different, unusual species each had their own rules. True, too, Geoffrey had told her nothing specific about the man, had only come to her aid, when she was afraid. The pair didn't like each other, but that might be related to Clarissa; she really didn't know. Tomorrow, she would have to ask the angel to find out.

Gerrard stood, seemed ready to leave. Lydia wasn't certain whether she were relieved or curious, only hoped that she weren't being duped into the latter emotion.

"I'm not the enemy," he assured her quietly. "I just want to make certain *they*," he shrugged his head toward Damian's units, "don't win." His eyes darkened. "None of us will be safe, if they do."

With these words providing an unpleasant sort of shudder, his leather duster billowing in the breeze, he walked down the steps from the balcony to the first floor and took the path between the buildings and the woods, before disappearing into the night. She hated to admit that he looked damn good doing it.

She could only sigh after this, closing and locking the door, her mind drawn back to her past, the vampire's words haunting her. It was a wonder that she could ever have believed that the worst was over after only that one night of her near-sacrifice. How unlikely was that? She had the demon brand on her back, her attempts to burn it off only covering the truth. Maybe it was too much to hope for salvation to ever come so easily.

This disturbing thought took her into the deeper part of the night, pacing the apartment. Only when the cats started to stare pointedly did Lydia finally give up, reclining on the sofa.

Somehow, the place held the most comfort for her of anywhere in the apartment; the reason wasn't difficult to find. It had been here that Geoffrey had kissed her, had kept her close. If she breathed deeply, she could imagine his scent. That alone allowed her to gain a little bit of rest.

This reason noted nothing about the fact that her bedroom was currently occupied by an industrious imp, but the less said about that, the better.

Instead, she lay on her side, Eveningstar joining her to perch upon her knees like a lion surveying the savannah it alone ruled. Tiger could just be heard discussing the imp's progress in the other room. Somehow, the surreal normality of the scene comforted her even more thoroughly, encouraging her to drift.

The change was immediate, as it so often was for her. A wrinkled face peered down into her own, gaze demanding, as soon as she was asleep. "So . . . Geoffrey is treating you well?"

The sight of the little old lady shouldn't have been a surprise. She had been a constant in her dreams for as long as Lydia could remember. "Um?"

The Lady seemed to take that as an answer. "Feh— Angels." She stood, still staring, hands on her hips. "Lovely, sensitive creatures, when they're good — don't get me wrong. But romance? Phooey."

This was how these dream conversations normally went, Lydia always on the losing end. She felt the need to defend him. "It's not like he's meant to be my lover." And, even if he were, he was certainly succeeding in seducing her.

She chased that thought away, as she watched the old woman's eyebrow rise, as though she had heard it, too. Lydia wouldn't have been surprised. "I'm just happy that he's willing to protect me."

"Ha! That's what he lets you think he's interested in? *Protection?*" The Lady shook her head, focusing on the distance, her words half-murmured. "Some of his plan, I see. The Bad Ones need their lesson." Her voice dropped again, eyes sad. "Too many victories they've had lately." The silence of her one long breath seemed to last at least eight days. "Much too many."

Something pulled her back to her listener a moment later, her gaze calmer. "Still, that boy . . . " The words drifted, as she stared into the distance. "He's a thousand years too young, that one. Got a lot to learn. Nothing but work, work, work, all the time." Her look returned to the younger woman. "Where does that get you, I ask?"

As usual, Lydia had no answer. After all, this was her very first job. Of course, it weren't as though she had spent the earlier years of her life in play. More like survival. She just shrugged. If her usual experience with this dream character were true, she wasn't actually looking for anything besides confirmation, anyway.

The woman proved her mental point, continuing, but her gaze was suddenly piercing. "You've got to teach him what he needs, Lydia. You hear me?" She leaned down again, and the indigo-haired woman got the distinct impression that she darn well better do as she was told. "You've both got to learn."

"*Hey!*"

The shout made her jump, waking her thoroughly. She even displaced the cat, who managed to land on the floor with supernatural grace, and a definite glare for the indignity.

Alvin had her manual alarm clock in hand, shoving it toward her. "You deaf or something?" Eveningstar looked like she might object to the imp's rudeness but seemed to think better of it, given her recent ill treatment. "This thing's been waking up the whole complex for the last five minutes." The castle enthusiast leaned in. "You planning to go to work, or what?"

It occurred to Lydia that the imp was doing no better a job at staying unseen than he had before. She hoped that aiding him wasn't considered one of her duties.

This latter idea didn't last long, however, the memory of her dream taking precedence. Her gaze was distant, as she murmured, something about the warning haunting her. "She said I had to learn." That wasn't a surprise, really. There was a lot she didn't know. But something about the way she had said it . . .

The imp blinked at this non sequitur. "Who did?"

She glanced back to him, could see his look of *Is this dame crazy or what?*

She sighed, continuing. "The little old lady in my dream." Nope, that didn't sound nutty at all. Riiiiiight.

The imp blinked once more—this time, strangely, in obvious and total disbelief. "Th—*the* Lady? She *talks* to you?" His gaze sized her up disparagingly before meeting her eyes again. "*You?*"

Eveningstar, apparently, had gotten over being miffed, her claw scratching threateningly along the floor.

The imp took her message, holding back a little, but stared at her, dumbfounded. "I'm just saying — *her?*" The claw cut in even deeper, and he sighed, giving up. "Yeah, yeah. All right."

Lydia was just pleased that she hadn't paid a security deposit. The cat's lessons would have been costly, otherwise.

This wasn't her major reaction, though, her life just getting stranger. "How do you know her?" Alvin's wasn't the typical response to figments of the imagination.

Of course, this didn't tell the whole story. Given the other details of Lydia's life, she knew there was a good chance the images weren't entirely fictitious. Geoffrey hadn't been. Neither were the cats. She stared into the distance. But where little old Jewish ladies fit into the grand scheme of things . . .

She didn't get as far as an answer, Alvin glaring at her for her previous assumption. "We all know her, toots." But this only got him a two-claw reminder to stay quiet.

Wherever this was going, she had no time for it. Tiger taught her that by licking her paw in very close proximity to the clock, before staring at her meaningfully.

Lydia shook herself from her musings. "Right. Thanks." She stood up, carefully avoiding treading on any of her housemates. It didn't take much to guess that that would be considered bad form, all around.

The small scene behind her dispersed, as she moved to get ready, Alvin retreating to his closet, the cats taking up posts on the couch to watch her, as she passed between rooms. Even hearing her pour food in their bowls apparently only made their ears twitch. They seemed determined to see her out the door.

It took a few minutes, but she did leave eventually, glad that she just had to walk across the parking lot to work. If she had had to commute, she would undoubtedly have been late. She even missed waving to the hounds, only saw the back of Lon's car, as he was pulling off down the street. *Ah well*. At least it was helpful having an angel for a boss. He certainly understood the concept of forgiveness.

Sadly, it wasn't Geoffrey she found at first, Gail sneering upon seeing her. "Good job, Freak. Now, I've got to do *all* the work around here."

Lydia wanted to answer, but the other girl moved unpleasantly close, eyes glowing, nearly giving her a chill.

"Damian's going to be *so pissed*, when he returns." Her grin was carnivorous. "I can't wait to watch."

Patience — it was a heavenly quality. The angel's assistant remembered this, refusing to be needled.

The man behind Gail interrupted, anyway. "Kitten, don't tease her." The blond girl preened, looking back to him with obvious delight. His smile was perfect and unpleasant. "You should never play with your boss's food."

Such words alone would have killed any warmer feelings Lydia might have had toward him, but she didn't need them to finish the bad impression. Yet, she also knew that she was supposed to find him stunning. Any other woman probably would have. He was tall and cool and elegant, his suit probably designer, his nails manicured without seeming fey. His dark hair was slicked back perfectly, his green eyes glowing in a way usually only found across a warm bed in a romance novelist's dreams — every inch of him clearly sculpted for fantasy. He even outdid Gerrard in his air of sensuality.

But none of it worked for her. All she could see was the cruelty in his eyes, the cunning in his smile. It didn't take much to guess that all of it must be part of his natural lure. Just what he was she had no idea, although his predatory nature was never in doubt.

Gail purred back to him, her look inviting. "I'd rather have *you* taste me, Roderick." She leaned even further in to him.

Lydia felt like gagging.

To her surprise, someone else voiced her opinion. "Ugh. How very obvious."

The assessment came from the unnaturally elegant woman sitting in the chair outside the tenant manager's office. Lydia tried not to stare, but it was difficult. Even models couldn't look that good, these days. The woman's long, inviting legs were crossed, her black pumps dangerously high. The rest of her ensemble came straight from a '40s movie star photo shoot, the dress hugging every, sinuous curve. Her long, wavy auburn hair could beg a man to touch it, her face classically beautiful. Even Lydia felt drawn to her. She was the sort of woman whose picture many a poor soldier had kept pinned to his wall in wartime, the only thought of home and desire he had needed. It would have been entirely impossible not to notice her.

Their two visitors actually seemed rather well matched to one another, each of them the height of romantic dreams. But they clearly felt nothing for each other. That fact was not only shown in the way they each kept solely to the angel's and demon's respective sides of the office but in the looks they threw — hers all disdainful dismissal, his a scheming lust for her blood. There was no question that they knew each other only too well.

Her words, though, had thankfully broken up the little scene Gail had initiated with her own visitor. The girl glared at her, Roderick smirking behind her back. Only Damian's assistant couldn't see the pair's utter disinterest in the blonde, as she faced down the woman. "Like you can talk with that outfit on, you miserable harpy."

The perfect girl grinned, apparently thinking that she had won a point, although the woman's look clearly showed her endless boredom at the taunts. Gail's finger ran down Roderick's side when she moved beside him, the man allowing her touch with a grin, however little attention he was actually paying her. "You're only jealous, because you can't have Roddy."

Such a claim was only too ludicrous, on every level. Even a bystander like Lydia could see that.

The man Gail was pawing — Roderick, apparently — gave a most unpleasant little smile, his hand lifting her chin to capture her gaze. "My dear." His look only pretended to be warm. "Haven't I warned you about using that name?"

"But Roddy . . . " the blonde girl pleaded, in the most disgusting manner. His index finger traced lingeringly along her throat, right down to her breastbone, his smile widening, as he seemed to contemplate taking it further.

"Two years, three months, five days," the glamorous woman commentated.

Gail looked a little startled, pulling away uncertainly.

The woman only smiled. "Do drain her dry, Roderick. She's even more tedious than the last one."

Ah, Lydia understood now, her eyes widening, as the word escaped in a whisper. "Succubi."

The beautiful redhead smiled at her. Thankfully, for many reasons, there was no malice in it. "No, dear. Succub*us*. I'm only one woman." Her head nodded over toward the male visitor. "*That* boring creature is an incubus."

The woman's smile hadn't faded, eyes friendly. The look was unusually warm, given Lydia's lurking fears about her kind. Still, she lectured herself. The succubus *was* on Geoffrey's side; Lydia bit her lip, berating herself. She had to learn to stop being so prejudiced, especially against beings she had no knowledge of at all.

The woman's, possibly unintentional, lesson was learned by the tenant manager, even if Roderick looked extremely displeased. "I hate that term, Hattie. There's simply no sex to it."

The succubus only rolled her eyes in response. Apparently, there was some disagreement about terms within the ranks.

"Um, Roderick," Gail drew his attention again. This time, Lydia noticed, she was keeping a little distance. "I can help you in here." Gail clearly couldn't decide whether to simper and invite or avoid completely.

Lydia would have found this amusing, had she not found Roderick so especially repulsive.

Gail seemed determined to change her mind, though, glaring back at Hattie. "If that *shrew* will excuse us."

The redhead rolled her eyes. "Go away, you tiresome, tiresome girl."

The blonde started to storm away in a huff.

"But Roderick." Hattie's words continued when Gail could clearly still hear them. "Do leave a few bones. Damian does like to have his fun."

It was at this point that the truth dawned on Lydia, making her feel rather shrewish. The woman was trying to warn the demon's assistant. Vapid and cruel as Gail was, Hattie wasn't willing to simply watch her die.

Lydia felt distinctly churlish now, invited the woman into her office, assuming that she must be there to meet with either her or Geoffrey. Mostly, she was just wishing that she would learn. Werewolves, cat people, ghosts, or succubi — they were just people, of varying sorts. The angel's existence alone showed that God must have some sort of purpose for all of them.

She began to wonder whether she herself belonged on Damian's side, as her eye caught the change to the name plaque on her desk, which now read simply *Lydia*. She wondered when that had happened — far too distracted these past couple of days to notice — as she took a seat across from the elegant woman, but her real thoughts were still elsewhere. Her presumptions, her prejudices, had shown themselves too many times these last few days; her sigh was barely repressed. Why Geoffrey protected her at all was a mystery.

Hattie paid no attention to the fact, her gaze distracted. "Not to be rude, but why on earth do you have those?"

Lydia followed her look and saw the flowers, wilted already. Granted, they did seem more like something you'd find moldering in a tomb than a friendly gift, but that truth alone was all too telling. No matter, she found it difficult to get rid of them.

"They were a present," she responded weakly. She didn't really want to say that they were the first she'd ever received.

This wouldn't have been easy to explain, invited too much attention. Yes, she had been saved before in her life, had been inexplicably protected, but more material gifts were rare. Her parents hadn't celebrated Christmas but a rather twisted version of the winter solstice. And her birthday? The only reason she could remember that was because she had occasionally needed it to fill out school forms. Her parents had only provided what clothing suited their purposes, a place to sleep — if that could be managed past the chanting — and enough food to keep her alive. There hadn't been any friends. Those who had looked on her kindly had only done so briefly. Her parents *always* found out. Then it only took one single spell before all such hope would vanish again.

This fact made her want to keep the deadly blooms, surprised as she was that the water feeding them hadn't eroded the glass by now. It wouldn't have been unlikely, given how poisonous they all were.

Still, as evil as the intentions of giving them had been, they *were* a gift. It was hard to turn down the only flowers she had ever received.

She hadn't answered, then, saw no reason to lay her miserable girlhood out before a woman who undoubtedly had more than enough problems of her own.

Thankfully, she was spared the necessity by the appearance of her boss. "I'll take care of them." He lifted the bowl carefully before carrying it into his office.

Despite herself, Lydia wanted to cry.

The angel's eyes were so kind, when he returned. "I'll bring you better ones, from now on."

Oh. The very idea made her heart contract a little, made it difficult to keep back the tears. Flowers from Geoffrey were the most blissful gift she could imagine.

If he even noticed their visitor, he didn't show it yet. He simply came to Lydia, whispering a "Good morning," before placing a blessed kiss on her temple. It took quite a bit of effort not to cry from happiness.

It was even more of an act of concentration to remember their guest — Geoffrey's kiss, seemingly chaste though it was, sending very interesting tingles to rarely used places.

The other woman was almost laughing. Lydia tried not to guess why.

The angel smiled at the succubus before gazing back to her. "I see you've met Hattie. She's one of our oldest . . . "

The woman raised an eyebrow at him, and he laughed.

"Sorry. One of our most long-term residents." His head tilted toward his assistant, whose chair he stood by, hand on her back. "This, of course, is Lydia."

"That was never in doubt," the elegant redhead smiled, and Lydia was almost relieved not to understand the deeper levels to that statement, certain they would have done her no credit. The woman reached out her hand. "Pleased to meet you."

Lydia shook it warmly, even though she was rather uncertain about the woman's powers. A little part of her, part she wasn't at all proud of, couldn't help remembering that Roderick had apparently been able to steal several years from Gail just by his brief touch. The rest of her mind lectured her about her own experiences with prejudice, however. There had been more reasons than her parents' spells for why she hadn't made any friends.

Hattie, to Lydia's dismay, clearly saw her battle, her smile somehow remaining. "I've taken nothing from you, I assure you." Her teasing gaze went to Geoffrey. "But if you want to kiss her again, I can probably get a meal just from the contact high."

"Hattie," he murmured, shaking his head. But his hand wandered slowly along the back of Lydia's neck, as though drawn by pure instinct, putting those earlier shivers to shame. She had a sudden, vivid fantasy of pushing him into the other room and having her way with him, for hours. The tip of his thumb ran up just under her hairline, and she couldn't quite hold back the gasp. No man should be able to stoke that sort of reaction that simply.

She could see that her boss was staring pointedly at the succubus, but the woman only shrugged in response. "Nothing to do with me, dear boy." She sat back in her chair, watching.

Lydia had a lot of trouble focusing.

"Now, if you don't want her to spontaneously orgasm, you might want to stop touching her."

To Lydia's surprise, it seemed to take a bit of an effort for him to stop. The notion of pushing him into the other room was growing stronger all the time.

Hattie raised an eyebrow, as his hand trailed along Lydia's back. Sadly, a moment later, he pulled away.

She couldn't stop the whimper that escaped her at the loss, the angel pulling a chair up nearby.

Hattie was barely repressing her laugh. "Have some mercy on the poor girl—" Her eyes moved down for a moment before he took a seat behind the desk. "—and yourself, Geoffrey." Her look glowed. "There's only so much you can get away with in public."

Lydia was having a lot of trouble paying attention, her fantasies of the man beside her incredibly, wonderfully graphic. She suspected that the succubus was telling the truth, when she said she had nothing to do with that. After all, Lydia had been thinking about him constantly since at least the first moment they had met. It wasn't like she required a lot of outside encouragement to go further.

Whether Geoffrey noticed the state she was in or not wasn't entirely clear, but he did change the subject. His eyes were kind, glancing over her before refocusing on Hattie. "Why don't you explain a little about yourself? Lydia's still learning."

This was only too true. Lydia leaned forward onto the desk, her hands in her hair, pulling herself back together. She didn't like where her self-analysis took her, once she did. Professional, she wasn't, but, thankfully, the succubus seemed to understand.

As her earlier behavior came back to her, a little of her distraction with the angel wore away in sorrow. She hid her face for a moment. "I'm sorry for my doubts." Her look returned to the woman. "I'm an idiot." She shrugged but knew no excuse was really good enough. "I'm just a little lost."

Thankfully, Hattie shook her head, as forgiving as Irena had been. Lydia knew she didn't deserve it but was grateful, nonetheless. "It's this modern world. They don't raise their children right."

This had certainly been true of Lydia's life, but she knew that wasn't what the other woman meant, as she went on. "Once upon a time, people knew we were all real. Of course," she shrugged, "they also wanted to kill us, so it wasn't entirely without its problems." Her smile was genuine. "Hiding the fact that we exist has probably been the safest path we could have taken, in the end."

She undoubtedly saw that Lydia was feeling lost, continuing. It was for the best, any distraction from her own failings welcome. "Let me tell you about us."

Lydia nodded, waiting, as the succubus went on.

"You know the legends generally?"

She nodded again, the whole stealing-life-through-sex thing pretty clear to her.

"The bad ones you can easily imagine, then."

Roderick passed by the office at that moment. He almost stopped to leer, but Geoffrey's gaze moved him on.

Hattie ignored him gracefully. "For the rest of us, we simply find methods of exchange that won't harm."

This was too concise a description, left Lydia blinking.

The succubus went on. "Take last night, for example. I met a young man in a bar who was two days away from death."

Lydia's gaze widened, understanding from the woman's look how literal the description was.

"He had pancreatic cancer that had metastasized. He was a good man, if depressed."

She had to admit it, despite her sorrow for the young man in this tale. She wasn't getting it.

The succubus' description didn't stop here, however. "I offered him a night of pleasure, which he was able to perform far better than he had imagined." She shrugged at Lydia's look. "I fed off the cancer. It's a living thing, as well, in its way." Her smile widened. "I'm happy to say he faces a whole new outlook on life today."

"Wow," Lydia murmured before blushing. She had assumed that being a "good" succubus would simply involve abstinence.

Her assumption, apparently, was obvious. "Sex is life, to my kind," the woman smiled. "There are many more opportunities than you think."

Despite herself, Lydia was a little nonplused. She looked over to Geoffrey, wondering, even if she said nothing. She had very little experience in this area. Lyle had been so guilty after their one night together, but that wasn't much to go on. She had never really imagined that a creature who seemed to exist on such constant, casual sex would be on the angel's side.

She didn't get an answer to this puzzle yet, Hattie rising. "I see you have things to discuss. I just wished to introduce myself." She smiled down at the woman kindly. "Don't feel too bad about your questions. Ignorance breeds fear." She nodded a goodbye to Geoffrey. "That's why you're here to learn about us, instead."

Lydia could say nothing to this truth, as much as she realized a moment later that she should have thanked the woman for stopping by. When Geoffrey took her hand, even that thought evaporated. Processing anything more than, *Yes! Yes! Yes!* was a little difficult, with him nearby.

He didn't seem to notice, or possibly didn't care. "There are many types of God's creatures, Lydia. They all have their own needs and limitations." The tip of his finger traced a delicate line over her palm, his gaze following. A moment later, his heated eyes met hers. "As well as their own desires."

She couldn't respond. Something inside her head was sizzling, as his fingers entwined with her own, their palms as intimate as his look. As supposedly chaste as the move was, it did *not* feel that way.

"God gave all the creatures of earth five senses as well as a mind and a soul. All of them can receive intense pleasure, which is another of the creator's gifts."

His hand cupped her cheek before stroking slowly along her face. How that was supposed to help the lesson, she had no idea, given the fact that her brain cells seemed to have spontaneously combusted.

"There's also the ability to perceive pain, which teaches us avoidance. Nothing that uplifts us and supports the soul is evil." His thumb skimmed over her lips in a light, sensual kiss. "But God didn't give us bodies hoping for us only to know torment."

There was definitely no pain to be found in his touch, the angel's fingertips now skimming along the line of her jaw, then farther down along her neck. It was so difficult to think, much more to come up with any sort of an answer.

He didn't force her to. "Every creature has to find its own sort of fulfillment." His hand cupped the back of her head, starting to pull her close. "For most of them, part of that is love." His next words were a breath against her lips. "There's no penalty for doing what God wants."

He caught her then in a kiss softer than last night's, but every bit as intimate.

With anyone else, the words would have sounded like a monumental justification, but not with Geoffrey. She could only whimper, every part of her turning liquid in desire. She could nearly hear the sloshing. When she moaned against him, everything but her soul and sense of him on hold, he turned her head, his hand tender on the back of her neck. Then she lost all knowledge of anything that happened at all.

There were probably several minutes of such heated, utter contentment, nothing else quite real in her joy. When he pulled back at last, she thought she heard his groan, discovered her arms around him, holding him close.

His look was burning, as he stood up, pulling himself away. "Perhaps you'd better tell me about your conversation with Gerrard."

It was a sudden change of topic, the man a universal tease. Still, when he stepped away, propping himself against the file cabinet to watch her, she could see all too clearly that she wasn't the only one being tormented. Her eyes widened, not at all meeting his own. *Oh my.*

She heard his shuddering breath, drew her gaze up to his with a great deal of effort. She had no idea whatsoever why he kept doing this, his own desires for more quite apparent. It wasn't like she wasn't willing to help him out.

She sat back in the chair with an effort, trying to calm herself, to find some explanation. She would just have to trust that he had some reason to keep pulling away.

She had forgotten about the messages in her dream now, her brain too passion-dazed to analyze. She didn't question how he knew about the vampire's visit, either, her experiences with Geoffrey all her life, even before she had fully understood his existence, making that clear. She was only confused by one point. "Do you need to ask? Can't you just . . . know?"

He closed his eyes for a moment, seemed to be holding himself back. "It's best if I'm not in your mind just now." His gaze was heated, when it met hers, and she started to see his point. The absolute intimacy of having him in her thoughts seemed enough to do her in, as well. "Besides, I want you to be able to tell me."

Something about this request caught her heart, though she couldn't entirely have explained it. Perhaps it was just the fact that he wished to hear her, as she shared her ideas. Whatever it was, she started to answer willingly. But then Gail emerged from her office, and they both saw the wisdom in not talking here.

Her boss sighed, moving toward his own, inner office. "Come with me."

She tried her darnedest not to think in double entendres.

Still, the sight of her unpleasant colleague took a little of the feeling away, Gail looking rather worn. She thought she saw a hickey on the woman's neck, also saw her smile. Geoffrey closed the door behind them. Maybe she had found some, minor compensation for the risk.

Her eyes met with the angel's, as he passed her, the look he gave making her want to take a few risks of her own.

He seemed to be contemplating the same thing, walking stiffly. She noticed, as they sat on either side of his desk, that the flowers he had brought in were gone. She didn't even bother to ask where they went.

He managed to refocus the conversation, his eyes serious, if still very warm. "Gerrard."

She took her cue, although she wasn't certain how much he needed to be told. "He came by, tried the same stuff again." She saw his anger rise — rushed along, almost fearing for the vampire. "He finally gave up when he understood that I wasn't interested."

Which had only taken an hour or so.

She didn't mention that, another fear emerging. "He did tell me to be careful."

The rage that had showed so briefly was dismissed again, Geoffrey releasing a slow breath. "Damian." His glance traveled along the desk. "Gerrard's afraid, too."

It wasn't a question, so she didn't answer, moving onto other concerns. "He told me a little about himself." If any of it could be believed. "He said that Clarissa was dying, when . . . "

She didn't know how to put it, didn't want to hurt him, had seen his fondness for the woman.

The angel just nodded. But his gaze didn't seem to support the other man. "There are worse things than death."

He didn't go into detail, but her past allowed her to guess some of it. She had never feared death, that night in the basement. She would gladly have welcomed it, to save her soul.

It took a second to draw herself back, purposely calming her breathing. She pressed him, then, needing to know. The vampire had made no promises not to return. "Is he dangerous?"

There was no answer for a moment, his stare distant. Finally, he sighed. "Not in essence."

That didn't tell her much. She waited, was rewarded with more, his gaze returning.

"Vampires feed off blood." He shrugged vaguely. "That's neither good nor bad. Every creature has to eat."

She pondered this, realizing, a second later, an unpleasant fact. It weren't as though she were a vegetarian.

Geoffrey seemed to have heard the thought. "Even plants can feel, Lydia." His look went deep. "Everything mortal comes to an end."

Oh. She guessed this was true. It wasn't like any creature could survive without eating something else. A fear within her deepened. But that only made the possibilities seem that much worse.

The angel understood, as usual, his gaze somewhere on a bookshelf. "He can't make you cross over, not without your soul's permission." The look moved even farther away. "For that sort of change, you have to desire existence before all else."

Oh. She saw this fact in his expression, understood another, as well. It hadn't been Gerrard he had disapproved of that night. Not entirely, anyway. It had been Clarissa, who had chosen to continue on in that highly altered fashion, rather than accept the peace of death, the predestined end of her life. Lydia understood, a little, knew that it was a choice she could never have made; her sigh lingered. But she didn't know where that left any of them now.

It took him a while to refocus on her, shaking his head. "If he comes to you again, and you need me . . . "

She nodded, had known all along. "Of course." There was no way she would let any vampire take her soul.

He seemed mildly satisfied, rising. She didn't know what he was thinking, until she heard his soft breath behind her. There was a long moment, before the words came. "I don't entirely want to share you." It was a guilty secret, clearly. His fingers just brushed against her back, before he moved away, pausing by the door. He stayed there a moment, as she breathed very quietly, afraid to turn for fear that he might never say the rest. "I shouldn't be able to understand greed so well."

Lord. Her heart was pounding, her need for him immense. She understood completely.

He pulled himself away, opening the door. "I should go check that Roderick hasn't done too much damage."

It was with this intention that he left her, breathing heavily, wondering what on earth to do. Certainly, she finally understood his reluctance to act any further on his desires. Given her fantasies, her rising need to possess everything he was, she sympathized, her heart and soul pounding. It just shouldn't be possible to want someone else this much.

Chapter Ten

It had been a morning to remember, but the rest of the day proceeded in what Lydia was starting to think of as a routine. A phoenix who had finally managed to harness the intensity of her resurrective fires turned in her keys, ready to move out to the desert to start again. Butch, their newest werewolf, needed a plumber to be called, having unintentionally clogged his drains with fur. She was even introduced to a revenant who was having trouble convincing herself not to go back to visit her family.

The latter of these, Carrie, had taken a good few hours of counseling by the angel, along with whatever general support Lydia could manage. Mostly, she had ended up pointing out the obvious. No matter how great their grief at her loss, her sudden reappearance from the grave could only have proven a nearly fatal shock to even the most loving family.

It wasn't that Lydia was unsympathetic to her tenant, of course. As much as she tried to settle herself into her own new life, she too felt terribly disconnected. In many ways, it wasn't a particularly new sensation. Never before had she had much of anyone to even try to connect with, Lyle probably the closest there had been to a real, flesh-and-blood friend, and he had just been in it for the demon. Now, strangely, she did seem to have some neighbors who cared, even if none of them could exactly be called normal.

This truth had revived her somewhat, knowing she too could never achieve such mundanity, despite her many efforts. The strange comradeship was even beginning to teach her a feeling she thought must be happiness.

Still, these, various events hadn't been the whole of her day. After the revenant had returned to her apartment with one of their newer tenant ghosts for company, Lydia had looked up to her doorway to see a man glowering, murmuring some of the more blood-and-death

Biblical passages. She had recognized them instantly. Her own parents had been quite fond of Revelation.

She was getting used to the job now, had instantly tried to connect. Despite the fact that she had felt a bit disturbed by his presence, she had started to talk to this man-of-the-cloth, not certain what he was but deciding that he must be one of Geoffrey's. Apparently, she had been quite wrong.

Her invitation had been all the man had needed. Just as he had started coming into the room, pointing at her, screaming, the angel had run out of his office, somehow reinforcing the web of shining lights over the door. With their glow, the man was, thankfully, cast back into the outer office.

Although enraged, he was eventually consoled by Gail, left, muttering, with her arm around him. Lydia had been left shaking all over.

There had been a reward for her fears, however. The angel had stood holding her for quite some time. Still, he had done nothing to explain, had released her only with a whispered, "Trust your instincts." Even hours later, she had no idea what any of that had been about.

The fact that she simply accepted all of these odd encounters — answerless as she was — showed what a huge series of changes she had been through in just these past few days. Now, she numbered an angel, a ghost, some talking cats, and a couple of werewolves as, at least potential, friends. She'd met others, as well, who were very pleasant acquaintances. As motley a bunch as they all — herself included — were, they were the closest to warmth and love she had ever known.

She was thinking about this truth — about the entire day — as she started to make her way home that night. Geoffrey had even let her go with a light, but very tender, kiss, his eyes glowing their eternal warmth.

But, as thoroughly as she had cherished it, as much as she was starting to accept what her "typical" day at work might entail, a fear did follow her — the messages of last night's dream entirely forgotten, replaced by Geoffrey's confession that morning. She understood his concerns only too well. Somehow, it felt very selfish to want him so desperately.

It wasn't that Lydia had much experience with such emotions, even less with their fulfillment. Even if Geoffrey might, somehow, return her desire, she wasn't at all certain that any of her fantasies would be good for him. According to what little she had heard about them, angels weren't even supposed to be such physical creatures — and she was certainly no prize worthy of falling for.

The night became darker the closer she got to her apartment. The more she considered this fear, as well, the more depressed she became. It was a nearly monumental feat just to drag herself across the parking lot to, what passed for, her home. The knowledge that she would be greeted by two over-observant cats and a disdainful imp didn't exactly hurry her along. Whatever answers there were to find, they didn't seem any more likely to emerge with an audience.

She was just pondering this depressing idea, when a cheery voice suddenly sounded beside her: "Hi!"

Lydia startled, as Sybil glowed her usual, happy blue. Whatever parts of this job she might get used to, sudden appearances probably weren't among them. They had certainly never gotten her anywhere good before.

Despite her growing despair, the tenant manager did manage a sort of smile. "Hi." She wasn't certain what the woman wanted and had no idea what sort of conversation to make with a ghost. As usual, she made a flailing attempt. "Is your job done for the day?"

"Job?" the spirit blinked, confused, before her usual animation returned. "Oh, the counter! My shift's over, yes. I just came by to see you."

So much for that conversational gambit.

Lydia did her darnedest to look welcoming, still making her way home. "Do you need me for something?" She couldn't think what. Sybil wasn't even one of her tenants.

The ghost looked thoughtful, as though presented with the idea for the first time. "Well, the new werewolf downstairs howls a bit in his sleep, but I suppose they all do, at first. And the new cat person keeps pacing over to her door and then retreating again." She shook her head before looking back to Lydia happily. "But it takes them all a while to settle in, doesn't it?"

It was certainly taking Lydia a while. She was beginning to wonder whether she was even meant to.

The thought of willingly leaving Geoffrey, however, even if it might be for his own good, seemed impossible. It had taken her whole life to actually meet him. Even if she did seem to present some sort of strange, unpleasant temptation for him . . .

There was a huge gasp, as she felt something cold and . . . well, ephemeral pass through her body. When she looked back to Sybil, one arm of her blue dress was covered in black gunk.

She goggled at the ghost, who was making an almost-comically-disgusted face, as she examined the stuff. "Geoffrey was right." She let out a sigh. "That idiot preacher did leave some behind."

No matter how much Lydia thought she was catching onto this place, she always appeared to be wrong. "Um, what?" she blinked.

"This," Sybil motioned, raising her arm a little. She looked up, obviously saw Lydia's total confusion. "It's just the usual. Hate. Fear. Lust."

Lydia was blinking.

The ghost screwed up her face. "Um . . . bad vibes?" She shrugged, apparently giving up. "Whatever you want to call it, certain people carry it around with them like a virus." Her gaze wandered back to the stuff. "They'll hide behind anything to try to spread it around."

The ghost now seemed sadder than Lydia had ever seen her. Prying into what Sybil was thinking about didn't seem a good idea, though, especially given what Geoffrey had told her about the woman's death: a stepfather, an axe, lots of blood. Even a couple hundred years ago, such evil wasn't hard to find.

Lydia was trying to put these facts together, as she watched the woman. All afternoon, she had been doubting herself, and her effect on the angel, had even begun to wonder whether he wouldn't be better off if she left. Now, she understood. That hadn't been her idea — not entirely, anyway. True, she wasn't completely certain why the angel bothered with her, but she trusted him to know whether physicality and angels were supposed to mix or not. In many ways, she thought, heating a little at the memories, he had already answered that question. Her head shook, staring at the horrible, oily stuff on the ghost's arm. Now, all that remained to be explained was . . .

"Why was he here, anyway? Just what does a preacher have to do with us?"

Sybil finally stopped staring at the goo and looked up at her, smiling. "Depends on the preacher." Her eyes seemed rather distant, glazed with possibilities, before she pulled herself back. "Anyway, there are a couple of churches around that know something about us. I could take you to a service, if you'd like . . . "

Lydia didn't even let her finish, her palm up. "No. Thank you." She tried to smile. Maybe her parents' little services for the devil weren't exactly the norm, but their fervor — and every local church's assumption that she was either crazy or damned — had cured her forever of any desire for religion.

Sybil looked disappointed. In Lydia's experience, every devout person did, when such invitations were turned down.

A moment later, the nonmaterial woman shrugged. "Whatever you'd like. There's a church downtown that caters to us, though. Let me know, if you change your mind."

This wasn't likely to happen, but the information did fill in a blank for Lydia, one she had purposely been ignoring before. When she had first arrived in Decatur, she had seen a church whose sign had read, "Church of the Living Dead." She had thought it only a parable, before now. She supposed she should have known better.

It took a second to pull herself back from these memories, the black goo rather disgusting. "And that preacher today?"

Sybil scowled, unusual as that was for her. "His church boasts itself as 'Sign Watchers.'" Her head shook. "They're waiting for the end of time, or something. They don't even know what we really are. Whenever they see someone who's not white and attracted to the opposite sex or who's female — especially female — they go a little crazy." She finally refocused on Lydia. "His own prejudices are so immense, he can't even see how unusual we are." She shrugged. "Probably for the best."

This explained a fair amount but left Lydia with a few questions. "Sybil, how did you know about . . . ?" She pointed toward the goo.

"Oh!" Suddenly, most of the ghost's usual animation returned. "Geoffrey asked me to look into it."

Surprisingly, this answered nothing. "So, Geoffrey couldn't handle it himself?" He was an angel, after all. It sort of seemed like his area.

The ghost just smiled, back to assuming that everything she said was entirely obvious. "It would hurt him, silly. All that hate . . . "

She looked back to the stuff, shuddering a little, before pulling herself together, her smile at Lydia warm. "It's not the same for me. For me, it's just . . . " She stared at the gunk, seemed to be searching for words. "Icky."

It was with this pronouncement that she left, apparently to get rid of the substance. Lydia didn't want to know where. She was just very glad that it was gone.

She returned to her apartment, glad to be back, found the cats waiting, their tails twitching as usual. She wondered for a moment if she had forgotten to put down their food this morning, but eventually remembered the truth. Her hand dug into her purse, finding two, slightly squashed, and rather stale, doughnuts.

She unwrapped them and put them on the floor, as Eveningstar's eyes glowed more widely. "Sorry I forgot yesterday."

The cat clearly wasn't listening. The kitty confection fiend was back.

Lydia watched, barely managing to get the door closed around her, as the Persian gobbled. Tiger just observed in amusement. "Alvin got another couple of turrets done today."

Lydia had no idea what the proper answer to that might be. How did one praise an imp? "Um, good for Alvin?" she tried at last.

There was a small "Hmph" from the other room, but it sounded rather pleased.

For some reason, watching an elegant feline turn into a ravening donut maniac was rather hypnotic. It was only as the cat finished, walking away to preen herself disdainfully, that her observers finally returned to themselves.

Tiger took the initiative. Lydia hadn't managed to get any further in than the door. "Have you thought about the Lady's words yet?"

"Um, what?" she blinked. She hated the realization that this seemed to be becoming her catchphrase.

If the tortoiseshell were annoyed, there was only a small flick of her tail to show it. "Your dream. The . . . advice you were given."

"Oh!" It had been a long day, many events getting in the way of contemplating it, not the least of which being her own fear that she simply wasn't good enough for the angel. She didn't know how to deal with it or who to discuss any of it with.

She looked down at the cat. "Um, Tiger?"

The animal waited patiently, as Lydia slid down the wall into a crouch. It was difficult to have a heart-to-heart talk with a cat.

"Do you think it's okay for a human to be in love with an angel?"

The tortoiseshell just watched.

"I mean, is it okay for an angel to . . . ?"

The cat interrupted, looking her slowly up and down. "How much of that gunk did the preacher get on you, anyway?"

It *was* an answer — for a cat. Lydia didn't take the hint. "But is it okay for an angel to . . . "

There was a knock on the sliding glass door. Tiger sighed. Lydia wasn't certain whether it were in annoyance or relief. "It's your nightly vampire visit. Why don't you go discuss this with him?" She strolled away to perch on a table that gave her a clear view of the patio — and their visitor. "If you must."

Lydia, again, wasn't really listening, too surprised by something else. "These are *nightly*?" She had barely noticed that night had fallen fully, so lost in her musings.

The cat ignored her, forcing her to wander closer to the glass door, glaring at the vampire.

"What?"

To her surprise, Gerrard actually looked rather sheepish. "I just want to talk."

It took a moment to decide, but Lydia eventually approached him. Tiger was watching everything. Eveningstar was apparently still off somewhere pretending that she had never in her life been anything less than perfectly elegant.

The present cat murmured, "Invite him in, and my claws take out his heart."

"I heard that," the vampire glared, as Lydia opened the balcony door.

Tiger's head lowered to her paws, watching intently. "Good." Her tail flicked.

Her visitor's mouth was open to respond, when Lydia interrupted. "Okay, the usual. You're not — and never will be — invited in. I have no interest whatsoever in becoming a vampire."

His mouth opened further to respond.

"And why the hell are you here, anyway?"

There was a moment when it continued to hang open, before he gave up, retreating to his, rather dirty, lounge chair. His black leather duster flapped out dramatically, as he lay down, staring up at the sky. "You know, this is getting to be rather comfortable. It's like an open-air therapy session."

The possibility of a vampire with a psychiatrist made perfect sense to Lydia, but it wasn't a role she relished.

She pulled up a chair, sitting near the door, ready to slam it if need be. "You didn't answer my question."

For a moment, it was almost like the night before. His eyes turned to her, the light in them immense, his hand gesturing in a tortured fashion. She could nearly hear the indie rock soundtrack behind him. "Can't I come see my lovely Lydi—"

She raised an eyebrow, and he smiled, shrugging.

"Oh, never mind." He went back to gazing at the stars. "I think I like your porch."

His listener was blank-faced. "I'm thrilled. And your purpose in being here . . . ?"

He was silent for a moment, the only sound his fingers thrumming on the arm of the lounge chair. Finally, he spoke. "Lydia, have I ever told you how I met Geoffrey?"

She had to admit it. She was intrigued but had no intention of telling him that. "Since I only met you a couple of nights ago, I'd say no."

Surprisingly, he fell silent again. Perhaps he required a desperate audience? "Does it involve the gallant deeds of knights and crusaders?"

Like there was anything noble about that.

"Or the counselors of kings?"

Ditto.

"Or . . . ?"

"I was the town drunk," he admitted finally, before an awkward pause overcame them both. "It was a rogue crossing over. I wasn't even dying." His finger tapped against the arm of the chair. "I think I was just easy prey."

"Oh." Even she didn't know what to say to that. "So, not quite so dashing a story."

He was examining his fingernails casually. "It's not exactly a babe magnet, no."

Despite herself, she was intrigued——but part of her wondered if she weren't supposed to be; she didn't say anything for a moment. Maybe this was the new-style vampire, the poor, abused boy you were supposed to feel terribly sorry for — until he took out your jugular.

She tried to refocus. "And Geoffrey?"

He was silent for a while. She wondered whether he were just making her wait. "There's a second, before you cross over, a decision point. It's quite a conscious moment." Apparently, his nails were fascinating. "You can either stay as you are, die, and move on in spirit to whatever awaits you, or you can continue to live on, changed."

This was far more about his species than she had ever known before, which wasn't surprising, given her general lack of interest.

He let out a sigh, either at her usual imperviousness or his memories, staring back to the stars. "You're not alone then." His eyes traced a constellation. "I suppose we never are." He seemed to pull himself back, glancing somewhere to her left. "In my case, the angel with me was Geoffrey." There was a shrug. "He made the next life seem quite appealing, really."

Despite her usual lack of interest in his kind, the story made sense so far, explained the angel's sadness over the vampires, as well as his wariness of them. It took a moment to drag herself back. "Then, why'd you choose this one?"

This silence was longer, more profound. "I don't know, exactly. Many of us don't. It's just . . . " His gaze retraced the stars. "Maybe it's disappointment at what's been so far, a desire for more." He went back to his nails. "Being a vampire can get you nearly anything — money, power, sex. Especially these days."

She continued to watch him. He had given up on his nails. "A real panty-dropper, huh?"

"Totally." He smiled at her for a moment. "That's why you're so unique, Lydia." His look traced over her hair bemusedly. "One of the reasons, anyway. You don't fall for the tall, dark, and tortured thing. You demand more out of your partner than that he look good at a party."

"If you confess your undying need for me again, I'll puke."

Gerrard only laughed. "Wouldn't dream of it. Geoffrey would kill me."

The silence returned, Lydia left to ponder in the dark. "Why are you here, again? I assume you don't make a habit of such impromptu therapy sessions."

His smile broadened. "It's an interest, more than anything else. Most people choose basic physical survival, no matter the sacrifices made for it." He shrugged. "Some are even eager to." His look upon her deepened, a little uncomfortably. "The ones who truly choose soul over body are rare." His smile was slightly wistful. "I just wanted to see what it looked like."

She wasn't entirely sure whether she should be flattered or embarrassed, especially given her far-less-than-ethereal fantasies about Geoffrey from the first moment she'd met him.

She just blushed, instead, glancing away, as Gerrard stood, walking over to her. His voice was soft, evidently understanding her thoughts. Embarrassingly, they probably weren't that difficult to guess.

"He's been waiting for you a long time, Lydia." His gaze deepened, as she managed to connect with it. "Human form has no idea of that kind of time."

She couldn't help it, was blushing furiously — mostly thinking about all that she *really* wanted from the angel. But she couldn't say it — not to a vampire, especially.

To her surprise, Tiger broke in. "She's afraid that wanting to jump Geoffrey makes her a bad person." Lydia's cheeks were deep red by the time she glanced over at the cat. "Silly girl," the feline added.

It didn't help her embarrassment any that Gerrard was chuckling now. As much as she was trying to concentrate on him enough to make certain he didn't try anything — like coming in the room — she was just far too mortified to look at him.

His voice was rather warm. "I don't think Geoffrey waited that long just hoping to hold hands."

She forced her eyes back to him reluctantly.

"Not that he wouldn't settle for that, if it were what you wanted, but still . . ."

She gazed at him for a minute more, cringing too much to speak.

To her surprise, the vampire actually looked kind, as he leaned toward her. "I don't know all of your experience, but I do know one thing. Sex and soul are not mutually exclusive." He shrugged, when she looked at him plaintively. "They can be, but not always." His smile was actually genuine. "Why don't you trust your instincts, for once?"

Despite herself, she had to laugh, the mutter half to herself. "I've been getting that advice all day." But she hadn't particularly antici-pated — or wanted — sex counseling from a vampire.

The bloodsucking fiend in question just shrugged again, looking like he was about to go. He turned back, though, seeming a bit wor-ried. "I'm sorry. I just have to ask." He moved closer once more, star-ing. "What on earth happened to your hair?"

The question made Lydia pat her head, wondering just how di-sheveled she actually was. Surprisingly, not too much. She stared at the man, clueless.

Eveningstar filled in the rest, apparently having recovered her cool enough to return to them. "He means the color." The *Idiot* at the end of the sentence only came out in her tone.

"Oh." Lydia tried to look at a bit of it, but it was too short, only a vague blue blur caught out of the corner of her eye. It wasn't some-thing she liked to talk about. "Um—"

Tiger explained when she didn't. "The demon."

This only made Gerrard more confused, his look quite comical.

Lydia had to laugh, a sudden revision of that night making her life far more humorous than it was. "It's not like the demon was into hairstyling," she smiled.

If only.

The look faded a moment later, as the reality returned, although there was a bit of a pause, before she could force herself to answer more fully. "It turned gray." It was clear to all that she wasn't talking about the demon.

"Ah." The vampire seemed sad for a moment, until the confusion returned. "So the blue . . ."

"I dyed it," Lydia shrugged. Her visitor looked thoroughly non-plussed. "Not blue." She rolled her eyes. "Not intentionally." Her sigh was lengthy, before she refocused on him. "I was trying for blonde."

She held up her hand, before he could ask. "This is just how it came out. Apparently, I'm not cut out for a career in cosmetology." There was a shrug. "I decided to cut my losses." Thus the indigo-haired weirdo was born.

To her surprise, Gerrard looked sad, his eyes roaming over her. "Why not let it stay gray?" He shrugged. "It shows maturity."

Lydia just glared at him. "Too right." She had no desire to look 120 yet. She only felt it, most days.

The vampire didn't stick around for any more fashion tips, waving his goodbye rather than arguing the point. It was almost a shame. The way his coat billowed, as he jumped down from the balcony was the stuff of movie posters. Lydia shut the patio door. If only everyone could look that good naturally.

She just stood there for a moment, admiring, her gaze tracing over the unknowable woods, even long after he was gone. It was only the emphatic stare of a cat that brought her back. "What?"

If Tiger had had eyebrows, they would have been raised. "Enjoying the view?" She clearly wasn't referring to the trees.

The woman flushed, scrambling for answers — for herself, as well. "I like his coat."

The cat's pointed gaze continued. "So did Clarissa." With that barbed truth, she jumped off the table, leaving Lydia to wonder at herself.

Granted, this wasn't a difficult state to put her in, her parents having trained her for it from the cradle. But this was a far more serious accusation — to her mind, at least.

Was she falling for Gerrard? Was it all just part of his plan? While admitting to being the town drunk didn't *seem* like a standard pick-up line, Lydia didn't have enough experience to know for certain. Maybe he was just tailoring his seduction better than she had feared, knowing her too well. She had always had a prejudice for the underdog.

She returned to her chair, finally remembering to lock the patio door. She only wished she had some steel reinforcement — and maybe some garlic.

She was staring into the night intently now, her earlier worries back with a new, terrifying twist. She had always known that she wasn't good enough for Geoffrey — what human could be a match for an angel? — but the cat's question was truly making her wonder. Yes, she thought constantly about her boss, but that wasn't anything like enough. If she were shallow enough to be blown away simply by a guy who looked intriguing in leather, she didn't have any kind of right to think that she could ever be good enough for the one she loved.

There were several facts she was ignoring just then. Little as she wanted to admit them, some of them did sneak through.

The first was inspired, to her embarrassment, by a mental flash of what Geoffrey might look like in a leather duster. It took at least three minutes to settle her heart rate down from that one. As determined as she was to berate herself, she had to admit that Gerrard's last impression was a pathetic imitation in comparison.

This was the beginning of her dismissal of her fears. Mostly, though, she couldn't ignore one obvious fact. She had loved Geoffrey even before she had met him, when she had had no idea of his looks. Given his pedigree, the physical side of him was more a costume he wore, anyway, could probably be changed at will. She supposed that applied to everyone, on a certain level.

While she had to admit that she was glad he hadn't changed it yet, always quite happy to watch him, it wasn't his looks that attracted her. Damian shared a lot of those, after all. The thought of the demon only made her want to run, screaming. No, it was the soul of the man she loved that caught her most, holding her utterly spellbound. And that was something no vampire in a leather duster could compare with for a second.

She stood up, smiling, as this truth finally made a home within her. She even managed to beat down the part of herself that was pointing out that all of these insights had been spawned by a conversation with a cat.

When she made it back into the living room, she found Tiger perched on the back of the sofa, staring her usual cattish stare. This time, it clearly meant, *Did you get it yet, Stupid?* Lydia hated to admit that that was probably the translation 90% of the time, anyway.

She rolled her eyes, giving up on at least a few of her fears, heading for her bedroom. "Message received." Tiger just rested her head on her paws, but Lydia understood that she was pleased.

The night, finally, seemed to be at an end. Her — God help her — nightly vampire visit over, she was just about to change for bed, when she heard Tiger again. "You have a visitor coming." A moment later, there was a knock on the door. Cat ears were apparently quite useful.

Lydia was just heading over to answer it, when the cat interrupted. "Don't you want to see who it is first?"

She gazed back to the feline. The tortoiseshell had a point. Apparently, she was growing so used to this place that she was forgetting what dangers it could hold. As the fate of every tenant manager she had heard of before her seemed to show, that could be a stupidly fatal mistake.

She made herself remember this very unsettling fact, staring through the peephole even as part of her mind ran back. She had never been this incautious in her youth. Well, her younger youth, anyway, before her hair had gone gray. She had always stared quite timidly at her parents' visitors before being forced to let them in. Of course, knowing that all of them would have enjoyed seeing her heart on a stick had made trepidation an easy state to achieve.

She dismissed these thoughts with a blink, seeing her newest visitor — and newest tenant. She opened the door, curious. "Irena." She tried to smile, not certain yet whether nighttime visits were a typical part of her job. "Can I help you?"

The cat person seemed unsettled, as though she couldn't stay still. Lydia had no trouble believing Sybil's report of her usual behavior. "I'm sorry. I couldn't think straight." She clearly had to stop herself from pacing. "I just needed someone to talk to."

Lydia nodded, seeing no reason not to let her in. She was one of Geoffrey's, after all — one of hers, too. And she had never heard of any tales stating that such invitations became permanent with her kind, as they might with vampires.

She smiled, then, stepping back. "Come in."

Irena accepted, even if she seemed quite lost in her thoughts. Lydia closed the door, wondering whether she could really be of any use here. Despite her parents' intentions for her, she was not a supernatural creature, was rather pathetically human. True, she knew what it was to be shunned and unwanted, knew what it was to be alone and uncertain and friendless. But she didn't, as far as she knew, risk turning into a panther, if her sexual desires or jealousy got the better of her. How she might be able to counsel the woman, she had no idea.

She turned back to witness a scene she hadn't anticipated, the stare-off already in progress. Both cats were now in the living room, Eveningstar perched on the back of an armchair. The two felines and the, somewhat, woman simply watched, sizing one another up. Even when she offered Irena a seat, they remained unmoving.

Lydia finally slipped around her, making her way to the couch. All she could do after that was witness in silence and wonder how long such matches were expected to last.

Given the cats' usual propensity for sitting and watching, she began to wonder whether she couldn't go catch a nap but decided that would be more than a bit inappropriate. She waited patiently, instead. There really wasn't much else to do, with cats. Nothing else on the planet moved quite so solely to its own will.

To her relief, the staring contest did end eventually. It might have had something to do with Irena blinking. Whatever it was, the outcome seemed to please the cats, who both put their heads down on their paws, continuing to watch the semi-woman intently, as she brought herself back to the moment. "Um, sorry about that." She glanced around before apparently spotting something near the balcony door. "It's a cat thing."

Lydia discovered what the other woman had seen, when Irena dragged in the far-less-comfortable chair that had been left there rather than take a seat at either of the ones the cats had already claimed.

Lydia tried to smile, not understanding. "I figured as much." She would have thought that a panther would outrank a mere cat, but she supposed she didn't know much about cat society. Besides, Eveningstar was powered up by doughnuts. That probably gave her the strength of at least a hundred pumas.

There was much she didn't know, of course. It was still her job to learn.

She resolved herself to this task as much as possible, as she waited for Irena to begin, wondering once more just what she could help the woman with. Whatever it was, she only hoped that she were up to the task.

For a while, silence reigned. Lydia knew that she should have said something polite to start things off, but she had already given the only opener she could think of at the door. She could manage about a half dozen variations on, "Can I help you?" now, but those were about the limits of her abilities. One of the many things her child-hood hadn't taught her was basic conversational skills.

She waited to hear the cat person's concerns, then, hoping that she wasn't greeting her like the cats. What was fine behavior for a fe-line didn't exactly work for a person.

Irena was staring distantly at the floor. Just as Lydia was becom-ing desperate enough to try to think up some kind of opener, she spoke. "Do you think Butch likes me?"

Okay, that hadn't been a discussion Lydia was expecting. She blinked, entirely out of her depths, cursing her upbringing. If she had just had a normal girlhood, she would have had such conversations with friends at least a hundred times.

She struggled. "He, um, seemed taken with you." Or, at least, that might have been what that stunned stare had meant.

"Yes, I know," Irena sighed, relieving Lydia to know she had been right about something. "His scent was . . . "

Lydia was happy that she didn't continue there, not quite catlike enough to want to know.

The cat person looked up to her with a tormented gaze. "But he never talks to me!" The woman's long, perfect nails dug into the seat of her chair. "I've seen him at the mailboxes at least three times now, and I can barely get him to say hello."

Despite her attempts to be soothing, Lydia was trying not to smile. It had only been a day since the pair had moved in. Unless the supernatural community had a far more active mail service than the average human, the likelihood of either of them suddenly getting that much mail wasn't particularly overwhelming.

She didn't know how to point this out politely, however. Her mother would have just blurted it out. Well, maybe not, since the knowledge might have made the woman happy, but anyway . . .

Lydia nearly shook her head. She had no desire to follow her par-ents' example in anything.

She let out a small sigh, wrestling with this question, wondering what Geoffrey would say. Of course, she suspected that, angel or not, the woman would never have gone to him. This was what qualified as "girl talk." Too bad she had no experience with it at all.

She flailed away at helping the woman, then, looking for whatever knowledge she did have. "Um, his upstairs neighbor, Sybil, says that he howls at night."

Was that a helpful fact or not, and was she even supposed to repeat it?

"Maybe he's lonely?"

Irena considered this for a moment. Finally, she shook her head. "No, most werewolves do that, when they first turn. A friend told me that they're just appalled at discovering all the new places for hair to grow."

Lydia didn't even want to know whether this were true. It sounded a bit like an interspecies slander, but she had no way of knowing for certain.

She let it alone, then, focusing elsewhere, feeling a little inspired. "Have you approached him? Maybe he's just shy."

This brought the first real reaction, from all three felines—an aghast one. "Yield to a *dog*?!"

"Um . . . "

"It isn't done," Eveningstar informed her frostily.

This lack of options only left Irena seeming all the more depressed.

The Persian sighed, descending from the armchair to approach the forlorn creature. To Lydia's amazement, the feline jumped up on the cat person's lap. "*Here's* what you do." Her look made Irena lean down, the cat whispering in her ear. But whatever knowledge she imparted was a mystery to their observer.

Lydia could hear none of the cat's proffered advice, as curious as she had to admit she was, could only see that it was impressing her listener. Irena let out a little "oh!" every few seconds.

Lydia glanced over to Tiger, who watched smugly, and decided not to ask. This, too, was apparently "a cat thing."

Whatever was imparted by the feline, it seemed to have worked. She and Eveningstar exchanged a long glance, before the cat jumped down off her lap.

Irena rose, smirking. "Thank you for the help!" She waved, as she made her way toward the door.

Lydia was lost but rose to follow, knowing she wasn't the one the gratitude was for. She supposed there were some things she just wasn't meant to understand.

She did know, quite clearly, that she had had nothing whatsoever to do with any aid the woman had received. She considered suggesting doughnuts as a reward for the Persian but decided against it. Revealing such an uncouth secret would have probably won the feline's eternal enmity.

The cat person was half out the door, as Lydia spoke. "I'm sorry I wasn't more use."

Irena was smiling, as she turned to her. "No. I appreciate you listening to me."

She was about to go again, when a new question came to Lydia. "I'm always happy to, but I've gotta ask. Why did you think I was the right person to help you?" A thought dawned on her. "Or was I just the only person you knew?"

The latter seemed a far more likely theory, but it left Irena tilting her head at her curiously. "Because of you and Geoffrey."

Despite her attempts to be professional, Lydia's eyes widened, suspecting what she meant, wishing she were more right. "Me and . . ."

"Yes. Your scents." The head tilt increased. "You are together, right? Because the way your scents mingle . . . "

Suddenly, Lydia couldn't get the door closed fast enough. "Right. Tell me if I can be of any use to you." She managed a smile, closing out that deadly knowing head tilt. She didn't bother to add on, "unlike this time." That was clear enough to anybody watching.

She was still looking at the door long after it was closed, felt herself blushing furiously. It didn't help any that she knew she would see the two cats watching the second she turned around.

She drew in a deep breath, forcing herself to encounter their staring faces, both of them suddenly clustered around her feet. She decided to change the subject, before they could comment. "Thank you for helping her. I was lost."

To her relief, they didn't give the obvious answer. Tiger blinked once, looking rather innocent. "That's all right. Eveningstar has quite a bit of experience to draw from."

The black cat hissed before walking away regally.

The whole incident with Irena had already left Lydia confused and embarrassed. This didn't help. "What was that about?" she asked the tortoiseshell, as the cat returned calmly to an armchair.

"Didn't Glory tell you? Eveningstar's my mother." She seemed rather smug, as she started to curl up. "What's life, if you don't score off your parents occasionally?"

This wasn't the theory Lydia had expected to be left with. Of course, given the complete difference in looks between the Persian and her daughter, she couldn't exactly dispute the cat's claim. Eveningstar, apparently, had gotten around.

This was more than could be said of Lydia, but she wasn't certain whether she were happy with this fact or not. Shaking her head, she headed for bed — before remembering that there was an imp in her closet. While she knew that the small castle builder couldn't care less about her, it just seemed too weird to go to sleep, knowing he was there.

She resorted to her usual fallback, then, and lay down on the couch. The day had worn her out more than she had realized, the cats' sudden spat the final weirdness she could stand.

She fell asleep quickly, but only to once again encounter her usual dream visitor. This time, the old lady had her arms crossed, her foot tapping. "So I see you're not listening to me yet?" She snorted, glancing away. "Kids."

Lydia didn't have a real excuse. She knew it, as she gazed into her visitor's eyes. "I'm sorry. I just . . . "

The woman was having none of it. "Look, young lady, when you're given advice, you take it, understand?"

Lydia didn't know how to respond, apparently leading the older woman to shrug, her voice wheedling.

"I'm only trying to help."

Lydia knew this, as overly-emphatic as the woman tended to be.

She sat up, bracing herself, deciding to just ask about her fears. It was better than enduring the guilt. "But aren't angels supposed to be . . . um . . . "

She trailed off for a moment, the Lady's eyes intense.

" . . . pure?"

The question clearly didn't sit well with her visitor. "Pure? Pure!" There was a sudden, red light outside the window — a very disconcerting one. "And what do purity and physical intimacy have to do with each other, I ask you?"

The Lady stood up, pacing away, clearly agitated. "You think a man who never has sex can't be a serial killer? You think a couple in love can't be good, kind, decent people?"

Lydia opened her mouth but wasn't allowed to answer.

The Lady paced further away, hands up in the air. "Where do they get these ideas from? What idiot came up with *this*?" Her hands flailed upward. "Morons!"

Lydia really hadn't meant to upset the woman, especially since the red glow outside the window was becoming even more fierce. "I'm sorry." And she definitely was, part of her hating that she felt this way. It took a moment to confess the rest. "I'm afraid."

Her voice was plaintive, begging. It brought the Lady's attention once more, her look softening a little. It took her a moment to answer. "Fear?" She sighed, gaze maternal and understanding. "Eh," she shrugged. "Fear happens."

She came closer with this admission, calming the younger woman, the red light outside becoming a little less intense. Lydia was just glad she wasn't so upset anymore.

"But, little Lydia, don't fear something just because some . . ." Her hand gestured suddenly again. ". . . *moron* tells you to." Her finger pointed toward the younger woman. "*Love* is what matters in this world. Love is what keeps us from becoming . . . " She seemed to flail for a moment, pointing toward Damian's side of the apartments. ". . . those things." Her look softened once more, gazing at the girl. "Love is not something to fear."

Despite all her terrors, Lydia nodded, seeing her point. She only hoped she still did, when she woke up. "And Geoffrey?"

She had meant to agree, the fear slipping out. Fortunately, the Lady didn't seem to be offended this time, shrugging. "You, Geoffrey, you're not wrong together. You're right." She seemed about to poke Lydia in the skull but apparently decided against it. There was a long sigh, as she turned away. "I made both of you too darn humble."

This last part was only a small murmur, Lydia not certain she'd heard it right. She shook her head, trying to remember all she was being told, knew she needed to. Not only was everybody and their . . . well, cat, telling her the same thing, but she also simply felt it, knew they were right. Besides, the truth was so obvious. She loved Geoffrey, always had. If he chose her and she could bring him even the tiniest fraction of the solace he brought her, then all of it would be worthwhile.

She could tell the dream was ending, wondered whether Geoffrey had them, too. She didn't have time to ask, only got in one more question. "What is that glowing outside?" It was far too disturbing not to wonder.

The Lady suddenly seemed rather overly innocent. "That?" She gazed toward the window, as the light faded. "Eh, just a small fire."

She turned back to Lydia's shocked face, seeming almost guilty. Lydia was about to wake, the woman's image fading.

"If a lady can't burn a shrub or two in her old age, what pleasures are left?"

With that, Lydia woke up, shaking her head, hoping it would help the thoughts adjust themselves. It didn't, the crick in her neck not aiding her, either. She glanced down at the couch almost scornfully, standing at last, a new determination formed. *Industrious imps be darned.* If she was going to have dreams like that, she might as well sleep in her own bed.

Chapter Eleven

Switching to the bed must have worked. The next morning, she actually woke up on her own, no imps needed. While she could hear Alvin pottering away, he wasn't in her face. *A glorious way to awaken, indeed.*

There were better ways to wake, of course — one fantasy in particular coming to mind — but she tried to ignore it, for now. While she was attempting to remember the Lady's words, it wouldn't do to focus too much on what she'd suggested. Presumably, there was work to be seen to in the office that morning. Walking in and begging for sexual favors from Geoffrey probably wouldn't get it done.

She sighed over that unfortunate fact, stumbling out of bed and dragging herself over to the closet to search for clothes. When she opened it, the imp glared up at her. He'd been fiddling with a turret so perfect it gleamed.

"What?"

She stared at him, a new thought occurring to her. "How did I not notice you the first day?" She had a feeling that, even among imps, Alvin would stand out.

His look alone was an answer, and that answer was, "Duh!"

"Yeah, you were noticing *sooo* much when you moved in." Even worse, he apparently took her embarrassed silence for encouragement. "I could've started up a brass band and you would have said it was just the house settling or some other nonsense." He rolled his eyes. "Humans."

He'd intoned the word the way a '40s movie hero might have said, "Dames!" She only wished she hadn't backed up his stereotype quite so much.

She couldn't deny that she'd been deep in denial when she first arrived. Given how much so, it was a wonder she'd come this far.

Now that she was a bit better acclimated, she finally realized something else. "Did you put up all my stuff for me?" How she had failed to notice the lack of boxes, had settled in instantly to where all her things were kept, amazed her — and that said nothing of how her hotel bill had been paid and her suitcase delivered. She hoped it wasn't a sign that she just wasn't particularly bright.

The self-doubt was creeping in again. No matter what her resolve, it never went away for long.

She didn't get time to think into the tendency now, Alvin shaking his head. "Who else do you think might have done it — the cats?"

Actually, given what she knew about the pair, that didn't seem unlikely, but she supposed opposable thumbs would have made the work far easier.

Any tirade the imp might have given at her silence was cut off by the felines' arrival. The small, blue creature knew his place, abandoning any further disparagement of the animals to continue his adjustments to one of the castle's turrets. "Don't you have to go to work?" Even losing the opportunity to grouse was apparently better than facing the cats' disapproval.

Lydia saw his dilemma, smiling, a new appreciation of the turns her life had taken forming. "Thank you, Alvin." She unhooked a dress, her eyes warm, as the imp stared in amazement. "For taking such good care of me."

For once, she left him speechless, although she did notice, as she slid the door closed to leave him to his art, that his cheeks had turned a deep purple. Maybe those in his line of work didn't get much appreciation.

This wasn't much of a surprise, given the fact that he was supposed to be unseen. Even if such training wasn't going well for him, she was grateful to have him around. Unpacking could never have been this easy, otherwise.

She got dressed under the cats' watchful gazes, ready as she was going to be to face another day. But she was a little bothered by how easily she'd accepted the results of the imp's work. Surely, it should have dawned on her a bit more that all her things, as meager as her possessions were, had arranged themselves.

The thought made her more than fear for her intellect. Reasonable people couldn't normally expect that all work was simply done for them, especially if they'd never experienced such an arrangement before.

This question worried her, as she dashed through her morning preparations. She was just finishing fussing with her hair when the obvious answer occurred to her.

Intelligence aside, it wasn't as though the few days since her arrival had been calm and uneventful. Only her second night, there had been vampires. The third, there had been a warding-off, somehow, of a demon attack, not to mention the start of "vampire therapy." Given that such discussions had continued last night, it probably wasn't too surprising that she hadn't had time to notice anything smaller than that.

That was the excuse she was giving herself, anyway, not wanting to admit that it might all just be down to Geoffrey. Whenever she had a free second, that was where her mind tended to wander. If she came home to find, displayed in her living room, a giant pink elephant balanced on one leg with a sparkly umbrella wrapped in its trunk, she could easily imagine wandering right past it, caught only in fantasies of her boss. An angel outranked any number of other magical splendors every day of the week.

It was with this warming thought that she was about to leave the apartment, when she heard one of the cats clearing its throat. "Forgetting something?"

"Oh!" She turned around, grinning sheepishly, before starting to make her way to the kitchen. "Sorry about that." This whole having-cats-around thing was difficult to get used to. She frequently only half-remembered to feed herself. That she was responsible for them, too . . .

She was just drilling this fact into her head again when Tiger sat down directly in her path — an odd reaction for a cat waiting for food. "Don't forget to close the door." Her eyes glowed warningly. "You don't know what might get in."

Now, *there* was a nice, disturbing idea. Lydia returned quickly and closed it. And locked it. And said a small prayer near it. It couldn't hurt.

"Food?" Tiger asked, bringing her back to reality.

"Oh. Yeah." But the cat's warning had upset her more than she would have expected, her gaze on the door. It was only when Eveningstar sat down to guard the portal, managing at the same time to dislodge Lydia from her place, that she finally moved away.

The reminder haunted her the whole time she was in the kitchen, only half-noticing her tasks. Still, she wasn't certain why it was getting to her, especially now. Her life and soul had been endangered since the moment of her birth. True, Geoffrey's assistants tended to have short life spans. True, too, that Damian had, the night before last, tried to renew the mark the demon had left on her back — and her soul. But why did she suddenly feel so . . . ?

"Jumpy" was clearly the word she was going for. Tiger proved it unintentionally, when she reminded her of the time, Lydia spilling the whole water bowl she'd been filling in her fright, having to start all over again.

She did so quickly. Whether it were simply the fact that she needed to be more careful in general or something more — she was hoping for the former — she knew that she'd only feel really safe once she was by Geoffrey's side.

She finished the forgotten task then hurried toward the door, but she didn't get out as quickly as she expected. The cats blocked her, twisting again and again around her ankles, making it impossible to move.

It wasn't an unpleasant sensation but was a little odd, especially since they seemed to have pushed some sort of shed button. They only let her go after issuing dire warnings for her safety.

She intended to heed them, locking the door cautiously, glad the cats — and possibly even Alvin — were there to look after things. As much as she wanted to believe, whatever it was she was feeling was clearly not an illusion. Just the fact that the cats were temporarily ignoring their food told her that.

Furry ankles and all, she left for the day, wondering all the while what on earth was happening to make her feel so unsettled. Whatever it was, she only hoped that she didn't discover it in half the unpleasant ways she was imagining.

She'd expected many things, but her first omen was still an odd one. So lost in thought was she that she made it halfway across the parking lot before she noticed them.

Once she came back to her surroundings, she saw Lon blocking the way of a perky brunette. While the girl seemed all innocence and light and only too happy to see him, Lon was anything but. In fact, the door to his car was flung wide open, as though he'd gotten halfway through the lot before jumping out to stop the woman's progress. Despite her simpering, he didn't seem any too likely to back down.

Lydia wasn't entirely certain what to make of this scene, but she didn't think what she normally might. Lon's body language was almost threatening, would have encouraged her to go rescue the girl, in most other situations, but life in this place wasn't always as it seemed. For one thing, she knew Lon. For another, the girl seemed to be coming from the other side of the complex. And anyone who emerged from Damian's territory, no matter how innocent they might seem, was certain to be doing nothing like God's work.

She approached the pair cautiously. To her surprise, it wasn't just the hound's stance that was menacing, a feral sort of growl rumbling in his throat. While he was as outwardly human as ever, she could clearly see the sort of terror that might be felt facing one of his kind alone, at least were they to emerge from the demon's side.

She wasn't certain what to do, part of her wondering whether she shouldn't just run and grab Geoffrey — or call him mentally or something — but some impulse stopped her from going into the office just yet. Maybe the situation was too dire, although it didn't look it, what with that bright, wide smile the girl gave.

Lydia approached slowly, placing her hand gently on the hound's back. "Lon?" She wasn't certain whether she were trying to comfort him or draw strength. "Is there some way I can help?"

That was her standard offer, as little as it really meant to anyone yet, not having learned enough to be of much use.

The werewolf never took his eyes off the girl. "'Ashley' here wants to visit some of your tenants. But she doesn't belong on this side at all."

Lydia could have sworn his eyes were glowing so golden they were nearly alight.

"Hi, I'm Ashley." The girl held out her hand as though she were greeting her next best friend.

Lydia opted for caution and kept her hand on Lon's back.

When Ashley withdrew her fingers to pat her hair, it was with an *I'm sorry you're so rude* sort of smile. "I have some friends who live over here that I haven't seen in a while." Her look made it so clear she was in the right. "I just wanna say hi."

Lydia watched for a moment, wondering at this scene. Ashley really was the perfect girl. Of slightly indefinite, although youngish, age, she was dressed in what even Lydia could tell was the latest and most expensive fashions. Everything about her screamed of prolonged and extensive pampering, not a single long, glossy brown hair

dreaming of getting out of line. How she kept it looking that way
without a stylist on 24-hour standby, Lydia had no idea.

Her eyes narrowed, though. Somehow, this all seemed eerily familiar.

It took a second, but she did finally remember who it was Ashley
reminded her of. It was one of those popular girls in high school —
not the *most* popular one but one of her hangers-on, the one who
did the dirtiest of the queen bee's scut work. Sometimes, it was a few
days of pretending to be friendly in order to size up the competition
or look for weaknesses, before utterly destroying a newcomer. Sometimes, it was planting a stomach-churning rumor in just the right ear
so that everyone, student and faculty, would have irrevocably turned
against the enemy by lunchtime. She was a terrible breed, impossible
to ignore. She always knew what she was doing, and she always suc-
ceeded in her crimes.

This wasn't the whole of what Lydia knew of such women, however. They were also always the ones most desperate to hold a reunion
in hopes of reliving their former glory days, most Ashleys never getting much further than community college.

Lydia had had the misfortune of knowing a few of them in
school, even if their names had been different. She'd even seen the
grown-up version once, wheedling with the principal to allow them
to use the school gym on a Saturday so that all the "old girls" could
see the place once more. She'd never really put the facts together before, had only known the type as one to avoid whenever possible.
She almost laughed. It had never occurred to her how desperate such
girls' lives became once they graduated.

There was no doubt, given where they were, that this particular
Ashley was not the garden variety, but that hardly mattered. She
wasn't one of Geoffrey's. Lydia suspected that his tenants mostly understood a truth this girl never would. High school might seem eternal, but it wasn't. Good, bad, or indifferent, such experiences went

away with time. It was only the crazy and the suspect who held onto them forever.

It was with this new conviction that Lydia had the courage to stare down the potential intruder. While she didn't entirely understand the woman's danger to her tenants, aside from general annoyance, she trusted Lon's instincts. Besides, this girl was clearly one of Damian's. That alone told her everything she needed to know.

"No, I don't think so." Lydia met her eyes, unflinching. It was a bit of a victory, given the fact that she'd never willingly met the eyes of an Ashley in high school. "You probably have friends on your own side." Her tone said that she doubted it but suggested that it might be a good idea to try to cultivate some. "Go talk to them."

Such an affront was not what Ashleys were used to. She was just about to press her point, looking Lydia over disdainfully, when her eyes stopped at Lydia's ankles. "Is that . . . cat hair?"

Lydia looked down, nearly laughed. Yep, she was furry today. "Definitely." Whatever the cats had been up to, she had no intention of apologizing for them.

Fortunately, that seemed to be the turning point. Their potential invader stepped back. Whether the reaction was caused by witnessing such a fashion faux pas or confronting the reflected power of the beasts, Lydia had no idea but was glad for the victory either way.

Ashley planted her feet for a moment, further forcing a smile at the pair. "I'll come back another day, then." She leaned toward Lydia just a little, not trying to hide the evil in her eyes. "Maybe I'll bring some friends."

She left, flicking her long hair over her shoulder, as she walked away, but her words lingered unpleasantly. Lydia wanted to ask Lon about them but decided against it. If she let herself, she could easily guess their meaning. Damian had already hidden little, and the general feeling in the air today supported what she suspected of his intentions. The demon still wanted her. Her shudder ran deep. And, if that creature got its way . . .

She didn't understand the full implications of such a victory for Damian's side, but she didn't really want to. She looked at Lon, instead. "Thank you for dealing with her. Sorry I was late." She didn't even realize that she was taking responsibility for the full protection of Geoffrey's domain.

The hound seemed to, however, or so his smile said. "Don't worry about it." His look traveled to her ankles. "I think the cats saved us this time."

"Mm." She nodded, but her mind was elsewhere, her gaze following the woman's retreat. She needed to know. "So was she . . . a demon?"

Lon shook his head, as she refocused on him. "Not really. She's quite human, but she's fully aware of what she's doing."

Lydia knew she should be getting to work. So should Lon, for that matter. Still, she needed to know. "Which is what?" Besides trying to invade their side.

"She doesn't actually know any of the people over here. She's just trying to reestablish the hierarchy she was part of before, with herself at the top this time. All she needs is someone vulnerable enough to let her do it."

She didn't need to question this, the first part already obvious. High school and vulnerability went pretty much hand-in-hand. After all, teenagers were stuck there for around seven hours a day, five days a week, for four years of their lives — and all of that during their most physically and emotionally awkward stages. The ones with even marginal outer confidence could easily rule everything.

Why the woman wouldn't want to try on her own side of the complex was obvious, too. Ashleys only devoured their prey symbolically, but most of Damian's residents . . .

She shook off the idea, not wanting details, another question arising. "If she's human, why did you say her name that way?" She had nearly heard the air quotes.

He smiled. "Only because it's a type. At her age, it's Ashley." He shuddered. "She could just as well be a Brittany or a Brook or an Amber." There was a shrug. "The names are almost meaningless. The type never changes."

Lydia understood, was about to suggest that they head to work — she was probably late by now — but Lon went on. "Besides, it's more than that." His gaze was distant, tracing worriedly over the complex's other side. "If she does well enough, wounds enough people deeply enough, she might not always be human." The look became even more fearful. "Deals can always be made."

It wasn't the first disturbing notion of Lydia's day, but she wasn't thankful for it, nonetheless, her own gaze cast doubtfully over Damian's little kingdom. "I should get to work." But even she noticed that she wasn't exactly running.

The pair just stood there, staring.

"Yeah."

A long moment passed. Finally, Lon took out his cell phone, pulling up the first name in his call list. "I need to tell Hugh to go visit Lacy. Newly-turned werewolf," he supplied, as she watched him curiously. "The girls definitely have it worse. Ashley might have destroyed her."

Lacy. It seemed an odd name for a werewolf, especially given the nearly joke names of the other ones she had met. But what did she know? She'd been introduced to her first hound only three days ago. Expert, she wasn't.

Lydia was just about to wave a goodbye to Lon, thankful for his help, when she saw his expression. After a moment, he put down the phone, cutting off the call.

"He's not answering."

She hadn't realized werewolves could turn that pale.

She didn't know what was happening but suspected from his tone that it wasn't good. She also knew that she wasn't going to be able to help just standing here. She needed to get to work. Maybe Geoffrey could aid them.

She touched the hound on the arm as a goodbye, left him staring worriedly at his phone, before he began to obsessively redial. Something about the way he stood there, car abandoned, as his look of morbid fear grew, made the gnawing sense that something was very badly off today start roiling deep inside her, nearly painfully. While she wanted to believe that the other werewolf was merely busy or in the shower or something, the feeling of the day — the way the cats had acted — made her doubt it. The anxiety grew greater. All she knew was that she needed to see Geoffrey. She didn't have any possible answers outside of him.

She nearly did run this time — wanted to, anyway — but she was just beside Damian's domain. Maybe it was her imagination, but from every window she could feel the eyes watching; the chill caught her, her hands rubbing over her arms. As much as she needed to get inside, she had the distinct feeling that her every movement counted, and any greater fear than she was already showing was a very definite point for the other side.

The office looked almost empty, as she approached. No Gail hanging around outside, no immediate succubi waiting to meet her. The fear grew icy, her steps speeding up, despite the eyes. The lights were on, at least, even if no one was about. Of course, as far as the demon's side went, that was fine with her.

She entered her office, desperate to find Geoffrey. The last thing she wanted was encounters of the filthy kind.

The first thing she found, fortunately, was nothing of the sort, even if they didn't answer her immediate problems.

Geoffrey had kept his promise. A beautiful array of flowers waited in a vase for her — deep blue roses. She bit her lower lip, nearly in tears from the gesture, the contrast of the love they held a sort of shock after her fears. It was the first really good thing to happen to her all morning.

She calmed a little, then, leaning down to smell them, searching for anything like equilibrium. The scent alone was overwhelming and rich, her eyes closing. It wasn't like any other flower she had come across, was something out of heaven. Her hand stroked over them, luxuriating in their silkiness, a warmth starting in her heart, as the truth sank in. For the first time ever, someone had brought her roses. Her smile was deep, lost to the moment. And that person was Geoffrey. Nothing else quite seemed to exist.

Unfortunately, something else did — a something she would rather never have met.

His beautiful voice was barbed. "I see the bitch is back." The feeling of him hovering in the doorway was enough to fix her in horror where she stood.

Lydia could say nothing, was trying to find the power to move.

When she finally did, with a steelier bit of will than she had even realized she possessed, she didn't notice that she had unintentionally pulled away a petal in her hand. She managed to turn to the demon at last. "Damian." She stayed as outwardly calm as possible, even managed to raise an eyebrow. "I see you've been able to return."

To her dismay, the demon continued to move in. She was unconsciously sending out a serious SOS to the angel, as their nemesis went on, giving up on all, even sarcastic, greetings, getting down to his real truth. "You're going to regret what you did. We're going to see to it." His eyes said that nothing he told her was meant as an idle threat. "You and all of your 'friends.'"

It was a terrifying moment. Most of Lydia wanted to run screaming, but there wasn't much of anywhere to go. Besides, she knew anything like retreat wouldn't help. Evil like this had to be faced. Turning your back on it was always a deadly idea.

She managed to be professional, then, making her way around to her chair, clinging to the petal. To her relieved delight, the feeling of its silk in her hand gave her a little strength.

She took in a deep breath, countering her enemy with the only weapon she could muster: flippancy.

"Are all your threats so stereotyped, Damian?"

He clearly wasn't pleased.

"What's next? 'I'll get you, my pretty. You and your little dog, too'?"

It was only a second later that she realized what she had said, her heart nearly stopping. The demon's smile said everything. "How about your hounds?" She was holding the petal so tightly she was nearly crushing it. "Or your cats?"

The first question had upset her, made her want to run. The second, surprisingly, was enraging. She hadn't realized how protective she was of them, before then.

She said nothing, figuring that if any creature alive knew how to take care of itself, it was the cats. She only told him the truth, the one she felt to her soul. "I won't let you win." Her gaze spared him nothing. "Not you, or your master, or your minions."

The declaration seemed to disarm him a little. It had her as well. "Minions"? Where the hell had that come from?

She didn't have time to think about the choice for long. Geoffrey — to her delight — appeared behind her tormentor. The demon seemed to know he was there even without looking, his gaze on the flowers. "You really are a showy bastard, you know."

Geoffrey moved past him without any apparent effort, although the demon didn't seem to yield an inch. Damian was pointing to the flowers.

"Blue roses?" He sounded disdainful, meeting the angel's eyes. "There are limits to flamboyance, even for a son-of-a-bitch like you."

Geoffrey, apparently, saw more in these words than a simple taunt, his chin rising. "We're all children of the same creator, Damian." His gaze burned. "Even if you've forgotten her."

The demon's eyes were cold flint. "As I said."

This was the last insult the angel seemed ready to bear, pointing toward the door. "Leave." With that pronouncement, Damian was tossed back violently into the outer office, the door slamming in his face. The lines against them had never shone more brightly.

Lydia felt herself shaking, only half-understood what was happening, her heart hammering wildly. Geoffrey took her by the hand, leading her into his office, before she could ask or say anything. It was only after his thumb drew some sort of pattern on her forehead that she finally began to calm.

It took a few moments before words returned. "Hugh," she got out at last and saw the worry in his eyes. Apparently, it *was* as bad as she had thought.

This truth did nothing to settle her, Geoffrey starting to take her other hand. He opened it, only to show the crushed petal.

She was horrified to see it there, started to explain. "I'm sorry. The flowers are beautiful. I love them. I didn't mean to . . . "

He stopped her rambling in the most wonderful way, his lips pressed lightly to hers. It not only kept her from blithering. It took away her breath.

He didn't seem disappointed with her but also didn't explain. "I'm glad you like them." For a moment, there was almost a smile — but what he did next obliterated whatever passed for thought.

He had taken the petal from her, had pulled back the collar of her dress a little, making something inside her go a little funny. Now, his warm fingers slipped that lost blue fragment over her skin, until he stopped it above her heart. She wasn't even certain she was breathing, her eyes lost in his. Sadly, a moment after that, he removed his hand, but the petal remained where it had been.

Why it didn't fall, she had no idea — mostly missing his touch — but she knew that this was no time to focus on such desires, especially when he told her the rest. "Sybil's also gone, a few of the others, too."

Her gaze widened, the horror setting in further. Apparently, she wasn't the only one the demon wanted.

His look was so sad, as though he bore the weight of the entire world. There was a pause, before he sighed. "There's no other way." His hand raised to her forehead once more, placing his fingers there, closing his eyes. "You have to know." But she was in no way prepared for what she saw.

The images had a nearly physical effect, came to her in a series of overpowering fragments.

Wings. There were wings, feathers, flowers.

She couldn't understand, let out a whimper, which grew into a gasp. It was a bombardment of sights, too many to process.

There were voices, as well, a cacophony of them, drowning out thought, painful to hear. There was clashing, fighting, screaming.

But, somehow, Geoffrey was there, too, primary among every sight and sound, his presence the only constant, rooting her, keeping out the insanity that would otherwise have engulfed her.

Just when the constant barrage of visions seemed far too much, when she was about to scream, did it end — and she was left with only one fact for certain, gasping for breath. Geoffrey was now an absolute presence in her soul, as she was in his.

She didn't understand the vision, could only feel its ancient truth. Still, she knew she could have learned anything about her beloved at that moment with a single thought, could have explored his every emotion, memory, and desire.

But it was all too much, the tears in her eyes, her words a whimper. "I'm scared."

His hand was on her cheek, his gaze, his love, so knowing.

"I don't understand . . . " She was afraid to finish.

His touch was gentle, even as the images, the sounds, flapped through her brain, threatening to drive her mad.

"It's all right," he soothed. His gaze roamed over her so tenderly. "I have no intention of letting you go."

That wasn't what she had asked, but it did answer a large part of the fears.

He drew her to him. "Let them come to you, as they will. Don't block them." His first kiss was light, worshipful. "Let yourself know, and we'll win." The next was searching, passionate. "That's all either of us need to survive."

She didn't know whether he was talking about the kisses or the knowledge she somehow now had and didn't have — the memories that were there and inaccessible at the same time. By the third kiss, she no longer cared, her arms around him, lost in all he was, feeling some part of him flowing through her soul.

She had no idea what was happening but no longer minded. His touch told her the truth. He was there with her, no matter what. Whatever the odds, they would win — together.

She lost herself to him, treasuring it all. There might have been a million other concerns, but for that instant, that was all she needed to understand.

The pure sensory overload of the moment was enough to demolish much of her senses. Even the flapping and screams he had released in her memories became nothing but a dull roar, echoing in the background of her thoughts.

It was a surprising, enticing moment of discovery. Still, when it was about to become truly intense, Geoffrey's kisses more and more passionate, the door to his office flew open, slamming into her shoulder, the one with the repressed demon mark. That, sadly, was the end of that — for the moment, anyway.

It was a terrible way to be woken from such a dream, the pain intense. Lydia gasped, tears in her eyes. She'd almost forgotten — well, had tried to forget — just how much the wound hurt.

Their intruder didn't seem to notice, was screaming, nearly out of breath, her eyes and hair wild. "Sybil!"

Lydia couldn't take in much but her own agony. Her legs were threatening to give out, only Geoffrey's efforts keeping her standing. The pain was immense, seemed to be invading her body somehow, taking over every inch — a hideous, molten evil snaking its way through her blood. She only dimly heard the woman's terrified voice somewhere in the background.

"Geoffrey, Sybil's gone! She was supposed to . . . I tried to call out . . . went by her apartment . . . Gone!"

A very small part of Lydia's mind realized that she was missing some of the words. Maybe she was passing out? But that hadn't happened before — not even in the horror of that one terrible night when she'd been supposed to be sacrificed. Why should it be now?

The torment didn't let her think into this too far. It seemed to be exploding through her head, a ghastly display of images suddenly accompanying it. Some were from that traumatizing night. Others, she didn't recognize. But she almost thought that she saw Sybil there — and Hugh and Damian and . . . Clarissa? Her mind went almost entirely blank, only one element certain, burning within her, a fire out of Hell. It took a lot not to let out the scream she was holding.

The demon. He was back.

She wasn't sure how long she was in that state, lost track of any outer reality. All she could hear was the demon's voice — or the one, at least, it had borrowed for the occasion — calling her, telling her that her soul was his.

She didn't answer, willing him away — back to whatever inferno he came from. She only wished it would work as well as it, somehow, had with Damian. After all, she was finally making friends, had people she could trust. The horror was nearly overwhelming. Why couldn't she, just for once in her life, be allowed to be happy?

The thought could easily have turned into despair, but fortunately, she was saved. She didn't realize how, until she finally came back to herself.

All she knew for a moment was an all-encompassing image of a wing flapping, one she felt she recognized, one she adored. It was accompanied by a scream, that of someone protecting their most dearly cherished beloved.

After another gasp, reality returned. Geoffrey and the stranger stared at her worriedly. That was when she realized she was weeping.

The real world continued to slowly come back to her between sobs. The angel had his hand on the skin of her back, his palm pressed over the demon wound as though he were willing her to live. He'd apparently loosened her dress enough to let him do so. The tiniest fraction of her mind — the only one not entirely overtaken — wished that he had had very different reasons to do the same.

Mostly, she was sitting there, sobbing in torment, in rage. She tried to focus on Geoffrey's strong, worried eyes, eyes that seemed to understand far too much about the situation.

"What did you see?" Something in his tone and his serious gaze made it clear that he understood at least a good part of what was happening to her.

This fact should have comforted her, given her strength. She tried to tell herself that, to calm down, but another emotion erupted instead. "He wants me." Her breaths were shaky. She hated every bit of what was happening but couldn't stop it. "That goddamned demon wants me again."

The look of sadness on Geoffrey's face made her angrier. She hated herself for that feeling but couldn't hold it back. "Why? Why is it always me? What makes me such a fucking prize for them?"

There was a flap of wings in her mind, but she pushed it away, not really wanting the answer. Part of her knew damn well that she didn't want the demon to be targeting anyone, wanted it gone for good, but she couldn't let the rage go. It had a life of its own now.

"I'm useless. I'm ugly. No one human's ever wanted me, but I'm some sort of demonic party favor, every monster's favorite toy."

Geoffrey and their sudden visitor stared at her sadly, only making the hurt grow.

"What in the hell sense is that supposed to make?"

She could feel the fury growing, moving through her. Despair rose with it. It only grew more intense when Geoffrey took his hand off her back, probably disgusted with her. The tears had calmed for a moment, replaced by dry, angry sobs, but the torture remained, the patterns of her life utterly unbearable. Why, oh why, couldn't she be wanted by something *good* for a change?

She didn't want the angel to go, couldn't stand to see him withdraw, as much as every part of her fully admitted that he had a right to. There was nothing about her that could attract anyone with sense or soul. There never had been, as her parents had known only too well.

Still, something willful moved her, her hand catching his retreating wrist, even as she turned away, *desperate* not to lose him. When his left hand pried hers loose, her eyes closed tightly, wanting to give way to the despair for good.

She was waiting for the tears to start again, certain nothing would ever exist now but pain and futility, when she felt Geoffrey's fingers entwining tightly with hers. With that sensation, the torment started to leave.

She looked up, afraid of finding only vague angelic sympathy for a doomed soul. Instead, she saw a very odd sight.

There was a hole in the room, a small circle of light that wasn't part of this universe. She knew it, even if she couldn't say how. It was heavenly, held love and peace and hope — and he was feeding into it long strands of glutinous black oil.

For a moment, she could do nothing but watch, stunned, entirely uncertain where the substance came from. When her head turned further, she discovered the hideous answer. All of that evil was coming out from her back, straight out of the wound.

A lone sob escaped, as she stared, horrified. She wanted to believe that the damn wound was responsible for it, that it was the demon's infection that caused such emotions in her, but she couldn't. All the pettiness she'd been spouting a moment before — as understandable as any rage at such a demon was — had also been coming from her. She was the one who'd come up with, "*Why me?*" and not, "*Why would this happen to anybody?*" She was the one who had, at the return of a demon who'd already — apparently — stolen at least two of her new friends, begun to feel sorry for herself.

It wasn't right, and it wasn't good. But it was all a part of her, nonetheless.

She hated this fact, hated everything it probably said about her, even as she let go of all the vile emotions Geoffrey saved her from. She couldn't meet his eyes, looked instead at their visitor.

The woman was watching the process in amazement. Lydia couldn't blame her for that. She was dressed all in black, in a minister's outfit, looked perfectly put together, other than her slightly disheveled hair.

Lydia could only half focus on the woman she hadn't been introduced to, but the apparent minister was a good distraction from her shame. Several cinnamon-dyed ringlets had escaped the woman's attempts to pull her hair back, kinking up at angles she clearly hadn't intended.

The color was nice, though, went well with the rich shade of her skin. Too bad this wasn't a better situation for them both.

The woman seemed to have calmed somewhat since she'd first come in, wasn't screaming anymore, at least. Granted, Lydia had been a bit too distracted to notice when she'd stopped. Her dark, worried eyes watched Geoffrey.

"Did I cause that?" She didn't give him time to answer. "Sorry. I'm just—" She visibly swallowed back a sob. "Sybil."

The stranger had gone off in a reverie of her own, leaving Lydia with only one certainty. Maybe she hadn't nearly passed out before. The visitor was so upset that she couldn't get out whole sentences.

Lydia couldn't blame her. If someone tried to take Geoffrey or to harm him in any way—

She cut off the thought, tamped it down into the deepest, most unreachable parts of herself. It wasn't simply that she didn't want to think about it, although that was certainly true. It was more that she feared what she would do if that ever happened, all she might be capable of. She could clearly imagine tearing apart the entire world to find him.

There was a deep breath, as she tried to evaporate the idea. Whatever the demon's plans, they obviously involved her utter torment. She didn't want such a possibility to exist anywhere inside of her for that creature to be able to find.

This truth had passed through her in a matter of seconds. She only hoped that she'd hidden it away quickly enough.

Geoffrey was answering the visitor by the time she came back to herself. "It's not your fault, Erika." He sounded sincere but a little out of it, utterly soul weary. "It was just bad timing."

Lydia had been trying not to look at him, not to show him her guilt, her ugliness. But the rasping sound of his voice scared her, finally reminded her of Sybil's words yesterday. The ghost had come to remove the same sort of oil because it would hurt Geoffrey if he touched it. Lydia's soul ached with the thought. That possibility was the most painful one of all.

She did let out a little gasp with this realization, finally refocusing on him. He was just tucking the last of the gunk into the rip in reality — or whatever it was — placed his hand over the light for a moment to clean the last of it from his fingers.

Horrified at what she had somehow dragged him into, her heart sank. She could only wish that she could ever just be a comfort, and not a burden, to anyone who helped her.

Watching Geoffrey, she worried. He was standing but a little shaky. Small, bright lights seemed to be escaping from him, as though he might evaporate, could disappear completely if she chose the wrong moment to blink. She almost started to cry again at the thought — because she would never survive without him here.

She wanted to do something for him, was desperate to help. The guilt was the smallest part of it. She realized she'd been holding his hand all along and clung to it more thoroughly, willing him to stay with her, wanting to beg him to accept her love. There was nothing on earth to live for without that.

Fortunately, Erika helped in this quest, pulling around a chair, placing him beside Lydia. Geoffrey took it gratefully, slumping into it, holding Lydia's right hand with his left, even though that caused her to half lean in to him.

She wondered over this for a moment, thought for a second he might just be too tired to be thinking clearly, when she realized the truth. He was afraid of touching her with the other hand so soon after using it to rid her of all that evil. He was afraid of infecting her again.

Her heart ached, her fears for him immense. He was an angel, after all. To have to encounter all of that naked pain and enmity and to have it all coming from the woman he loved . . .

Strangely, she accepted his feelings for her now, knew they were the truth. For one thing, nothing else could have hurt him that badly.

She felt the truth, somehow, just from the bond they shared in their touch, as though his emotions were seeping into her warmly. She worried for him desperately, aching for the depths of his pain.

Obviously, he was in pretty bad shape. For one thing, she could see small points of light starting to emerge from his shoulder blades, knew they were the start of wings — that he was starting to revert to his true nature a sign of just how hurt he was.

She didn't know exactly where such a breakthrough would lead, was afraid that the wings' return might destroy this sweet form, leading him back to heaven, away from her. Her heart seemed to cry out. Selfish or not, she didn't want him to go. She didn't want him anywhere except where the two of them could be together.

She leaned further into him, caressing his back with her free hand, kissing the tip of his shoulder, willing him to stay. Part of her knew it wasn't a selfish wish. Not only did all his residents need him — now more than ever — but she was aware, for once, that he wanted to be with her, didn't want to go.

Some small part of her even wondered whether this wasn't really as dangerous a moment as it seemed. After all, he'd revealed the light of his wings fully before when he'd been encouraging poor Mandi to move onto heaven. Lydia would have very much liked to believe that this was no more serious than that.

Somehow, though, she knew the truth. This was more than that, much more. She sensed it in how still he was, in the furious concentration on his face. Part of her understood what he was doing, even if she couldn't have put it into very clear words. He had chosen this physical body for his work here, and for her. It wasn't the truer part of who he was, as, she supposed, such outer shells weren't for anyone. But, for an angel, such a choice took much more effort than your average human to maintain.

For a second after this, she had to hold back her gasp, a new thought moving through her, realizing that she'd already had this theory proven by Geoffrey's polar opposite. She had, somehow, dismissed Damian's physical form earlier, had triggered some sort of shift in him. True, he'd been able to return in it — or one just like it — a few days later, but she didn't want the same to happen to Geoffrey. Among a million more personal concerns, she suspected they didn't have that kind of time. Whatever the demon who wanted her was planning, he clearly had no inclination to delay.

She needed to keep the angel, then, had to have him near — and not simply because she wanted no life without him; she held his hand tightly, the other roaming over his back. He was still shaky, seemed to be fighting to remain. She felt the tears coming, her fingers trailing up into his hair, begging him not to go. All she could do was show him her love, give him whatever strength she might have. That was the only way she knew to keep him here.

She followed that inclination, her lips kissing over his shoulder, then along his back. It seemed to help but clearly wasn't enough.

She dismissed the despair, refused to embrace it. This was far too important. She just had to do more.

She had no conscious plan, moved only with what she felt. One path became clear to her, too. When she approached the point of light where his wings threatened to grow, she imagined all of her love, her desire, her admiration of him, tried to focus it intensely. Then, her fingers rubbing over the same point on his other shoulder, she kissed him there and did her best to transfer to him everything she would always feel.

It seemed to work, the change immediate, his gasp echoing through his chest; his head had fallen back, whole body shuddering.

She pulled away a little to gaze at him and saw the right hand he'd been holding clenched so tightly open. From it oozed a small puddle of that terrible oil, snaking its way out. When it reached the surface of his palm, he let out a shaky breath, tossing his hand up, flinging the oil away, seemed to be performing tricks with it. First it was a snake, then a butterfly. Finally, it disappeared into a small flicker of heavenly light no bigger than it was.

With this, he let out a very deep sigh of release. Then the most wonderful thing happened. He turned and held Lydia tightly in his arms.

He was back with her now, hers completely; she understood without doubt, could feel all his relief and joy. The truth flowed through her, warming her to her soul, as Geoffrey kissed her cheek tenderly before trailing down along her neck, sending her into de-lighted shivers of her own.

He loved her, and he was safe. Her nails pressed into his back just slightly, as he found the spot where her neck and shoulder merged, placing there a soulful kiss. Oh, yes. Nothing else mattered at all.

She was crying again, lightly this time, very happily. It was only when Erika cleared her throat that Lydia opened her eyes, remember-ing that they had an audience. To her shame, she'd forgotten entirely about the woman.

She pulled back reluctantly — felt a tremor of delight that Ge-offrey seemed far less willing to comply — to see not only Erika but Hattie. The succubus had one delicate eyebrow raised, almost seemed impressed.

"Sorry," Lydia murmured. She couldn't help noticing that Geof-frey didn't bother to apologize.

She felt strangely proud of this fact but decided now wasn't really the time. Too much was happening. Erika was also clearly in distress. This probably hadn't been at all what she was expecting when she came to them for help.

If Erika was disturbed by their behavior, she didn't show it. She just looked desperately at Geoffrey, murmuring, "Sybil."

Hattie seemed disappointed, head shaking for a second.

Geoffrey moved them back to their more pressing concerns, although he was still holding Lydia's hand in both of his. "I know about Sybil. Hugh's also been taken. Gladys and Melanie have disappeared, as well."

He turned back to Lydia, even though, given the seriousness of the situation, she hadn't actually planned on interrupting to ask. "Two more of my residents — a siren and a muse." His gaze was intense but brief, reminding her wonderfully for a moment of what had just happened between them. That singeing second over, he looked back to their visitors. "We're going to get them back."

Lydia was glad that he was so certain, even though she wished she didn't already know one part of his plan. She supposed it couldn't be avoided, however. Facing down the demon was the only way out.

This was only part of her reaction. The other, very small, thought she wasn't at all proud of. *A siren called Gladys?* Maybe men didn't care much about names.

She flicked away the idea as unworthy of her, refocusing on the conversation. Geoffrey was looking to Hattie, as she explained her sudden appearance. Lydia tried to focus, reminding herself firmly that just staring at him wasn't going to get them out of this.

"They tried to take me, too. Some nonsense with a bunch of horny frat boys." Hattie rolled her eyes disdainfully. "Roderick has never even *begun* to understand my taste in men."

How such a lure could tempt *anyone* was beyond Lydia, but she didn't bother to address it.

"I'm worried about Lacy. She's in my building." Hattie aimed that last part at Lydia before returning to the angel. "We've gotten to talking lately. Last night, she seemed . . . " She stopped for a moment, staring off in the distance, seeming to search for words. ". . . jumpy.

It was like she kept expecting some visitor she didn't want." Her gaze went back to him. "And she was getting angry."

She didn't really need to say the rest; even Lydia got it. The results of an out-of-control werewolf didn't take a horror film buff to figure out: death, destruction, and lots and lots of blood.

She was as worried as the rest of them, as a few, winged memories flashed in her mind. Wouldn't that be just the sort of homecoming a demon would love?

Fearfully, she focused back on Geoffrey. To her small bolt of delight, he put his arm around her, giving her even more strength, as he addressed their two visitors. "We're going to get through this." His eyes were so strong, only a hint of the sadness evident. "But be prepared. It's only going to get worse from here."

This truth terrified Lydia, especially since she feared that she was going to be at the center of events.

Some small part of her started to rail. If she hadn't come here, these people might be safe. If she just had the sense to keep to herself, no one but she would have had to suffer.

That inner voice went on, trying to get her to hate herself for it — but for the first time, she refused to listen. Wherever she'd gone, the demon would have followed. Wherever that had been, there would have been innocents in the line of fire. Demons were like that. Unlike some attempted hiding places, too, this one would work. Nowhere else she could imagine would be quite as prepared for the coming battle as this one.

The women in front of her proved the point, Hattie gazing over to the minister. "You ready for this, Erika?"

The latter's dark eyes flashed. "If they hurt one ethereal hair on Sybil's head, I'll show them what real Hell is." Her eyes focused on the angel and his assistant. "They're not going to win."

Lydia was relieved by such shows of faith. She only wished that she felt so confident herself.

Despite her knowledge that this was inevitable, every time even the smallest flash of that night in the basement came back to her, it terrified her so badly she wanted to run. And hide. And whimper. How she was supposed to not only survive — as she had barely managed that first time — but save all these other people . . .

Thankfully, Geoffrey chose then to lean in, half-whispering in her ear. "We're with you."

She tried to remember this — her love for him, at least, assured.

"*I'm* with you." He kissed the pulse point where her jaw met her neck, calming her further. "You'll never be alone again."

Her eyes closed, soothed somewhat, the truth that came from the angel so very intense. It was only once she opened them, saw Erika's confusion, that some small part of her realized that he hadn't been speaking in English.

Hattie confirmed the rest, looking at Erika. "Aramaic." She shrugged. "Not the sexiest of languages."

But, given that it had been spoken by her angel, no one could ever convince Lydia of that.

The love, the comfort Geoffrey gave her so generously had quieted her considerably. Still, she could hear a small echo of that Linda part of her freaking out over the fact that she had somehow understood the angel's words, could now apparently comprehend a language only the heartiest of Biblical scholars had even the tiniest acquaintance with.

Not only did she not listen to the voice; she dismissed it completely, could nearly feel it blinking out of existence. The very thought made her happy. She had no use for such nonsense anymore. The world, as she had understood since birth, was a far wider and more magical place than your average human gave it any sort of credit for being. Besides, she had some larger, supernatural problems of her own now, and they would never get solved by pretending they didn't exist.

A small part of her wondered when she'd even started to believe in such delusions. She certainly hadn't in her childhood, had never been capable of enough psychosis or self-destructiveness to think that the things her parents conjured up weren't real.

She supposed it had all happened after her encounter with the demon. Maybe with everything she'd had to fear apparently gone, it had just been easier to fit into the remaining world by adopting their more fervent hallucinations of normality.

These truths and theories passed in a moment, as she gazed lovingly at her angel. She almost wanted to release all the memories he had given her immediately but understood, somehow, that it wouldn't be wise. She didn't bother to question the knowledge. Wherever those images were taking her, she would let them unfold naturally, as Geoffrey had suggested. That way, whatever good they were supposed to do wouldn't be undone.

She accepted this fact instantly, listening to the succubus' next question. "What do you need us to do?"

Like a general preparing for battle, Geoffrey started to deploy his troops. "Go with Erika. She'll need some help in her preparations, and I'm not certain how many of her human parishioners are ready to listen."

Erika rolled her eyes in acknowledgment, but the succubus was waiting.

Geoffrey looked grim, as he told her the rest. "Don't worry. When you're needed, you'll know."

It occurred to Lydia that it would have been nice not to understand just how dire a warning that was, but there wasn't time to fantasize.

"And you?" Hattie wondered.

Geoffrey's look didn't change much, only a tinge of sadness invading it, as he stood; since he was still holding her hand, Lydia followed. "We need to visit Lacy."

The pair before them was about to take their orders, preparing. Erika stopped, though, returning. "I take it you're Lydia."

She nodded, about to apologize for their unusual introduction — for her distraction on a million different levels — even though she was well-aware it wasn't really either of their faults.

Before she could, Erika reached behind herself, unfastening a necklace on a silver chain; Lydia hadn't seen it before, the majority of it hidden beneath the woman's clothes. A moment later, Erika was fastening it around Lydia's neck. It clearly wasn't a gift she'd be allowed to reject.

It wasn't like she would have, anyway. Lydia looked down to see a cross, an ankh, and a Celtic wheel of life on three separate, small pendants. One thing her childhood had given her was a thorough training in various religious and supernatural symbols. Her parents had enjoyed subverting them far too much for her to miss their various meanings.

When she glanced back up, Erika was shrugging at the angel. "They can't hurt." Then, she left with Hattie before Lydia even had a chance to thank her.

Geoffrey watched the pair go, sighing, before gazing down to this new gift. When he reached out to touch the pendants where they hung against Lydia's breastbone, she felt a tingle reflected through her entire body. Even the objects he held seemed to glow. Sadly, a moment later, he let them go, after slipping them out of sight under her dress. Then, he zipped up the material from where he had earlier disarranged it to remove that gunk from the wound on her shoulder.

She let out her own sigh, not entirely pleased at being so covered up around him. She would have liked far more pleasant reasons for him to be touching her skin.

This was the thought of an instant, soon forgotten for many reasons. To begin with, there was a sweet moment when Geoffrey just stood there, gazing at her, his hand caressing the back of her neck. She almost thought he would kiss her again, until he let out a shuddering breath, pulling away. "We need to go." He didn't seem any happier about it than she did.

Part of her wished she could argue, but there was no way to. They were facing down a demon, after all, one who was clearly drawing together its forces, preparing for attack, stealing all her friends to do so. No matter how tempting it might be in the short-term, none of them would be aided by Lydia losing herself in Geoffrey's eyes now.

She kept this truth firmly in mind, as he led her out of the office. But she was only able to give one, brief smile at the blue roses, before they were out the doors and headed toward the apartments.

She'd expected Damian to be hanging around, had certainly thought that he would have wanted to take a few more opportunities to gloat, but he was nowhere to be seen. It wasn't at all comforting to think about where he might be, instead.

They continued on, the angel leading her toward Lacy's building. But, halfway there, he stopped dead, staring off into the distance in shock. When he glanced back to her, he caught both her hands, gripping them tightly. "I have to go."

She could see the fear in his eyes, tried her best to quell her own rising terror. Anything that made angels afraid was too horrifying to ponder.

He seemed to know what she was thinking but clearly didn't have the time to reassure her. It was even more disturbing to think that he might not have any sane fact to quiet her with. "Lacy's in apartment 692. Calm her down. I'll be there when I can." His hands squeezed hers one last time, and then he disappeared.

She had known that he was capable of this, of course, but it was a little disturbing to see in the flesh. She understood, too, that he could probably be in several places at once, shouldn't need to leave her like this. Whatever he was going to face was too important to focus only part of himself on, his whole force and soul required. He needed her here to back him up.

She took on the task with more strength than she had ever really experienced before, refused to feel abandoned or scared. Uttering one message to her beloved, she knew he would hear. "Protect yourself, Geoffrey. I won't accept you being sacrificed." Her message sent, she nodded — and then went to face an angry, unknown werewolf all on her own.

Chapter Twelve

A week ago, Lydia would have laughed, if rather nervously, at being sent to soothe a disturbed werewolf while the demon who stalked her rounded up everyone she cared about just to torment her, but she had more sense now. Her head high, she went to find the woman, knowing the truth. She *would* get through this. She couldn't force Geoffrey to keep his promises to watch after himself and not do the same for him in return.

The first task didn't take long, Lacy's apartment soon located. Lydia used the knocker to rap on the door, not as loudly as she could have but enough to assure attention. "Lacy? I'm Lydia, the tenant manager."

There was no sound from inside besides a rather low growl.

Geoffrey's love — the messages of those images she had yet to decode in her mind — kept her in place, refusing to be cowed. "I'm sorry we haven't met before, but I need to talk to you."

Only silence this time.

"It's important to everyone's salvation, including your own."

The door opened forcefully, a wild-eyed woman glaring. "What the hell do you want? Can't you see when a person needs to be left alone?"

Lydia wasn't so certain of that, Lacy looking to be teetering very close to the edge of a breakdown. Her blond hair was frizzed and wild, didn't seem to have been brushed in days.

Her voice rose, glaring at Lydia. "Why can't you all just leave me to my damn misery in peace?"

That the woman was nearly out of control was hard to ignore. Even her nails seemed to be growing steadily, turning into hardened claws, ready to put out someone's eyes. Lydia could hear them starting to dig further into the wood of the door.

But, strangely, she wasn't the least bit frightened, felt only the most intense sympathy. "You poor thing." She put her arms around her tenant, drawing her close, as what could well have been a growl sounded in the woman's throat. "You must have suffered so much."

It wasn't an act, her absolute, immediate empathy and love for this suffering soul apparent even to the tortured woman herself. She tried to hold onto her rage, but it couldn't last for long. The growls continued for only a second before turning into a moan, then a series of snuffling sniffles, and finally broaching into sobs. By a few moments later, she'd half-collapsed, taking Lydia with her.

"Shh," Lydia soothed, her hand stroking over the Lacy's hair. "It's all right."

The woman gave up, started bawling against her shoulder.

Lydia kissed her temple, feeling all of her tenant's pain, aching with it, returning it only with love. "We won't let anyone hurt you again."

They stayed like this for quite some time, neither of them questioning, the werewolf letting out loud, wracking sobs, weeping out all of her misery. Somehow, Lydia felt it, could nearly picture it, but every time she was about to, it only brought back other, hideous memories of her own.

It didn't occur to her — as it certainly would have a few days ago — how strange she must have looked, embracing this total, half-crazed stranger, kissing her temple, promising her that good would triumph. She even forgot to close the door, not concerned with appearances.— but that would prove to be an almost-deadly mistake.

It was a bright, perky voice that announced this fact to her. "Am I interrupting?" It seemed so innocent — but it also sounded like the precursor of Hell.

Lacy had been calming, the tension and rage draining steadily from her under Lydia's absolute sympathy and understanding. But now the werewolf stiffened, growling once more. The transformation took no time at all. Lydia could feel coarse hairs starting to appear through the shirt on the woman's back, felt a claw almost dig into her shoulder.

Lacy pulled it away just in time, backing away. As she did, Lydia could see her teeth growing pointed and canine, her eyes starting to glow gold, as the shift began.

But seeing it made something inside Lydia burn. *No.* She wouldn't let this go the anywhere their intruder intended.

Lydia was utterly unruffled, felt only a mild revulsion for Ashley; she hadn't even turned to acknowledge her yet. Just as Lacy, now in wolf form, was about to spring and attack, Lydia placed her hand against the wolf's brow, her voice soothing. "No. Please." Her thumb stroked a pattern up along her fur. She was pleased to see Lacy's eyes calm slightly, to a darker shade of yellow. "Let me."

It took a moment, but there was a small nod of Lacy's furry head, giving Lydia her chance.

Apparently, Ashley saw one as well, began to speak as Lydia turned to her. It was no more than a vague vowel sound before her hand raised, her voice clear. "You will never harm her." Lydia took a step closer, their intruder appearing extremely startled. "You will never come near any of us again."

That moment saw the change, a permanent one. There was a flapping of wings through Lydia's mind, her hand nearly performing on its own. A second later, a pattern of glowing light filled Lacy's doorway. It was an exact replica of the Celtic wheel of life Erika had given her earlier — and it proved very effective, indeed.

The instant the light was there, their unwelcome visitor was tossed back from the portal, just as Damian had been propelled earlier by Geoffrey. Some small voice within Lydia said that she should be surprised by this new power, but she knew how foolish it was. After all, she had started to recognize something in that vision, had allowed herself to at last. She knew whose some of those wings belonged to now. Two of them were hers — and no demon would take them away from her again.

She continued to approach the intruder, walking straight through the pattern of protection on the door without disrupting it in the least. Ashley looked like she wanted to be brave but was apparently about to go into hysterics, was simply cowering in the doorway across the hall.

Despite the feelings Lacy's pain had evoked in Lydia earlier, there was no sympathy here; she gazed down, implacable. "You will leave, Ashley. You will go and not return to this side, ever."

The woman was shaking but seemed about to try to argue. Ashleys were always bad about admitting defeat.

"Do you walk on your own, or do I send you flying?" It was clear to all concerned that this was no idle threat.

To say that the intruder had lost was a bit of an understatement. She wasn't gracious about it, either. Glancing around Lydia at her attempted prey, trying to sit up a little taller, she did her best to appear the injured party. "But I was just trying to tell you that . . . "

This was as far as she was allowed to get. The pointing of Lydia's finger dammed the breath in the intruder's throat. Even Lydia didn't know whether that were from this rediscovered power or simply from unconquerable fear on Ashley's part.

She didn't bother to ponder it, pointing instead toward the front door of the building. "Leave," she commanded. And, to put it mildly, their intruder was forced to do just that.

It wasn't a pleasant trip for her. The screams made that obvious.

She was being tumbled in midair, battered by the glowing lights, as Lydia followed her outside. Even as the woman struggled, she was propelled far across the lot to land in a rolling, battered heap on the perfectly manicured grass of the demon's side of the complex. It was quite clear she wasn't coming back.

It took Ashley a second to get back to her feet, and her whole demeanor changed, the trip apparently doing her little good. Her inherent violence and viciousness was clear in her eyes, even from this far away. Her shrieks of fury rang loudly through the parking lot and probably the surrounding neighborhood. "You're dead, Lydia! Every single one of you is going to get sucked straight down into—"

The last word was unheard, if obvious, Lydia having formed another glowing barrier, a huge one, this time in the middle of the road that divided the complex, protecting all of Geoffrey's tenants and residents. She, and several others who stood by, astounded, could see Ashley continuing to rage and shriek on the other side. But now they didn't have to listen to a single word.

The woman's petulant display continued, ignored completely, as Lydia started to return to the tortured werewolf. Several tenants, only a few of whom she knew, stared, in varying combinations of awe, shock, and happiness.

She walked away from them, back toward Lacy, until a sudden thought made her turn back on the front stairs. "Geoffrey's given us a home here." Several of them nodded. "I know you'll all help me to defend each other."

She didn't wait for an answer, but she could see that all of them agreed. She returned to the building, and the apartment, shutting the doors behind her.

Poor Lacy was still on the floor, looking less canine but now naked and more than a little intimidated. She was staring at Lydia, her breathing clearly unsteady. She didn't wait long to tell her what caused her fear. "Your eyes."

Lydia just tilted her head, not understanding.

"They're glowing."

The fact didn't faze Lydia much. She'd known weirder. "Oh." She pondered for a moment. "What color are they?"

Lacy was staring, dumbstruck enough for them both. "Gold." She looked closer, seemed to be in awe. "Burning gold." She leaned in. "But there are little flecks of . . . deep green there."

The woman seemed utterly stunned. Lydia wasn't, anymore. So, they were the opposite of Geoffrey's. That was interesting.

A small part of her wondered whether she might be in shock, told her she shouldn't be taking this so calmly, but she ignored it. Her hair had already gone through a few major changes. What was an eye color or two, as well?

She continued to approach the werewolf, who, after a minute to adjust, thankfully, didn't seem frightened or angry anymore, just immensely tired. "I need to sit down," she muttered. The fact that she was already on the floor, and naked, seemed to have entirely slipped her notice.

Lydia couldn't blame her, knew she had been through a lot — and werewolves probably got used to the naked thing pretty quickly. She just smiled, taking Lacy's arms to help her stand before leading her over to the sofa.

The werewolf went without complaint, resting her cheek against its back; her words were barely audible, as Lydia sat beside her. "Why is it always this hard?"

When Lydia just watched her calmly, Lacy sighed.

"Why are some people born to suffer?"

For one of the very first times in her life, Lydia didn't agree with this statement — but she suspected this wasn't the time for a theological debate.

She led the woman to talk instead, understanding that she just needed someone who would listen. "How did you become a werewolf?" The tenant closed her eyes, making Lydia's heart ache, as she suspected the rest. "That bad?"

Lacy gave a small snort. "Yeah . . . 'bad.'" She only barely seemed to force her eyes open, giving way to a distant stare. "Imagine being violently attacked by some stranger. You're hurt in . . . " Her voice failed her for a second. ". . . *every* way. Then, just as you think he's finally killed you, that you might *at least* be free, you wake up in a morgue to discover that you're something very different." A small sigh rose from her, the pain in her eyes contagious, her voice nearly disappearing. "And entirely inhuman."

It certainly wasn't difficult to find sympathy for the woman's plight. All the events she had hinted at were hideous enough. Lydia took her hand, squeezing it gently. She guessed there might be a reason why no one went on about wanting to be a turned into a werewolf. They didn't have the cachet of vampires. She managed to repress her sigh, a random thought creeping in. At least there was *some* sort of psychosis society didn't seem to suffer from. Maybe that was a good sign for humanity.

She continued to listen, then, as her tenant went on, spilling out her pain. "You can't see your family and friends anymore. You can't go back to school. Everyone thinks you're *dead*. And, to top it all off, you aren't even allowed *that much* peace." Lacy had to swallow back heavily, the torment clearly unbearable. "You're given a new name, forced into a new home, and then you have the utter *joy* of discovering hair in places hair is simply *not* supposed to grow!" She was sitting up now, eyes desperate. "Can you tell me how the *hell* that's fair?"

Lydia didn't answer, suspecting that there was no real way to, anyway. She just took the woman slowly in her arms and held her close. Although she suspected that her tenant's complaints had travelled from the unspeakably grim to the mildly ridiculous, she decided to focus on the latter. The pain of the former could only ever be endured with time and comfort. "I guess being a werewolf gives a whole new meaning to 'bad hair day,' huh?"

Despite the seriousness of her problems, Lacy did laugh, Lydia's empathy clearly calming her. "You've got *no* idea." The laugh contained a small sob, but she managed to hold it back.

Lydia kissed her temple, and Lacy sighed, putting her head on her shoulder. For a moment, it seemed to be enough just to have somebody who would try to understand.

They stayed like that for quite a while. Lydia didn't realize how long, until she noticed that it was growing darker outside, more than it should be. She tried to hold back the slight dread, knowing again what was coming, what she had to do.

"I need to take you somewhere." Lydia noted, as she pulled away, and Lacy nodded. "I need to make certain you're safe."

Lacy seemed unlikely to argue anymore, questioning only what she needed to. "Do I need to take anything?"

A fear had started somewhere in the back of Lydia's mind, but she tried to hold it back, knowing it would do them no good. "Just put on some clothes, and grab your purse, if you want it. What the demons are planning shouldn't take more than a night." *One way or another.*

The instructions made Lacy glance down. "Um, yeah. Forgot about that." She looked back up. "It's weird how quickly naked becomes normal, after you're turned."

Lydia just smiled and waited.

It only took Lacy a minute or so to prepare, leaving Lydia to her thoughts, unpleasant company though they were. She wasn't looking forward to the coming battle, but she accepted what needed to be done. Despite her fears, she was well aware now that she was the only person who could do it.

It only took a few minutes before they were out the door, Lacy locking the place up behind them. Despite — or maybe because of — the oppressive atmosphere the night gave off, Lydia kept up the conversation, wanting to distract the werewolf's mind from the deeper parts of her pain. It wasn't like either of them would be aided by pondering the future, at the moment.

"What's your full name, Lacy?" Lydia could see a few of Damian's residents gathered on the other side of her protective wall, glaring at them, hoped to keep the werewolf ignorant of the sight. "I'm pretty new around here, I'm afraid."

The last part of that sentence wasn't just politeness, but Lacy either didn't notice or knew better than to comment, a deep sigh emerging. "It's really stupid."

The sigh grew deeper, as Lydia waited. Given the ones she had heard already, though, she wouldn't be surprised.

"Lacy T. Roat."

Okay, that one went even further than Lydia had imagined, deciphering the not-exactly-hidden pun. "Lacy Throat?"

The werewolf nodded.

Lydia shook her head. "Who names you people? And what sort of sick comedian is he?"

Lacy laughed, as they turned their backs to the demon's side of the complex. Lydia noticed the woman's eyes, though, saw that she was actively attempting to keep from looking over there; she was proud. *Good for her.* She was going to make it through this, after all.

Lydia tried to take this good news as an omen for them all, attempting to focus on Lacy's words. "There's an alpha werewolf, at least a few for each city, I hear." Her smile actually continued. "Mine's not too bad, really. He's just got a really warped sense of humor."

This went without saying. There was a pause in the conversation, as Lydia led her visitor up to her apartment.

The lighter air disappeared, once they reached the door. She had to catch the werewolf's wrist to keep her from retreating. "No. It's all right." Or, at least, that was what she was going to tell herself.

It was a little difficult to believe such a theory with what appeared to be a bloody, upside-down pentagram on her door. It didn't bring back good memories. She had seen such signs before, had even been bled to create one; she took in a deep breath, calling forward all her newfound, formidable strength. But they weren't going to harm her or anyone she loved any further tonight.

She refused to think about whose blood this little message from Hell might be derived from. Especially since Geoffrey had failed to return, she knew it was better not to know. Some things simply had to be faced. Agonizing over the possible catastrophes beforehand would guarantee no one's safety now.

She kept this fact strong in her heart, as she held her palm over the doorknob, watching the glowing lights she emitted purifying it completely, before she tried to enter. She already knew that, despite her earlier actions, the door would be unlocked. Their enemy had been anything but slothful today.

When she was finally able to open it, her heart was pounding a little, trying her best not to be afraid of what she would find. Damian's threat continued to plague her. When she discovered two cats and an imp staring up at her worriedly, she had never been more grateful in her life.

She left the door hanging open, leaning down to hug them. The cats, anyway. The imp wasn't the touchy-feely type.

Of course, cats were pretty notorious for not allowing such displays, unless they themselves initiated them, but today seemed to be an exception. She even detected slight purrs.

The moment was brief, but it braced Lydia for everything that followed. The cats clearly knew it, watching her closely, as she rose, covered in their fur, to hold her palm in front of the deadly sign on her door. Then, with intense concentration, she began to erase it with the light.

This was not an immediate process, the minutes slipping away sluggishly. In the end, both cats sat on her feet, as she finished. She barely had the strength to do anything but lean against the doorpost, once she was done.

It was only with the cats' directions, and Lacy's willingness to help, that the felines, imp, and werewolf got her to a chair. Once there, she could barely move. Fortunately, her tenant closed and locked the door behind them, came back to focus on her worriedly — but not with nearly as much concern as Lydia herself had.

Eveningstar lay purring on her knees, giving her strength, as one question continued to torment her. If just removing the demon's calling card had taken this much of her energy, how on earth would she survive his real attack, much less save her friends? And, if she couldn't save them, then Geoffrey . . .

She wouldn't allow herself to finish the thought, refusing to acknowledge the possibilities. While stupid, unfounded optimism probably wasn't for the best, learned helplessness would aid her even less. She had an entire lifetime of knowledge to confirm that.

She just sat there with her eyes closed, then, trying to regain her power. Lacy sat on the couch, watching uncertainly. A much friendlier-than-normal Tiger was on her lap — an odd fact, given the felines' general attitudes toward dogs — the cat purring under the woman's constant petting. Lydia didn't even have the strength to do such a thing with Eveningstar, although the Persian, happily, didn't seem to mind.

Finally, Lacy drew together the courage to ask about what was bothering her. "Who are you?"

Lydia just managed to open her eyes.

"Or should I say, what?"

This was a question far beyond Lydia, as much as parts of those images in her head were starting to make themselves clear. Still, she wasn't ready to discuss those, not with one of the tenants, anyway. With Geoffrey, yes, but he already knew. He had been there.

That recollection — the beloved wings, the voice shouting for her safety — flashed through her mind almost painfully. She had to close her eyes to the brightness of it for a second, before drawing in a deep breath, gazing back to the werewolf, cutting off more questions. "I don't have an easy answer for you."

Lacy looked like she wanted to press her further but didn't.

"I survived a demon attack before. I was raised, probably conceived, to be sacrificed to one." Lydia drew a deep breath, her gaze so sad. "Now, he's back."

Lacy still looked uncertain. "He plans to take you this time?"

Closing her eyes in pain, Lydia shook her head. "No." She didn't even want to think about the answer. "He plans to take everything."

The werewolf's eyes widened over this, but she didn't ask any more. Lydia was just glad that the woman didn't run screaming from the apartment. It was easier to look after her here, and she seemed to like the cats. That was good, might — if they were lucky — derail a few of the demon's plans. As to the rest of them . . .

Everyone was gazing at her now, Eveningstar from her lap, Tiger from Lacy's. Even the imp was a worried, furry, blue on the coffee table. He stopped wringing his hands the second she glanced at him, trying to look imperious. That was when she knew things were serious. If the demon could even distract Alvin from his castle . . .

She thought again into what she had just, only half consciously, said to Lacy, realized why they were all so worried — saw the truth. At first, she had assumed that the demon was just back for her, but after the events of this morning, she had decided that he was going after Geoffrey's whole side of the apartments. Now, she wasn't so sure that was all. Maybe he hadn't come to destroy the entire earth yet, but his plans weren't small — never had been. Now that he was back . . .

She began to see it, to understand much too well, wondered how far it all went. Ashley, apparently, had said too much. The demon *was* planning to destroy them, to obliterate their influence, replace it with his own. The angel's people, residents and tenants, were a force for good in this world — or would be, in the tenants' cases, once they learned to cope with their various problems. Somehow, they provided a bulwark against the demon's encroachment, made certain that his will couldn't be done, not entirely, anyway. By wiping out the whole of Geoffrey's side, the demons would win a huge victory.

What was that old quote? Something like, "All that is required for evil to conquer is for men of goodwill to do nothing"? If the demon won, there would be an even greater silence infesting the city than before.

She started to grow angry with this possibility, couldn't believe that they would try this here — anywhere, really. She had always hated seeing anyone hurt, the good and innocent most of all. Perhaps it was just her twisted upbringing that had brought out her passion for justice, but it was a part of her, nonetheless; her blood flowed more quickly through her, the strength returning. No — she would not allow any of these decent, loving people to be harmed.

Lacy was staring at her eyes in wonder, and she supposed they must be glowing again. Good. Because now she saw the truth, knew what lay ahead. She even saw the demon's methods. He was taking one person from each of the apartment's couples — stealing Hugh away from Lon, Sybil from Erika, and — most likely — Geoffrey away from herself. He planned, no doubt, to make the free ones choose: their beloved or the safety of everyone else.

It was a typical evil, clever ploy — or would be, normally. But not today.

This time, too, the demon would not win. This time, even the mark it had left on her would be expunged. She, and all of her friends, were going to save the prisoners, protect Geoffrey's domain, and help humanity along with it. They couldn't be stopped. They were going to save the goodness in the world, no matter what it took.

Such an absolute resolve would have seemed rather insane to her, even earlier today——but now everything was changing for the better. With those intense memories that her angel had begun to reawaken in her mind, the world was finally making sense. Maybe many of the details were a little fuzzy, the immediate paths they would take toward their victory unclear, but one fact was definitely revealing itself.

Geoffrey was not the only one who had once had wings; she felt one of her shoulder blades start to glow. She too would never turn away from all those who needed her aid.

This fire burned within her, as she looked down at the Persian in her lap. If such a thing had been possible for the creature, the cat would have been smiling. "Finally figured it out?"

Lydia laughed quietly. "I'm starting to." She would have said more, but there was a desperate knocking on her patio door. It didn't take ESP to figure out who that would be. Her nightly visit had begun.

While she was well aware that this would not be the usual bit of vampire therapy, she was resigned to the intrusion. Eveningstar looked pleased, jumping down from her lap. Lacy's obvious terror only seemed to be calmed by a decided increase in the volume of Tiger's purring.

She herself no longer had any fear. The demon mark on her back might have blotted out one of her wings — probably stolen for the demon's own uses — but that Linda-like constant terror was finally gone.

She might not be all-powerful, didn't even know whether she had anything like the brute strength her opponents clearly possessed, but she was well aware that she had one quality they would never know: love. Against such strength and protection, the demons' hateful malice seemed paltry, indeed.

She went to her back door as she had the previous few nights, although with far more confidence this time. She even opened it, knowing the vampire wouldn't try to barge his way in; he wouldn't dare. Besides, she knew exactly why he was here. It fit the whole pattern of the day. All she needed to do now was save them all.

"Clarissa — she's gone!" Gerrard's words were out, before Lydia had even completely opened the door. He looked truly panicked, his usual, stoic charm having fled. "You don't think she ... "

"The demon," Lydia interrupted, nodding. "Probably." It wasn't like she was the first.

The vampire contradicted her assumptions, however, pacing away to tug at his hair. "How could she?" He seemed almost like he might cry. "She knows I love her. I don't want anyone else." His hand covered his face. "How could she think ... ?"

Lydia tilted her head. "You think she went willingly?" That would certainly be a first.

Gerrard flopped down on the patio chair, nearly turning it over; he didn't even seem to care about how flustered he appeared — a first for her interactions with his kind.

He was staring at the ground, distraught, his voice barely audible. "She was jealous of us."

Lydia almost interrupted to ask him to explain that last word, but he continued before she could.

"I've never shown an interest in anyone besides her, not since she's known me." He was wringing his hands. "She thinks I ... "

Despite the fact that Lydia wanted to be annoyed, she managed to fight it off. "She thinks you're in love with me," she finished, when the vampire apparently couldn't.

He nodded, not looking at her.

Lydia sighed, her shoulder thumping against the doorframe, as she crossed her arms. She was half a second away from saying, "Why would *anyone* believe that I could be in love you?" when she managed to hold it back. The man was in enough pain without her rejection to add to it.

It weren't as though he were paying attention to such details, too lost to his own misery. She asked another question, instead — a far more serious one. "She would help destroy everything, because she lost you?"

The latter part of that assessment clearly wasn't correct — the vampire showing that — but this wasn't her real intention.

Her visitor's stare became more hollow, pondering. "I don't know. I wouldn't have thought so." A little fear started to show. "But lately . . . "

She left the man to this question, sighing, wondering if she could ever have done the same. But the answer was all too obvious. No — not ever. Even if Geoffrey had never wanted her, she would never try to hurt anyone else — especially the person he might love.

Her heart ached just thinking about it. How could anyone think that destroying something precious to the one they were infatuated with would make that person suddenly love them—or even simply not despise them? How could anyone want to harm the person they claimed to love?

True, had Geoffrey never cared for her, it was possible that she might have tried to harm her own life; her eyes closed on another sigh. But she was only now beginning to see what a crime against herself that would have been.

She had never treasured her existence much, up to now, had never been concerned with dying, only with what her parents might contrive to do with her soul after death. While Geoffrey was right — there were far worse things than death — she saw how she had been processed, growing up, the lie she had been taught to believe.

She had thought that she was entirely without value, her presence on this planet an unfortunate fluke. Now, she understood the truth.

She did have a place and a purpose. All of them did — each of the residents, every one of her lost and tortured tenants. That place might not always be clear — the world might even try to convince them that it didn't exist — but it did. Hers was to be here in this moment, to save them all, was to finally be reunited, as she at last recognized, with Geoffrey. Clarissa's might well be to be with Gerrard — although she hadn't seen the two of them together long enough to say for certain. Whatever it was, it wasn't — as Lacy, and she herself, had once believed — to suffer endlessly; she sighed, looking up. Now, it was her biggest purpose on earth to help save them all.

She wouldn't be alone in this task; she knew it, even as she gazed into the vampire's eyes.

He had moved soundlessly, as always, was now standing directly in front of her. She knew very well what he had wanted to do, and why, his fangs showing all-too-clearly.

She just shook her head, her hand on his cheek. "My blood will be of more value to you in *my* veins than yours."

He could have ignored her, could have stolen it — or tried to — but he didn't.

"We're all needed in this fight."

It was another decision point for the vampire. She witnessed it in his eyes, the struggle clear. Just as he had once had to decide between death or life-in-death, now he could either steal or give.

He seemed to reach a conclusion a long moment later, nodding, as he took her hand in his. She smiled. He could either join or walk alone — and he had finally understood that. The end he sought could only be found in their mutual struggle.

She retrieved her hand, nodding in return — knowing his thoughts, telling him the rest. "They have Geoffrey, as well. Several of the residents, too." The information clearly unsettled him, but she only went on; he needed to know. "One of each pair."

He seemed to understand, tortured by what his own partner's intentions might be, his eyes closing. "Clarissa."

She just nodded, waiting for him to refocus on her, her voice confident. "We all need rescuing, Gerrard."

Apparently, he understood, nodding, as he turned away. He did look back for a second, though, glancing between her and the table. "Ah," he murmured with a smile. Then, he left to begin his own preparations.

It was only the last part of this conversation Lydia didn't understand, as she closed and locked the patio door. She looked back to the table, saw Eveningstar lying there, watching her interestedly. "Well?" she asked the cat.

The Persian seemed pleased. "Your eyes." She said no more, waiting, leaving Lydia to blink.

For a moment, she felt profoundly clueless. Then, she noticed it. The cat's golden eyes were exactly the same as Lacy had described her own as being.

"Ah." There were a million other messages to the similarity, but she didn't have time to ponder any of them, at the moment.

Eveningstar made no objections to her ignoring the subject, simply watched, as Lydia spiritually barred the door, another Celtic wheel etched deeply into the handle. After a moment, she glanced up at the rest of the glass there, sighing. When her finger flicked toward it, the pattern expanded, flying out into an uncountable number of wheels all across the glass. That should prevent any immediate break-ins, at least.

It wasn't her material goods she was worried about, of course, was only the cats and Lacy. Well, the imp, too — although she suspected that anyone who tried to take Alvin anywhere would be facing a very ornery blue furry thing, indeed.

Eveningstar followed her human, as she went back into the living room. Lydia took a second to check that the pattern she had placed was also visible over the windows here, before turning to the little group she had gathered. "I guess it's time."

Her words were nearly a cue. Outside, an alluring, female voice called out to her. "Ly-di-a." There was a dramatic pause. "Ly-di-a."

That was pretty much what she had expected, although she couldn't say that she was exactly falling into a vampire-induced trance.

Both the cats joined her, wrapping again and again around her ankles. When they had shed themselves thoroughly, they paused by her toes. Eveningstar's eyes were glowing. "Fight well, sister."

Tiger looked at two particularly large balls of fur on her shoes before gazing at her proudly. "Tell Glory hello."

For a moment, Lydia was a little choked up. While it seemed an odd reaction to such a furry presentation, she understood the cats' deeper intent.

She crouched, picking up the largest of the balls of hair and tucking them up her sleeve. Then, she hugged the cats, kissing them both on the cheek.

They forbore it with the sort of restrained dignity only felines could produce. "Look after Lacy," she requested, rising. She noticed a blue blur with his arms crossed from the corner of her eye. "And Alvin."

The imp seemed about to tell her just what she could do with her protection but stopped when she smiled at him, his cheeks going deep purple.

She leaned down and petted both the cats once, waved to Lacy, and then headed down to meet the eerily-calling voice of Clarissa — and to finally face her fate.

Chapter Thirteen

There was nothing much that could surprise Lydia anymore. Even the demon's minion was the one she'd predicted.

Clarissa waited in the parking lot, dressed all in her usual black. How the woman had gotten through Lydia's wards, she didn't entirely know. Perhaps it was the fact that the vampire had once worked here; maybe it was the generally better nature of the man she was in love with. It was possible, too, that the demons had simply cast aside Lydia's beginning spells like cobwebs, allowing all of their progeny to roam.

The latter of these possibilities was by far the least preferable, but she didn't have time to ponder it. Besides, one look at the buildings around her showed that her symbol covered them all. That, at least, explained why the woman hadn't knocked on her door. Maybe the rest of the tenants , then, were safe.

Clarissa started to plead with her, seemed so upset. "Please, I need your help. There's a—"

Lydia held up her hand. "I already know." She nodded, confirming the knowledge behind the woman's widened eyes. "I know where you need me to go — and who sent you."

Her escort seemed a bit sour after this but said nothing, as she led Lydia toward the encounter she had once dreaded more than any other. Still, Lydia didn't let her off that easily. "Gerrard loves you, you know."

The blonde woman stiffened but didn't reply.

"His only interest in me is curiosity." In some ways, she couldn't blame him. There were a lot of questions she had yet to discover answers for herself.

This finally seemed to require some sort of response, the ex-manager looking hurt, her voice disdainful. "Gerrard." They continued to walk in silence toward their predictable destination — Damian's side of the apartments — before she went on. "He's got eyes for every new vampire in the area."

Lydia couldn't argue, not knowing the man well enough. Clarissa could well have been right — although Gerrard had seemed genuinely upset at her defection. But maybe that was just possessiveness.

Still, Geoffrey had appeared to somewhat agree with the vampire's claim that he hadn't wished to see the woman die, had backed up some of Gerrard's feelings for her. Lydia wasn't around the pair often enough to judge for herself — had only seen them once together — and then it had clearly been Clarissa who was the most affectionate and worried. While it wouldn't help her, or her friends', cause much, there might be a lot of truth in what the other woman said. It would make a terrible amount of sense for why she was helping out the demons now.

They walked on to their fateful destination, Lydia so caught in her thoughts that she almost missed the woman's next, whispered words. "He doesn't look at me like Geoffrey looks at you." The hurt was evident in her almost-tearful eyes, her voice even softer. "He didn't wait for centuries for me."

These words were loaded, painful. Lydia nearly let out a small, "Oh," as the truth settled into her — felt a bit foolish for not figuring it out before. Clarissa wasn't jealous over Gerrard — or, if so, only a little. It was Geoffrey she wanted.

It made sense of everything. Sybil had mentioned something about it, when the ghost and she had first met — about how poor Clarissa had known about her from the start, had never felt settled with the angel because of it. The look the vampire had given upon meeting with her old boss had spoken volumes, as well. What Lydia had then taken to be shame now seemed more like rejected love. It was terrible, told her more than could ever be her business. She only wished there were something she could do to help.

She wanted to hold the woman, to console her, as she had done for Lacy, but she didn't attempt it. A nearly rampaging werewolf had been one thing. A scorned vampire who was leading her to her possible doom was quite another. Despite the woman's needs, she didn't want to be drained of blood, before she got near the confrontation she'd been born for.

There was more to it than that, as well. From her very shallow knowledge of romantic relationships, up to now, she fully understood that consolation from the chosen woman wouldn't make the rejected one feel any better. If anything, it would be rubbing more salt in her wounds. Clarissa had been injured enough already.

She settled for an, "I'm truly sorry you've been hurt," and left it alone, seeing the woman bristle. Lydia couldn't entirely blame her, knew if she had been in Clarissa's place, nothing would console her for losing Geoffrey — even worse, for never having him in the first place. Knowing that he was destined for someone else long before she'd been born would have been no kind of solace at all.

They'd crossed over the barrier between the angel's and demon's sides of the apartments a moment ago, Lydia noting it only in the fact that she could feel a sense of cold spikes invading her. It penetrated the center of her being, was one she'd only encountered once before, at least in this lifetime. But she knew that hadn't really been the first time, now. Oh, no. She and some of the demon's minions went extremely far back.

She accepted this fact, tried not to think into it yet, focusing instead on Clarissa. If there were some way to convince the vampire to stay on their side, to help Geoffrey rather than try to destroy the one who had rejected her, all of them would be infinitely better off.

Unfortunately, no clear path came to her for this. Lydia couldn't imagine that telling the woman that she had never been interested in Gerrard would help. Clarissa could interpret that as the victorious woman rejecting the only man who would take the loser. That this couldn't be further from the truth wouldn't matter. Saying that she hadn't been trying to tempt the vampire to her apartment, that he'd always come on his own, would be an obvious slap on the face — something out of a soap opera. To promise the vampire that she truly loved Geoffrey would be no use, either. It only flaunted their relationship.

She thought for a moment of saying, "No one wanted to hurt you," but it sounded too much like what a duplicitous man might claim to his discarded wife when trying to assure that she wouldn't ask for too much alimony, as he moved in with a much-younger prize.

It couldn't be helped. She only fanned the flames further with, "Geoffrey does care for you," and shut up. Even that was saying far too much.

A stray tear escaped down the Clarissa's cheek. Lydia ached inside, not knowing what to do to help but deciding it wasn't her primary battle. What lay ahead was far more terrible than any petty disagreement over a man.

They moved around the winding road that led to the back of Damian's side of the apartments then out toward the woods behind them. There was only a narrow patch of land between these buildings and those beyond, the ones that bordered a main road. Theoretically, any major activity should have caused attention. But she knew too well from her own days in denial that very few people would take the time to notice.

She was proven right, as they came up to another magical barrier just before the woods. The thing was no creation of Geoffrey's, reeked of evil and blood.

She paused for a second to take a deep breath of the last remaining free air, before she went to face the demon. Then, the barrier parted like a curtain, and she was on her way to face the creature she had always most feared.

She braced herself for the Hell that lay before her, reminding herself of the past she'd survived. She'd already endured a childhood full of the most loathsome horrors imaginable. The taunting, the physical abuse — at home and at school — had been the least of it. From the moment of her birth, she'd been told of her fate, knew that she was intended to be sacrificed to a monster, one who would steal and torment her immortal soul. Once before, she'd managed to fight that creature off, but the victory hadn't made him happy. Now, he was finally here to collect.

She understood this, as she walked into the chamber of horrors that awaited her. Despite the fact that she was prepared, it still left her in shock.

Clarissa was immediately pulled to the side by Damian, shook at his touch, despite her choices. Lydia didn't blame her but also didn't have the time to ponder her feelings — not with all the scenes of torment that lay before her.

It wasn't merely as bad as she'd imagined — was far, far worse. It was almost impossible to process the entirety of it at once, the suffering too overwhelming to endure. She'd only known about one of each pairing, had not expected both of them to be there, hadn't fully realized how late her arrival was.

Encaged, a bloody Lon crouched beside Hugh, who was unmoving. Both were wolves now, large tufts of their fur missing, apparently pulled off by something else with claws. Lydia wasn't certain how she could tell them apart in that form, having only seen them partially turned before, but she could. Lon's jaw was dripping red, as though he were bleeding internally. If that had been the only hideous vision, it would have been more than enough. But it was only the very beginning of the pain.

Not wanting to comprehend all she saw, she was still witness to it. Inside a nearby cage, another wolf, whimpering and terrified, knelt near a black panther. Both were grievously injured, the wolf apparently trying to lick the panther back into consciousness. Other scenes of horror waited in every one of dozens of cages. And all the blood and gore from them, as well as their sheer misery and pain, dripped down into a giant cauldron below.

Lydia wanted to say something, wanted to scream, to destroy forever every single being who had anything to do with this abomination, but she focused, instead, on pooling her inner resources, knowing they would all need every ounce of life they could manage to see them through.

She managed to look calmly at Damian, as he greeted her, his smile quite gleeful.

"Happy Halloween."

That had to have been the sickest, and probably the tritest, greeting she'd ever been given, which was saying a lot, given that her parents had been into displaying skulls and burning black candles. Even though she'd forgotten what the day was, up to now, their choice did make sense. Samhain: the time when the veils between the worlds of the living and the dead were at their thinnest. Apparently, that wasn't just an old wives' tale.

She'd had little way of knowing this before; her own parents had tried to sacrifice her on New Year's Eve. So much for predictability from the world of the damned.

She didn't want to look any further, didn't even want to think. She could see Geoffrey in the cage nearest her, if only out of the corner of her eye. That he'd been tortured seemed to be the least of his troubles. He had what appeared to be knife wounds all over him, was clinging to the cage bars. It was clearly taking all the energy he possessed to hold onto physical form.

She knew why he was struggling. If he lost that, they would lose their one chance together here.

Damian grinned at her, knowing her thoughts. But she couldn't look at Geoffrey at all.

She felt her love welling, its strength buoying her, giving her power, knew Geoffrey would understand her inattention. If she lost herself, as all the couples around her, apparently, had, gave over to simple mourning and despair, she'd have nothing left for this battle. The only way to survive was focus of the most unearthly kind.

She needed every bit of it, the scenes of pain and trauma on every side far more than she could endure. Almost the hardest to ignore was Sybil. She could hear the ghost screaming in the background — the sound eerie, haunting, its pitch rising into nearly a banshee wail. She knew what she was mourning, had seen Erika's body the instant she'd come in, the woman's neck twisted into a position a human could not endure and survive. The thought nearly paralyzed her. She hadn't even known Erika, and now she was dead.

Lydia closed her eyes for a fraction of a second, enduring the torment that pressed in on her from every side, the waves of it brutalizing. Her gaze burned, as it refocused on the minor demon. But she wouldn't allow the torture to cause her to fail.

She said nothing, then, wouldn't give the demons power through any utterance of hers.

And there were so many demons here — or their allies, at least. From every corner, she could see the hellish minions, Ashley and Roderick among them; probably all of Damian's tenants were here. They huddled around each scene of despair as though watching a particularly amusing — or arousing — movie. Sybil perhaps had one of the biggest audiences, although there were a good few watchers over Glory, as well, as she stroked continually over the body of a cat that lay much, much too still, tears in her dark eyes. For some reason, very few had joined near Damian's watch over Geoffrey. Perhaps not having a mourner near him took away from some of the fun.

It occurred to Lydia that she could be the one who would die, that Geoffrey could be the one to have to suffer the loss, but her prior history with the demon who would soon arise argued otherwise. Besides, that wouldn't have made this any better. She couldn't stand the thought of her poor beloved left behind to mourn.

Damian finally spoke. He seemed almost bored, one hand holding onto Clarissa. "Okay, same old, same old. I've given everyone here the offer before." His white teeth gleamed. "Let's see if you're any smarter."

Lydia doubted it, at least by the demon's reckoning of intelligence.

Damian looked almost pouty when she didn't react more. "I'll let Geoffrey go, if you'll sacrifice yourself to bring my Master back. I'll even help restore him to health."

He presented this offer as though it were genuine, and generous, as though he weren't helping to hold the entire world hostage. But, like her friends, she wasn't selfish — or foolish — enough to accept.

Her silence made the demon frown. Evidently, he didn't like being ignored. She supposed he expected her to attack, to scream and rail, but she couldn't see what good that would do just yet.

It clearly took him a second to restore his supposed magnanimity, before he went on. "How about this? I'll even throw in a few of your friends and their partners." His unpleasant grin returned, as he pointed, apparently thinking he'd found the right bargaining chip at last. "Maybe the preacher?"

Despite her horror, Lydia looked at the cage that held Sybil and her partner, her heart aching. With the others, there was no knowing for certain that they were dead, was some hope, at least, that, could they bring the needed miracle about, they could still save them. After all, many of them were not mortal. But Erika . . .

She took a deep breath, holding her determination together, even as she felt sick. Human flesh was much too fragile a creation.

Lydia didn't give in, as much as she desperately wanted to protect all of these beings — Geoffrey especially.

Damian seemed really ticked off, pushing Clarissa away. Lydia noted the sight of the vampire's briefly-brandished fangs with interest but continued to watch her tormentor. It would do no good to get distracted for long.

Most of the demons were leaving the cages to come watch her. She wondered whether she should be flattered.

"Fine," the head demon pouted. "We'll let the lot of them go." His smile became utterly sickly. "We'll even heal the stupid preacher. But you." His finger jabbed at her. "*You* have to be sacrificed."

This statement told her everything she needed to understand. Damian wouldn't have been happy, had he known.

She stopped looking at him, watching the cauldron, the blood in it now boiling. All of the demons and their friends gathered around, observing her. When Damian finally lost his cool, screaming, "What are you waiting for?" she glanced at him calmly before continuing to watch the boiling blood.

She understood now why she was the last to arrive, and she wouldn't let this moment go to waste.

"I'm not making deals with you, Damian," she answered finally, when he seemed about to start screaming again.

His tenants and residents looked both confused and interested. Before he could phrase an impolite answer, she went on. "You're not even real, are you?"

When she looked back to the demon, he'd turned a deathly shade of white. That answered the last of the questions she had.

The tenants were watching avidly now. One would have thought they were cats.

She knew she'd won any possible arguments with Damian when he started stammering, "Wh-what do you mean?"

She ignored him once more, moving toward the cauldron. The evening had gone on long enough. It was time to bring it to a close.

She needed to wade through a sea of monsters of every description to get there. And, unlike those Geoffrey protected, they *were* monsters, every one. Vampires, revenants, flat-out zombies, even a few she suspected of being ghouls — given the way they looked at the prisoners' wounds — tried to block her path.

Damian was screaming again. "What are you doing?"

Still, most moved aside, as she approached. Only a truly stubborn, and mangy looking, old werewolf refused.

It didn't take long to win that particular battle. She simply stared the mutt down until he retreated a step or two away, growling. She knew his plan even before he formed it, floated a quick Celtic wheel at him. "Don't even think about it, Fuzzy." His attempted bite turned into a whimper in a heartbeat.

For all the horror of this moment, she was no longer afraid. The memories Geoffrey had released in her saw to that.

She had free access to the cauldron now, was right in front of it. She refused to look at any of the tortured beings above it, focusing solely on what needed doing.

Damian let out a desperate, "Somebody stop her!"

No one did.

She raised her hands in front of her. The demon seemed too afraid to interfere.

Focusing on what she wanted, a clear blue light soon shone from the end of one fingernail. "I'm giving you what you say you want, Damian." She honed the light razor-sharp with her mind and then slashed the palm of her other hand. "I'm bringing your master back."

No one said a word; even Sybil's weeping had stopped. Lydia wasn't certain anyone breathed — for those whom that was required, anyway.

She only half-noticed the change, squeezing her hand into a tight fist, her blood trickling steadily into the cauldron. She was well aware that this was exactly what was needed to bring this confrontation to an end.

Her determination was steely, as she stepped away, the cauldron starting to bubble. "Quite the Halloween effect, isn't it?" she taunted Damian, as she came back to stand near Geoffrey's cage.

She had plans now, was going to see them through. She used the fur the cats had given her to quickly staunch the blood along her palm, healing the wound at least superficially with a wish. Then, she tossed the two clumps of hair and her blood up to Geoffrey. She didn't look away from the cauldron to see whether the rest of her plan would work.

It would have been difficult to do so, even had it been wise, the sight before them too appalling to look away from.

The demon rose. Although it started out covered in that horrible murk, the blood, gore, and misery congealed quickly into human form. Lydia thought that it looked like a cheap horror movie effect but refrained from commenting.

Finally, once most of the contents of the cauldron were gone, a man stood, hovering above it, dressed in white robes and a smile he probably thought to be beatific. He couldn't have been more wrong.

It was to Lydia that he spoke first, perhaps not surprisingly, given her latest actions. "Nice to see you again, little sister." His grin grew wider. "Did you miss me?"

Lydia could think of many a snarky answer but didn't bother with any of them, becoming more formal. "A brother such as you is very difficult to miss." She meant it in every possible way.

They continued watching each other for a moment, before Geoffrey broke in. That he had the strength to speak was impressive, might mean her plan was working. "Lucifer." The angel panted against the bars of his cage, clearly doing everything in his power to maintain human form. "You were never supposed to return. That was the deal."

Lydia had to act quickly after that. Lucifer had pointed toward her beloved, but even his most minor attack would easily destroy his current body.

She sent up a quick Celtic wheel that hovered protectively in front of Geoffrey's cage. "Forget about me?"

Her brother lowered his hand. "Never, sister, never." He seemed to have temporarily dismissed the angel, except for his words, for which she was thankful but watchful. "I'm so glad Geoffrey gave you your memories back." He took the opportunity of everyone's attention to lower himself to the ground, walking among them. "It makes this so much more interesting."

He came closer, smiling. None of the residents dared to block him. She remembered that look he was aiming at her now, remembered everything that went along with it — that terrible clash of wings. The screaming. The exile. His smile said he remembered it, as well — and had every intention of winning at last.

He began to speak, reminding her of all she already knew. "How could I ever forget my sister? We were the first, you and I. We lived in our mother's creation in the first days of existence. We watched as the worlds were created, as our companions were born."

He was close enough to touch her now — an awful thought. "We were even together when Mother created that—" He pointed at Geoffrey, but her wheel blocked any damage. "—*brat* to be with you." His smile looked more like a snarl. "And I never got either of your attention any more after that."

Lydia crossed her arms. She was tired of games — millennia and more tired. "That's your excuse, is it? 'Mom liked you more than me. I didn't get the attention I wanted.'" She shook her head. "Good God, you're like a three-year-old. You'd think that all of this time would have taught you *some* sort of maturity." She wanted to roll her eyes but settled on narrowing them. "Instead, you try to destroy her creations, all because you're not everyone's favorite pet."

The snarl was definite now, but Lydia refused to look away; even a second could mean disaster. "As above, so below, my dear sister." He moved even closer. "If you hadn't fought me, we would have won."

Now she was livid. "Won what? Death? Misery? Pain? Endless, pointless agony for every creation everywhere?"

He seemed to be smiling at the thought, and she *really* wanted to hit him.

"Besides—"

"Without her," a new voice interrupted, "the rest of you—" One withered hand moved in the classic *blowing up* motion. "—Kablooie."

This, finally, gained back the devil's attention, his eyes widening. "Mother."

Chapter Fourteen

The Lady, the one from Lydia's dreams — and her past — walked up to them. She'd gotten through Damian's barrier without a single struggle.

"Hello, Lucifer. I'd say I'm happy to see you here, but I think we both know I'd be lying." She leaned in to kiss Lydia's cheek. "You, Lydia, always a pleasure." She ruffled her hair. "You're such a good little girl."

The devil was seething now. Apparently, he'd wanted this showdown without an Oedipal struggle on the side. "See? See?" He really did look like a pouty 3-year-old. "You always *did* like her best!"

The Lady turned to him. "And is that any wonder to you? She always *helped*. She looked after all my creations. When she was lonely, I gave her a companion, and she *loved* him! Heck, love?" She threw up her hands. "More like she *adored him with every fiber of her being*!"

She turned back to Lucifer. "And *you*. What do *you* do when I suggest a perfectly nice angel you might want to spend a little time with?" She pointed toward Glory's cage. "You throw a fit and try to kill every creature in sight!" Her finger pointed toward him like a knife. "If ingratitude had a name, it would be *you*, my boy!"

Seeing a supreme being when she was pissed was not a healthy pursuit. Damian's tenants discovered this, when they were attacked by the combined inhabitants of all of Geoffrey's apartments, as well as a few dozen vampires, Clarissa included. Lydia wasn't certain whether she'd convinced the woman to join them — which seemed unlikely — or whether she'd been with them from the start, but it hardly mattered now.

Through the struggling turmoil, the screams, and the running, the domestic drama continued to unfold.

Lucifer was yelling like a petulant kid. "But you liked her better than me! You always, always, always liked her better than me! The only way I got your attention was when I *broke* something."

Given the devil's power, the force that his name still held around the world, it was better not to discuss just what this meant. There were too many examples in the clearing for any sane person to want to begin to ponder this now.

Geoffrey's tenants seemed to be getting the upper hand. Even the ones in the cages appeared to be stirring.

The Lady wasn't paying much attention. "So, when you break something, *I* have to go clean it up. And your sister here—" She pointed toward Lydia. "—She agrees to get exiled to the earth, and *away* from the angel who loves her, for a couple of thousand *lifetimes* just to try to restore the balance and clean up your mess!"

She shook her head in disgust. "Why do you think I stuck you down in the basement, anyway? You think I *want* my son to suffer? No!" she interrupted him, her gesticulations speaking as loudly as her words. "I just want you to stop being on the side of those who make the good suffer." Her hands were now above her head. "Why won't you *listen*?"

This seemed, to Lydia at least, a compelling argument, but Lucifer obviously didn't agree. He continued glaring at his mother, as the chaos continued all around them. Fortunately, the good side seemed to be winning, was even opening a few of the cages, doing what they could for their occupants. Some things seemed, for once, to be going right.

Lucifer might have sensed it but was certainly distracted, as he pointed toward Lydia, still yelling. "No, I *won't* listen, not anymore. I've finally got something on you, Mother. I've done something you can't undo." His finger jabbed at Lydia even more firmly. "She's got *my* mark on her! You can't bring her back to salvation!"

Thankfully, that was Lydia's cue. She had finally seen her way through.

Having edged over toward Damian, she was now close enough to catch him by the throat. "Wanna bet?" Then, finally, she reclaimed what was hers.

What happened next went by too quickly for anyone human to follow, but most of those watching weren't human. The moment she touched him, Damian seemed to blink out of existence, which was generally correct. An instant after that, there was a pissed off spirit standing behind God — and two very large, impressive wings of light on Lydia.

Lucifer had watched this process in shock, his jaw dropping. "How did you know?" His jaw worked for a second longer, as he fought for words. "I took away that memory from you that night." His voice raised. "*How the Hell did you know?*"

Lydia wasn't concerned about his rage, had finally gotten back what she'd first given up in order to restore the balance of life and then had stolen by her brother. The spirit who'd taken the energy of that wing to create the form of Damian was clearly livid, but said nothing. He probably knew he wasn't going to get much of anywhere by protesting, not with these entities, at least. He skulked a little away before being scared completely off by a very pissed ghost.

No one in the clearing asked what was happening. Perhaps they understood. Perhaps they just knew better than to interrupt.

Still, Lydia's new knowledge of what Damian was explained how she had had the power to banish him earlier. He had basically used the energy from a defiled part of her soul to create the body he had worn.

She didn't bother to notice whether everyone understood, just crossed her arms, glaring at her brother. "Knowledge is what Geoffrey does best, remember? He's spent the millennia I've been stuck on this planet watching over the world, learning everything he could."

Before the devil could think to stop her, she touched the cage the angel was in, sending a shimmering light to rush over her beloved. "He's always been a part of me."

The Lady was smiling brightly, understanding.

"I just needed to remember what he knew."

Lydia was well aware of what was happening; it wasn't only her eyes that were glowing. The angelic spirit was burning from her, radiating in waves. When Geoffrey joined her a moment later, his own, golden wings shining, they finally joined hands, and the light expanded. Soon, everything was flooded with it — and the troubles of everyone there would very soon be worked out.

The light altered everything it touched in the most wonderful ways. One of its immediate effects was that the very last of Lucifer's supporters disappeared, sometimes literally — blinked out of existence here to be replaced wherever they'd originated before Damian had pulled them together. The few remaining ones were quickly rounded up, placed in the already emptying cages.

They made for strange bedfellows. Ashley looked especially nervous at having to share a cage with the mangy werewolf and a particularly nasty looking vampire. That seemed to have been Lon's arrangement, his little message to the woman. He was certainly watching all of them intently.

This wasn't the only revolution. Their formerly caged friends, whose resurrections had already been begun by the combined magic of the cats' fur and Lydia's blood, began to regain their balance once more, seeming more themselves. All except Erika, but her change didn't seem to worry Sybil at all.

Lydia saw it briefly, as the light swept by the women, their spirits now embracing in a way they had never been able to before. They seemed not only happy but giddy, laughing gleefully, little, phantom tears running down their cheeks. Even the worst of their situations seemed to be resolving themselves.

These weren't the only recipients of the light's power. Lucifer's image appeared a bit thinner, as though he were suddenly a cellophane cutout of his former self.

He looked down, growling, clearly unhappy. "This is what I get for all my planning?" His audience just watched, letting him rage. He glared at Lydia. "I tempt those idiots you were reborn to into giving me your wing. I plant Damian here, split off half of this moron's realm . . ." He pointed at Geoffrey. ". . . to give to him. I gather together a hundred and more of the most loathsome creatures I can find, all so you might give me just a *little* of the respect I deserve, and you give me *this*?"

He was glowering now, pointing at the held hands of the angels before him. But, to put it mildly, they weren't backing down.

Lydia just smiled, a few of her former questions answered. His plan made sense of there being a bad side to the complex at all. She'd gotten the impression from Geoffrey earlier that places like this were supposed to be beneficial, not simple repositories of evil.

These musings were cut short by Glory, who interrupted more politely than his mother might have. "Oh, give it up, you old reprobate. No matter how many short-term victories you gain, you know you never win."

He glared at her.

"Why don't you let it go for once?"

Not surprisingly, the devil wasn't good at taking criticism. Lydia had never imagined an ex-angel hissy fit but was suddenly given a full understanding of what one looked like.

Lucifer was stamping his foot, bawling in fury like a 2-year-old. "I never get what I want! You never, ever, ever give me what I want!" He sniffled a little, playing for sympathy, as he pointed toward Geoffrey and Lydia once more, turning to his mother. "Can't you *at least* separate them?" His voice was sickly sweet "Please? For me?"

The Lady had had enough. She was rubbing her hand over her forehead like she had a headache. "You did the right thing by bringing her here, Geoffrey. I see that now. But *you*." Both her hands extended toward her eldest son like she was giving him a platter. "Why can't you do something good for *once*? Why can't you love just *one* of my creations? Instead, what do I get?" She threw her arms toward heaven. "Nothing but whine, whine, whine!" Her fingers went back to her forehead, her sigh immense. "I think you were better off in the basement."

This, of course, only helped in making him exceedingly sullen. He was stubbing his toe against the ground repeatedly, lower lip extended. "Don' wike it dere." He gazed up at the Lady through his lashes, eliciting another of her sighs. "It's *hawwwwwt*."

She covered her face.

Clearly, they needed a better option for him. He was only making trouble where he was.

Glory, stroking the recovered black-and-gray tabby cat in her arms, came forward. "I have an idea."

Everyone looked toward her, waiting.

"Why don't you put him in Wild Flowers?"

This got Lucifer's reaction, back to his former fury. "Middle management?!"

The angels around him watched silently, not contradicting.

"Figuring where to pop up a few daisies? Deciding when the buttercups are supposed to wilt?"

The silence around him continued, making him frantic.

"*No!* I'd rather go back to the basement!"

The Lady raised an eyebrow at him. "That can be arranged."

Apparently, the ex-angel knew when he was sunk, glaring at the ground. There was a moment of plotting, before he spoke again. "Maybe I can at least plague a few golf courses with dandelions."

The Lady patted him on the shoulder, taking what she could get from him. "I'm sure it would do them good." She glanced over at Glory, seeming apologetic. "Would you mind?"

The other angel sighed, nodding. "I suppose it has to be done." She gazed down at the feline in her arms. "Do you really want to go back like that?"

It only seemed to pout. "I like being a cat. You can get away with so much."

Lucifer looked intrigued, until his Mother put her hand firmly on his shoulder.

Glory didn't argue, entirely, but her look cut deep. "But it does make some things between us quite difficult."

The cat looked at her for only a second before jumping down. An instant later, it started to change. By the time Lydia had finished blinking, there was no longer a small feline standing there but a very large, well toned, ebony-skinned god among men.

"Yowza." The words escaped from Lydia before she even realized it.

Everybody stared at her, Geoffrey especially. She couldn't blame them. Semi-obscene Grace Jones songs were playing in her head.

She managed a shrug. "Just admiring the Lady's work."

Her gaze told her partner her real choice clearly. He gave her a smile, kissing her on the side of the head.

Lydia did wonder one thing, as much as she had now remembered. "Is that why the cats talk — they're really angels?" For all the weirdness she'd experienced in her childhood, that still pushed the strangeness meter to 11.

Geoffrey shrugged. "Both angels and demons can take on other forms. If they do, then they can communicate with humans. It applies to their offspring, too, if they inherit some of their angelic qualities."

Tiger, she supposed, was proof of that.

His look grew rueful. "It's why you should always beware of your dog telling you to kill people."

Which seems to go without saying, really.

It was also why the cats' fur had been such an effective anti-demon antidote. Both it and her blood were the stuff of angels.

Geoffrey continued over her mental wanderings. "It's easier to hear them when you're an angel, too."

This made sense of the main people she'd seen talking to them, all of whom were angels. Well, angels and a cat woman — but that made sense in a different way.

She'd also started to lose focus on what the felines had been saying after she'd expended so much of herself by temporarily banishing Damian. Evidently, the loss of so much of her angel energy had made it more difficult for her to understand them again.

The Lady sighed, moving the clean-up on from this discussion of feline cosmology. "Glory, you and Lucius will oversee Lucifer—"

"What?" the prodigal screamed.

His mother ignored him. "Don't let him get into anything too dangerous." She sighed again, her voice dropping. "Like the people on this planet need help to screw things up."

Nobody argued, the angels coming forward to escort their charge back to heaven.

Lucius frowned. "Can't get used to these legs. Four were so much easier."

Lucifer seemed to perk up. "Do you think maybe we can adapt a human or two? It might make an interesting experimen—"

The Lady pointed at him. "Boy! Flowers!"

Lucifer sulked again.

Lucius took his other arm, leading him away, but he was whining, as well. "Cats can be crabby, and no one minds. I could say anything. I could form immediate likes and dislikes without anyone calling me on it. I could . . . "

Glory sighed, but she seemed strangely happy. Lydia decided she was like a great general without a battle to fight. A couple of very willful men would have to do in a pinch.

"Boys, I've got a lot of work to do with you . . . " Glory's words disappeared, as they moved into the light.

That bright spot had opened just as it had earlier in Geoffrey's office, when he was discarding the nasty residue from inside Lydia. It closed behind them. All those who remained watched them depart.

Looking around, The Lady sighed. "Most things are back where they need to be, I see." Her gaze went to one particular cage. "But those two . . . "

The central crisis having been somewhat resolved, they moved on to the smaller catastrophes. The first was by far the most tragic, even if the pair they approached looked strangely happy.

Sybil and Erika were still holding each other. But the events that allowed them to touch hurt every one of the bystanders.

The Lady addressed them. "What would you two like now?" It took a second to get the pair's attention, even for her. "What do you want me to do about this?" She pointed at Erika's body.

It was, in many ways, a terrible question. Lon had placed a few of the group's jackets over it, but they all knew what lay below them.

"I can do something to bring you back, but there are difficulties." The Lady watched Erika's spirit carefully, as she explained. "Your body will always know. It'll be painful. A revenant's easier." She went on, as they watched her. "But then you're dead and alive, all at once." There was a shrug. "It's a little confusing, at first."

Butch was looking worried, as always, if far more human again. He was standing in front of Irena, as though to protect her. Fortunately for the sensibilities of all the people around them, someone had brought all the shifters some clothes.

While Irena seemed the stronger of the pair, she allowed his cautious stance, smiling. "Why can't you just bring her back?" He nearly retreated a step at the Lady's look but managed not to — mostly because his new partner was right behind him. "I mean, you're . . . "

He couldn't seem to bring himself to say the rest. Lydia didn't blame him. Getting snarky with God wasn't such a good idea.

Fortunately, the Lady wasn't upset, smiling gently. "Life is more difficult than you think. You set the processes going, you watch over them, but if you step in to overturn them too often, nothing good comes of it." She rolled her eyes. "Trust me. I've seen it done. Usually, those you did it for beg to go back where they were."

Butch was holding Irena's hand, seemed to be drawing strength from her, his eyes on that terrible pile of jackets. "But the minister . . . "

Lydia's heart tugged. He didn't even know Erika's name, but he was willing to fight God for her. She smiled at him. Irena had definitely gotten lucky there.

She was still holding Geoffrey's hand, the connection giving them something like the fortitude to face Erika's death.

"Are you kidding?" Erika was agog. "It was only after I got out of that thing that I realized what a pain it was. Breathing, digesting, keeping it warm enough, keeping it cool enough — good God!" She looked over at the woman in question apologetically, shrugging, holding Sybil's ephemeral hand. "I like it better like this."

It was clear why this was, the two spirits' joy in their union obvious. There were a few seconds before Erika looked around at her watchers once more. "I appreciate your concern, and I know you're upset at how it happened." She gazed back at Sybil so lovingly, taking both of her hands. "But I'm so much happier now."

Lydia wasn't happy with what had brought this outcome about but knew it wasn't her decision. From the looks on all the faces around her, she suspected she wasn't the only one who was forcing herself to accept.

The Lady sighed. "I guess I'm not needed, then." She turned to the ghosts. "Sybil, Erika, you look after each other, wherever you choose to go."

The pair nodded, as she gazed at the others who remained.

"The same goes for the rest of you. And you two." She came up to Lydia and Geoffrey. "Just love each other, all right? You've waited long enough to be together."

They nodded, not that she really gave any of them time to object. She just smiled and disappeared.

There was a lull filled with sighs, once she was gone. It wasn't every day God put in a personal appearance.

Much remained to be done — some of it rather gruesome. Once they lifted the many jackets, though, Erika's body was gone. Apparently, the Lady had done them one more favor before she left. From the looks around her, Lydia was not the only one who was grateful.

Erika and Sybil merely shrugged. They were the first to disappear — more literally than the rest — too caught up in each other to even say goodbye. The next to go were Irena and Butch, the cat person dragging her partner off toward the apartments after only the first step of the cleanup was done, Geoffrey finding more spiritual ways to dispose of the cages and cauldron.

The rest of them were left with a lot of stragglers, blood, and general bad feelings lingering. Even if Damian's barrier were gone, far too much of his spell's residue remained.

It was mostly Lydia who was forced to dispose of it. Since the demon's body had been created out of the energy of her wing — her spiritual strength giving the evil spirit who had possessed it power — it fell to her to try to clean up his mess.

It was exhausting, tedious work. Geoffrey tried to help her, but it was very slow going.

Unfortunately, the more the residue lingered, the easier it was for it to infect those who were left. It probably wasn't surprising that the vampires were the earliest to feel the effects — all of them remaining to help under their leader's orders, covering up as much evidence of strange activities as possible. But Clarissa seemed to be the first to break.

She'd been watching the two angels pausing in their work, Lydia's hands held so tenderly by Geoffrey, as he gave her the strength to continue. It was a loving scene but clearly wasn't one she wanted to witness.

"That's it!" Clarissa screamed, tossing down the rake she'd been using to remove the blood-soaked leaves. She stomped over to Gerrard, whom she had been managing to avoid, despite his many visual pleas. "Why don't you ever treat me like that?"

The demand left the vampire stunned, blinking at his partner. He raised a hand to her face, gaze so tender. "But . . ." He seemed to be searching for words. ". . . don't I always treat you well?"

"No," she grumped, to his obvious astonishment. "How many nights in the last few months have you left me to 'look after' some female or another?"

His surprise and hurt were evident. "But Trisha and Priscilla are newly crossed-over." His hand caressed her hair. "You remember how difficult it was at first. They're trying to understand everything. They need me."

"And I don't?" She continued glaring, as his lips moved without a sound.

She leaned further in. "Blue roses, Gerrard. He brought her *blue roses*." She was pointing at the angel. "I saw them when Geoffrey called me to the office last night to ask me to pretend to work with Damian."

Gerrard's eyes widened.

Clarissa's rage continued, "When was the last time you brought me flowers of any kind?"

Again, his mouth hung open.

"Do I get a box of chocolates? So what if I couldn't eat them!" she stormed, cutting him off, half-changing the subject. "Every time we *almost* get close, you run out to help some newbie or another or you're off talking to *her*." She pointed at Lydia. "She's already got her eternal lover, Geoffrey." Clarissa rolled her eyes. "Why does she need you, too?"

This was a lot for the poor man to try to answer at once — or at all.

Sadly, what he came up with wasn't very useful. "B-but blue roses don't exist in nature." He shrugged, when Clarissa glared at him.

Even Lydia winced.

"Well, they don't," he whined, before rediscovering a little of his backbone. "What am I supposed to do? Go steal flowers from heaven like Geoffrey does?"

Oh. Lydia gazed at Geoffrey, smiling. "You brought me heavenly flowers?" They had been that, certainly, but still . . .

Geoffrey's eyes were gentle, adoring, as he brushed a few, short indigo locks behind her ear. "I'd gladly do much more for you than that."

The two of them were lost in their own little world.

Gerrard glared at them. "*You're. Not. Helping,*" he growled before turning back to his own partner, about to plead once more.

Her anger was starting to turn into a pout.

Gerrard sighed heavily. "Oh, hell."

He grabbed Clarissa, pulling her to him, kissing her forcefully, passionately. Her fury held out for about five seconds under the tender assault before she placed her hands on his shoulders, giving in.

When the kiss broke quite a while later, everyone in the clearing watched. "I knew I should've just gone for the classy European with you. The sulky boy toy doesn't suit you at all."

She almost smiled at him, did when he went on.

"You'll get your damn roses," he growled, looking over toward his amassed, and amazed, followers. "Ned, you take care of the newbies."

"I hate it when you call me Ned," a boy near him sulked.

"I don't care. Do it." He looked back to Clarissa, smiling. "I have more important things to look after."

They left then, caught up in their own little world. Hugh and Lon waited until they were out of earshot — which was pretty far for a vampire — and then burst out laughing. The glares of the rest of Gerrard's followers didn't even slow them down.

Hattie arrived, looking elegant, as always. Just as she did, a loud, lingering howl rose over the complex. It made her smile. Hugh and Lon laughed harder.

Hattie's voice, as always, was sex personified. "I suspect the new cat person and her werewolf have just worked things out." She looked like the well fed succubus she was just by having been near the pair's building.

Lydia smiled at her, ignoring the guffawing werewolves in the background. "Are *you* all right?" Not having seen Hattie helping with the cleanup had made her worry.

The question sobered the succubus. She glanced over to Geoffrey. "I found Gail, I'm afraid."

Lydia could feel Geoffrey's tension, feared the rest herself. She'd been too distracted to notice that woman's absence before.

"Roderick got to her." Hattie raised her hand before they could ask. "She's alive, if only barely. She's probably only got another ten years left."

Lydia winced, as Geoffrey's arm surrounded her, giving her strength. While she'd never warmed to Damian's assistant, knew the woman capable of murder, as she'd tried once before with Geoffrey's previous assistant, it was still a bad ending. It would've been better for everyone if they could just have convinced Gail to try a better path.

Geoffrey shared her feelings, she knew, his fingers stroking over her arm so tenderly. "I'll see to her tomorrow."

Lydia sighed, sharing his tired resolve. Despite how far they had come tonight, there was so much to be done. The thought was exhausting. She put her head on Geoffrey's shoulder, trying to draw the energy to continue.

Fortunately, she was interrupted by their friends, the werewolves having finally stopped laughing.

"We'll take it from here," Hugh assured her.

When she opened her mouth to object, watching the grumbling vampires raking leaves in the background, he went on.

"Anything that requires you can get done tomorrow."

She wanted to argue, knew her duty now, but even Hattie told her the truth. "The rest of this residue isn't particularly dangerous. We'll keep a watch, make sure no one gets near enough to be harmed." Her smile became positively suggestive. "You two go enjoy yourselves."

Considering Lydia felt like she was going to fall down, this didn't seem a particularly likely idea, but Geoffrey pulled her toward her apartment before she could argue.

"Thank you." He nodded at them, then led her the rest of the way home.

They arrived to discover Lacy, Alvin, and three happy cats. A new one, a Siamese, was being stroked on Lacy's lap, looked like it belonged there. Lydia remembered it vaguely. It had been one of Glory's. Apparently, the angel had distributed them among the tenants before she left.

This meant, of course, that Eveningstar and Tiger were now with her for good. Her heart started to swell. While her two feline friends approached to greet them, the newcomer only narrowed its eyes.

"Welcome home," they purred.

For the first time in her life, Lydia knew she was finally in a place where she belonged.

Chapter Fifteen

To Lydia's delight, it turned into an even more interesting night than she'd expected.

She'd thought, at the most, that she'd have a chance to sleep in her partner's arms — lovely an idea as that was — but that hadn't been the case. Well, not at first, anyway.

She was thinking about this, as she lay beside her angel, both of them delightfully naked. She couldn't help her smile. Images from their night before returned over and over, nearly making her laugh — but not so much because she found anything funny. No. It was more a reaction to having too much happiness in her soul to have any easy place to store it.

Her lover looked much the same, although his eyes held far more absolute peace. Hers was more barely repressed giddiness. When her hand began to slide down his body, his smile deepened, even if he did catch her fingers.

"Stop that." He gazed at her adoringly. "There's a cat watching."

"There always is," she agreed, staring up at Eveningstar, who sat perched on a chest of drawers nearby.

If the Persian had had the shape for it, she would have shrugged. "It's what I do," she purred calmly, observing. There had never been a creature with less remorse.

The cat wasn't the only one staring at Lydia. Geoffrey's eyes wouldn't leave her, his look adoring and intense. One arm was around her, the other hand playing with the strands of hair he had hidden behind her ear. His smile warmed her through.

"You should let it grow out."

It took her a second to understand, too lost in watching him nearly shining with love beside her, as the morning light hit the bed.

He almost pouted, making her laugh. "I want more to play with."

The words brought back a flood of lovely images and the memory that he'd already given her everything she'd ever desired.

She brought the hand holding hers to her lips, kissing the palm tenderly before letting it go. Leaning into him, she smiled. "You'll get it, I promise." Her hand was on his cheek, thumb roaming over his lips, as she grew more serious. "You have everything I am."

They kissed then, their passion eternal, adoring, letting them both flow through the wonderful memories of last night and much of the early morning. There were no words to describe those moments — not adequately, anyway. There had been sweetness and tenderness, strength and need. It had been a reunion and a discovery all at once. And, among all the wild adoration, there had also been what he had once feared: a greediness that was never entirely sated. But she'd finally realized the truth. It was a hunger not for just one of them but for both — a hunger for wholeness.

The kiss lingered, becoming more intense. She'd discovered the part of herself that had been missing all along. She knew she wasn't the only one who never intended to let go.

"Oh, sorry!" a happy voice interrupted them.

They sighed, smiling at each other, their hands on one another's faces. But that didn't mean that they were truly any further apart.

Sybil and Erika stood at the end of the bed, as Lydia turned back to them. The longtime ghost looked especially happy to see the two of them together.

"Sorry to interrupt!" Sybil was chirpy as always. "We just wanted to let you know that we're going to be training my replacement before we move on."

Lydia forced herself to see that as good news, even as she felt her heart ache. "We're going to miss you." She even managed to smile.

She couldn't help the way she felt, but she did hear Geoffrey's voice in her head. That had been a wonderful new discovery for her, although it made perfect sense. There had been a great deal of such communication this past night, in fact — all of it glorious.

"157 years," he reminded her.

That was how long Sybil had been trapped on this plane of existence after her body had been taken away. True, she was so perky that she tended to make everyone forget about her misery, but the facts remained. She'd already waited far too long. That she and Erika were able to be together now and not another fifty or more years in the future was a boon for the ghost. Lydia needed to remember what was best for them, not herself.

The sight of the two ghosts together certainly made it easier. They were so obviously happy. There were times when their spirits almost seemed to merge as one person. They only stopped when they were clearly growing almost too distracted for Sybil to go on. "We'll see you again, eventually."

Erika was so close to her, both of them smiling. "We're going to spend some time on the other side together and then be reborn." The margin that should have been the edge of each woman blurred into one. "Together, this time."

That was beautiful news — and certainly well timed. Heck, if they both came back as women, and a couple, they'd pretty much be in vogue.

Lydia smiled at the pair, happy for them, as she felt Geoffrey's arm surround her further, hand stroking down her side. She realized for a moment that her breasts were uncovered but didn't do much about it. Neither cats nor spirits seemed particularly interested in modesty.

Geoffrey smiled at them. "Tell us before you go."

The ghosts nodded before they disappeared.

Lydia knew she should be happy for them, tried to be. She let out a sigh, leaning down to nuzzle against Geoffrey's chest, but he only kissed her head tenderly. "Don't be sad. There are far worse things in this world than the release of the spirit."

She trailed her fingers over his shoulder, until he caught her hand once more. A certain part of him twitched, and she smiled, her leg stroking up to cover him possessively, kissing his jaw on his sigh of longing. Finally, she answered. "I know." The sigh lingered. "I'll just miss them."

Sybil appeared before them suddenly once again — not giving Lydia much time to get nostalgic. "I forgot to tell you! Lacy said to thank you for sending her Elijah. The Siamese," she added, when Lydia looked blank. It seemed a long time ago since she'd been introduced to Glory's cats. "Although he doesn't seem to *always* be a Siamese, which might be why she's so grateful. Erika wants you to keep the necklace she lent you last night as a gift." She thought for a second. "Oh, and there's a small imp uprising in the next building, but Hattie's agreed to work on negotiations."

Eveningstar had her head on her paws, watching lazily. "Alvin and Tiger went, as well." When they looked back to her, she blinked. "They thought she could use the help."

Sybil smiled. "I think it's working so far." She waved a brief goodbye. "Just wanted to let you know!" Then, she disappeared again.

Lydia let out a sigh, glancing over to Geoffrey. "Is it always going to be like this?"

He was staring at the ceiling, seemed to be calculating. "Let's see. We need to finish the psychic clean up, find good tenants and residents for the other side of the complex." He frowned. "Or at least keep the bad ones under close watch, get ready for our traditional children's trick-or-treat event, and continue to do our best to help all of those who need us. There are also a few of Damian's people we need to resettle elsewhere. So, hopefully . . . "

He smiled at her, his eyes glowing — not even trying to leave the bed.

"Yes." He kissed her deeply, lovingly. "Always."

To join Katherine Gilbert's More in Heaven and Earth Newsletter

. . . and get behind-the-scenes info and updates on new releases, sign up at: http://eepurl.com/dCcccL

• • • •

To join her reader group to get exclusive details on future and current works, interact with her about her characters and novels, or have a chance to join her review group and get free Advance Reader Copies of upcoming works, sign up at: https://www.facebook.com/groups/11169120069919462/

• • • •

You can also find her at any of the following:
Facebook: https://www.facebook.com/Katherine-Gilbert-Author-102573417043950/
Goodreads: https://www.goodreads.com/author/show/18141907.Katherine_Gilbert
Bookbub: https://www.bookbub.com/profile/katherine-gilbert
Smashwords: https://www.smashwords.com/profile/view/KGilbertSC

About the Author

Katherine Gilbert was born at house number 1313 and then transplanted to a crumbling antebellum ruin so gothic that The Munsters would have run from it. She has since gained several ridiculously-impractical degrees in English, Religious Studies, and Women's Studies and now teaches at a South Carolina community college, where all her students think, correctly, that she is very, very strange, indeed.

Looking for a taste of Katherine Gilbert's other novels?

Here's a sneak preview of *Unearthly Remains*, another quirkily-humorous paranormal romance/paranormal fantasy, with a bit of a paranormal mystery thrown in for good measure. Here's what happens when two members of Supernatural Oversight (Det. Erick Lawrence and Sgt. Marilyn Jaye) get called in to investigate a murder at one of these supernatural rehabilitation centers:

Erick followed Marilyn to the door of a penthouse which seemed to take up the entire top floor. Odd noises were already coming from behind it.

He raised an eyebrow, as she turned to him seriously. "It's going to go against your entire nature, I know, but I need you not to comment on anything you see here."

His mouth opened to object, but she shook her head.

"Yeah, yeah, I know you think you've seen it all, but you haven't. Not yet."

She turned to knock, leaving him looking irritated, and then thought better of it, opening the door. For far too many reasons, there was no need to wait for an invitation.

Erick's reaction was exactly the one she had suspected. She tried to stop his look of shock with her own hard stare, but he was, sadly, a bit too bug-eyed to notice. She couldn't really blame him. It probably wasn't every day that mortals walked in on a full-on orgy.

This was one of the better ones, too, she supposed. No one here was shy or uncertain, no one left out. There were at least 35 people in the room, all convulsing and cavorting in one rolling sea of naked flesh. The sounds of their orgasmic moans were nearly deafening.

Marilyn didn't share her partner's amusement or interest, however—and none of the participants' apparent joy. She stood with her arms crossed, foot tapping, as a small man in a robe dashed up to her.

He had to be new. He looked at Erick speculatively and at her a bit worriedly, wondering. "Um, did you wish to join?"

She bit back the growl. "Just get him here."

The little man's look became beatific. "You wish to see our Master?"

Not really—but there was no avoiding it. Still, she couldn't say it. "I know he's here. Just get him."

She was already mouthing the man's response, as it began. "Oh, our Master is always with us!"

"I didn't ask for a sermon, just a summons," she growled. When her badge materialized, it glowed a sort of electric blue. She really was annoyed. "I'm a sergeant with Supernatural Oversight."

The sound of her foot tapping nearly outdid the nearby moans. The fact that she didn't give her name even caught Erick's attention, which was hard to do, given their current distractions.

She disapparated the badge and crossed her arms more fully. This little man seemed far too interested in her cleavage.

"Just get the bastard."

That surprised him. "Oh, but . . ."

She didn't let him finish, using a very old trick to make her voice fill the room. She didn't have quite the range of her mother's magical abilities, but she hadn't gone to a witch school for nothing. "NOW!"

She *was* pissed—it echoed.

Still, it got her what she wanted, a feathery light descending into the shape of a robust, older man. His steel gray hair had not a strand out of place, his deep blue eyes twinkling on seeing her, smiling at her angelically. "Now, Marilyn, didn't I teach you not to interrupt anyone's pleasure?"

She tried not to grind her teeth, ignoring the old barb.

The bastard.

Better to just get on with this. If he thought she'd already interrupted, he'd seen nothing yet.

"Hi, Dad. There's been a murder . . ."

Available at any of the following for just $2.99:

Amazon: https://www.amazon.com/dp/B07PJM9B45/

Barnes & Noble: https://www.barnesandnoble.com/w/books/
1130937720

Kobo: https://www.kobo.com/us/en/ebook/unearthly-remains

Smashwords: https://www.smashwords.com/books/view/931259

• • • •

Or you can pick up the short story prequel for free on StoryOrigin:

https://storyoriginapp.com/universalbooklinks/
ae69fb58-66a1-11e9-9b5b-b3150184f041